PLANET EARTH

Period of Crisis

BILL DOHERTY

Copyright © 2024 Bill Doherty
All rights reserved
First Edition

Fulton Books
Meadville, PA

Published by Fulton Books 2024

ISBN 979-8-88731-008-4 (paperback)
ISBN 979-8-88731-009-1 (digital)

Printed in the United States of America

For Nicole, my daughter, whose support has moved me to publish this book.

The day Sunday, April 28, 2041 (earth time representation), dawns with a grave stirring on Nevaeh, the sanctified stronghold of the universal omnipotent. Nevaeh, home to the Great One, located cross dimensionally some four hundred light-years from earth, is representative of all universal good as it stands alone as the cornerstone of all that lives. Two earth children have just arrived and their presence at the throne of the jeweled city, Melasurej, has more than caught the attention of its unique residents. Kelly Marie McIntyre and Robert Judson were just three years old. Two hours earlier they had been attending a children's party at the Montebello Day Care Center in West Los Angeles, California on the planet Earth in a country called America. Now they were standing before the throne of the Great One so many light-years away from their home. In a sudden display of violence, two souls had been wrenched from their children's bodies as evil men on earth vied to slay one another. As their loved ones swooned and shrieked over their bullet-riddled bodies, a cadre of ten angelic beings had escorted their spirits away. The agonizing pain of their loved ones had also traveled along with them and now hung as a cloud at the throne's front gate. Two hundred and thirty-one European Army commandos had just successfully raided and penetrated the inner city of Los Angeles with the express purpose of dealing as much death and destruction as they possibly could. Six huge naval warships sat out in the Pacific Ocean awaiting their return. Women and children were targeted as prime victims as an earthly warrior by the name of Marcus Jean Aurielle, chief of staff of the European Defense Command, sought to break the back of the American Revolution and resistance movement. The battle for America was in full swing, and no life was considered too sacred to spare. Everyone was considered as fair game, and the blood of Americans was spilling out onto its streets and soil at an alarming rate. The universal clock was rapidly ticking its way toward midnight, and the residents of Nevaeh were anxious to enter the fray. Chief Elder Helnoch, an adopted brother to the Great One's Son, had called for an immediate gathering at the throne just prior to the arrival of the young souls. Helnoch raised his hands and uttered a powerful cry, "No longer shall we tolerate our children to be treated as such. Gaze upon these two innocents. The Great One has stirred me to action. We shall begin now our mission of truth and justice."

The power of his voice spewed forth fire in the sky. The symbolic ensign of the Great One's son was as a laser lit and now blazed brightly over the entire Eternal City of Melasurej. No such call or sign had been simultaneously given since the residents of this jeweled intergalactic ship traveling through outer space had welcomed her most famous Son home from the planet called Earth some two thousand years prior. Blessed Chorsadesh and Lord Adamos were already in the city. Two days had their legions filed through the jasper walls of the heavenly city. They had been summoned some two weeks previously by Helnoch. The Great One was soon to conduct meetings to discuss the planet Earth problem. What was this Earth thing? The talk around Melasurej was that the earthlings were coming close to destroying themselves and their planet as well. The Great One was extremely distressed over it and apparently ready to take action to intervene. The arrival of the Earth children had added fuel to the fire, and the inhabitants of Melasurej were awestruck by the events suddenly thrust upon them. Melasurej, oh beautiful city. Its light was like to a precious stone, as it were a jasper stone, clear as crystal. And it had a wall, great and high, with twelve gates. On the east are three gates, and on the west are three gates. On the north are three gates, and on the south are three gates, now enhanced further with the addition of thousands of precious souls newly arrived from the most distant reaches of the universe. Thousands more were sure to come to heed the call of magnificent Helnoch. Who could deny or ignore his crying call? For was he not as beloved as an adopted son to the Great One? Following the fall of Lord Adamos, it was Helnoch who became as a companion to Him. It was Helnoch who walked and talked with the Great One. Mortal Helnoch, yes, was it not he who helped restore immortality to mortal man? Did he not keep the great hope alive?

At midday, this same day of the twenty-first, the news is given, an announcement from the throne. The illustrious Joshea, aide to Helnoch, declares, "Henceforth, seven days' time from this midday now, the Great One's Son shall arrive and preside with the Most high Himself over this gathering. Escorted by the warrior spirit Michel and his vast legions, our Holy One, as a Lion, shall enter our City. Preparations for His coming shall begin. Our universe is in great peril. Be prepared to take heed of momentous decision. Be prepared to go to war."

Thunderous voices applauded the declaration, and the city became astir with excitement. A single voice was heard to cry out over all others, "Our Lamb shall turn to Lion and lead us to battle. Beelzebub shall rue the day he sought to destroy us."

Yes, Beelzebub, Lucifersaton, the mightiest of evil and cunning spirits, the great deceiver. Was he not truly loved by the Most High in the early days? He achieved power and greatness as no other living creation. The entire universe still reverberates from his great deception of Lord Adamos. Lord Adamos, the innocent one, so cunningly stripped of his earthly birthright. The noble and worthy project of the Great One, to create humans and make them like unto Himself, was so evilly sabotaged by Beelzebub. Who dare betray the creator? What power could be so bold? This, like a son against his father, husband against his wife, wife against her husband, brother against his brother, sister against sister. The great conflict rages on throughout the universe, focusing through the centuries on planet Earth, home to that awesome creation, mankind. Wondrous good versus awful evil. Does not universal law and order dictate the ultimate solution? Soon we shall know for the Earth's peril is at hand.

United Republic of Europe

Founded in 2032 in Stuttgart, Germany, with membership as follows:

Permanent members: Belgium, Denmark, France, Germany, Greece, Italy, Luxembourg, Netherlands, Northern Ireland, Spain
Associate members: 72 nations in Africa, the Caribbean, Eastern Europe, America, Pacific Islands
President: Hans Rizarre
Parliament:

Upper Body – 100 voting members from the permanent membership
Lower Body – 202 voting members from the associate membership

2032 – European Republic appointed Hans Rizarre as president and Gustav Erikson as finance minister
2033 – EDC (European Defense Command) established with French general Marcus Jean Aurielle appointed as chief of staff
2034 – EEEC (Eastern European Economic Community) established with associate membership in the European market granted to Poland, the Czech Republic, Slovakia, Austria, Hungary, Romania Slovenia, Croatia, Bulgaria, Lithuania, Belarus, Ukraine, Estonia, Latvia, and Moldova

2035 – ECOWA (European Conference on World Affairs) established with chief goal to study the feasibility of enhancing the powers of the president of the republic

2036 – EECB (European Economic Crises Board) established to offset failure of World Bank and subsequent failure of American economy of 2036 with primary goal to protect European interests and bail out American banks

2040 – Hans Rizarre awarded emperor designation by European Republic

Chapter 1

And I went unto the angel, and said unto him, Give me the little book. And he said unto me, Take it, and eat it up; and it shall make thy belly bitter, but it shall be in thy mouth sweet as honey.

—Revelation 10:9 KJV

September 21, 2040
Laytonville, California, USA

Laytonville mayor, Phillip Redding, prepared to address a very secretive and closed meeting at the Laytonville Long Valley Health Center. Situated on Highway 101 in the midst of northern California's heavily forested region, Laytonville was seen as a kind of scenic gateway on the road to America's redwood forests. Mendocino National Forest, Eldorado National Forest, Tahoe National Forest, Plumas National Forest, Lassen National Forest, and Modoc National Forest provide approximately six and one-half million acres of majestic trees and wildlife amid awesome forests alive with the beauty and wonderment of all that Mother Nature has to offer located in central California running north from Sacramento through to the state of Oregon. The majestic trees amid awesome forests and sturdy people, some of lumberjack origins, provided an unusual and clandestine setting for a group of American patriots who were about to set a new course of destiny for a country that once was called the land of the free.

"I think, Mr. Jefferson, that your idea to resurrect the Sons of Liberty has great merit. There is no doubt that Mr. Rizarre's oppressive measures against Americans are at this point more severe than

England's King George III in his dealings with the original American colonies. However, as the mayor of our town of Laytonville and as chairman of this group of fine citizens assembled here, I have grave reservations concerning the safety and welfare of all our citizens. As you well know, twenty-one hundred residents of New York City were murdered in cold blood for merely voicing their distress over increased European taxation last week. It's obvious our own troops and government officials have sold us out. It seemed such a nice gracious life-saving gesture for Europe to bail us out three years ago when our monetary and banking policies collapsed. But who would have thought the price we would pay. Our own president and Congress have agreed to every measure the EECB—European Economic Crises Board—has established, and Mr. Gustav Erickson and Mr. Hans Rizarre traveled our country back then as if they were conquering heroes. Your ideas are commendable, Mr. Jefferson, indeed certainly honorable, but also certainly shall result in bloodshed and more misery for our people. I know for a fact that if the intent of our meeting here was known by certain officials in Los Angeles, all of us here most certainly would be arrested and probably shot without delay. I give you the floor, Mr. Jefferson. We shall at this point only agree to listen."

David John Jefferson slowly and deliberately moved to the front of the room. Since he had resigned from his seat in the United States Congress three years ago in 2037, he had been quietly moving toward attending such a meeting as this. He knew the crisis America was in more than most and the urgent need to act now before it was too late. He had ensured that the forty-two people present provided a good cross section of Americans from around the country. Two came from New York, one of which witnessed the massacre on New York's Fifth Avenue—Americans killing Americans. Jefferson was sure that this was what Mr. Rizarre had intended to happen. In addition, Ray Myers, a businessman from Orlando, Florida; Charles Dodson, a United States senator from Atlanta, Georgia; Peter Crastin, an oilman from Lubbock, Texas; John and Perry Byers, ranchers from Billings, Montana; Nate Jablonski, a car dealer from Cedar City, Utah; Phillip O'Dougherty, a freelance photographer with Associated Press connections from Utica, New York; John and Carolyn Steele and Abraham Leiskey, community leaders from Chicago, Illinois; Issac Pelensky, a city inspector from Los Angeles, California; and Juan and Maria Cruz from Miami, Florida.

The list went on to include twenty-seven other Americans who were considered key contacts in their respective communities. Heartening to Jefferson was the presence of Anne Jones. One thing he knew for sure was that she was, at this point, at age 45, a key contact person for a group of Americans that had been covertly active for the past five years. Well organized with many sympathizers throughout the country, they saw the danger America faced well before he did. Rare of beauty, sensitive in nature, she always left Jefferson in somewhat of an emotional disarray when she was around him. He had kept that as a secret of her buried deep within his heart. He had always hoped that perhaps there would come a day when he could be more open about it.

David stepped to the microphone and began an impassioned message designed to reach this select group who had assembled.

"Mr. Redding, I am grateful for your courage and kindness to me in allowing this meeting to go forward tonight. There is no need to mince words, so I will come directly to the point. Consider the following facts: In 2036 and '37, a number of Third World countries, in conjunction with a number of major European aligned countries, collectively conspired secretly against all of their United States of America treaties, policies, agreements, business transactions, loans and debts as a planned conspiracy engineered and instigated by certain high-ranking European government officials to make America fall into disarray. Over a ninety-day period, we saw company after company collapse and file bankruptcy, and we soon had more Americans unemployed than ever before in our history to include the Great Depression of 1929 and the coronavirus pandemic of 2020. This action resulted in the immediate collapse of thirty-six of the largest American banking institutions. This also resulted in the failure of four thousand, three hundred, and sixty-five additional United States banking institutions. The American Stock Exchange closed its doors and for six months, not a single stock exchange took place. No bullet was ever fired, or a war declared, but America was brought to her knees. Our own president Carlson and his congressional mates sold us out to the Europeans as they rushed to our rescue. No one suspected that it was Europe that was the prime mover for our fall. No longer are our elected representatives' servants of the people, but instead, members of an elite status group who are more prone to capture the so-called American dream for themselves than achieving it for the citizens they are supposed to represent. So I say again, our president and our Congress have sold us out to the Europeans. Gentlemen, consider this. In 2036, we faced a country crippling crisis and in 2037, the European Republic, under the guidance of Hans Rizarre and Gustav Erikson, were allowed by our leaders to bail us out, and America was mandated to become a subservient associate member of the European Economic Community. We, in essence, allowed a greedy minority interest of American politicians, supported by leading businessmen who saw themselves as perhaps on the sinking *Titanic*, with no regard for saving American women and children first, to quickly sign every legal document Mr. Erikson passed in front of them. It is true that in six months most Americans were back to work and our companies were restructured and our banks were reopened. Those few of us who questioned and opposed the backroom deals that were perpetrated upon us were shouted down and singled out as being 'un-American.' We let our president sign documents which allowed Europeans to control our banking policies, our business dealings, our military expenditures. We even allowed European generals to direct our military troops in the field. We gave up our sovereignty in 180 days, gentlemen, and it has taken our people three to four years to realize the repercussions of it all. Can you believe our tax dollars now go to the European Republic first and then are reallocated back to us as they deem fit? The American dream started out as a simple quest to allow a man to be free, to seek individual opportunity in the way he chose. We let politicians, American business executives, the American press and the television media change that dream. It soon became more than that job and that house with the white picket fence on the hill. Now it included sporty cars, drugs, video games, tons of money, blatant pornography, anything-goes lifestyles, the absence of responsibility, et cetera, et cetera. The sweetness of it all. Goodness, it all tasted so wonderful. Who would listen to those who cautioned the road we were on? Now we retch with indigestion. We vomit from the botulism we have ingested. There is no gray area here—we either stand up and recover our lost sovereignty or simply submit to madmen across the sea who are no more than sadistic bullies who will bury us as they see fit. That is all I have to say, gentlemen. Remember the original Declaration of Independence."

With that, Jefferson stepped aside and directed two men in the front of the room to suspend the banner he had prepared for the group to see.

> The Unanimous Declaration of the Thirteen Colonies of the United States of America.
>
> When in the Course of human events, it becomes necessary for one people to dissolve the political bands which have connected them with another, and to assume among the powers of the earth, the separate and equal station to which the Laws of Nature and of Nature's God entitle them, a decent respect to the opinions of mankind requires that they should declare the causes which impel them to the separation.
>
> We hold these truths to be self-evident, that all men are created equal, that they are endowed by their Creator with certain unalienable Rights, that among these are Life, Liberty and the pursuit of Happiness...that to secure these rights, Governments are instituted among Men, deriving their just powers from the consent of the governed...that whenever any Form of Government becomes destructive of these ends, it is the Right of the People to alter or to abolish it, and to institute new Government, laying its foundation on

such principles and organizing its powers in such form, as to them shall seem most likely to affect their safety and happiness.

Jefferson continued on with rising emotion and passion.
"There is no need to go further. The time is here. Abolish it! Destroy the cancer that creeps among us. Sons of Liberty, Minutemen, Patriots—call us whatever you will. We must now begin to strike back and recapture the birthright our ancestors died to secure for us. I believe we now have the monies, supplies, and armaments to move. I ask for your support from all of you who have gathered here this evening."

A large clamor arose in the small room as several of the gathered attempted to voice their opinions. Suddenly, the six foot-seven-inch frame of Philip Redding appeared at the rostrum. Wisely selected by Jefferson, he was a man who commanded immediate respect. At age 55, he was in excellent physical condition and a retired US Army colonel. In Afghanistan, he became an honored American hero. As a twenty-six-year-old United States Army Ranger lieutenant, he was awarded a Silver Star for heroic valor in the field of combat. With half of his platoon cut off from his main company, Redding personally laid to rest thirteen battle-hardened Al Qaeda insurgents. Redding was as a wild man as he alone charged up into the surrounding hillside. His bloodcurdling screams sent chills through the spines of his men as he simultaneously threw smoke and hand grenades and fired his automatic rifle seemingly in all directions. In a span of seven minutes, he alone had cleared the hillside of every trace of the enemy. He was shot twice in the left shoulder and another flesh-tearing bullet tore through his left side. As the smoke cleared and quiet returned to the hillside, injured, he returned to his men and merely calmly stated that God Almighty had spared them for the moment and that they needed to quickly thank Him and move on. His fellow platoon members would never forget him. However, the only ceremony that ever honored him was held in a clearing outside of their Kabul, Afghanistan military camp forty-five days later when two hundred and twenty US Army soldiers and US Marines witnessed his receiving a Silver Star for meritorious action above and beyond the call of duty. In America, the only thing ever close to a ceremony for Lieutenant Redding was given him by two elderly Vietnam War veterans in the American Legion Hall near Laytonville in 2025, when they accidentally heard about his heroic efforts from another veteran. With tears in their eyes, they toasted his valor and bought him two draft beers. Such was life in America, and in a sad way, an indication of how we got to where we were in 2040.

"Gentlemen, and gentlewomen. Order please. We shall have order."

The room grew quiet amid an undercurrent of unrest.

"We shall conduct this meeting in a fair and impartial manner. Each individual shall have his opportunity to voice his or her opinions. We have nothing but time here, and everyone shall be heard as they wish. Mr. Curtis, Mr. Leroy Curtis from Los Angeles, you, sir, have the floor."

"Thank you, Mr. Redding. I say three cheers for Mr. Jefferson. Let me quickly speak to you on behalf of our Southern California coalition. We have already organized several of our black and Hispanic communities in Southern California. As everybody here knows, the European Defense Command abolished our right to open-carry and bear arms last year. Everybody also knows that the FBI and local police forces have confiscated every weapon they could find whenever given the opportunity, even going into private homes with bogus warrants and using them as a matter of public safety taking all the weapons they could get their hands on. Supply us with sufficient weapons, and we will gladly fight. I have nothing else to say."

"Thank you, Mr. Curtis. Mr. Lyle Swansen of Gadsden, Alabama, you now have the floor."

"Yes, sir, Mr. Redding. We in Alabama, as you should know by now, have been flying a new version of the Rebel Flag a bit lately, albeit mostly in the backwoods. As you might recall, the 'Old South' never cottoned much to outsiders coming in, no offense intended. Northerners, Yankees, etc., etc., let alone foreigners. Recently, in our 'New South,' we have established a new attitude, and, as a matter of fact, I don't think you've seen too many tax dollars coming out of the backwoods. You can believe the Feds haven't found half the weapons we've got put away. Quite frankly, you'll have very little trouble finding support in Dixie. It appears our main problems in this country lie along the East Coast, the large cities in the Midwest, and a real problem in the Los Angeles area. The country neighborhoods and rural areas of America will be our salvation. No power on earth can defeat us outside the cities. Our official group membership last month was polled secretly at 178,000 registered members taking in ten Southern states. With the threat of foreign troops in our midst, we have assembled quite an interesting cross section of membership. A new generation of Southerners that includes whites, blacks, Hispanics, Catholics, and Jewish folks as our brethren. In fact, any American who will join us is welcomed. I myself fought in the Iraq War for my country some years back. I wasn't no hero though. A good number of the men in my company were black folk. With my upbringing, I will say I didn't care much for it. However, I never did understand until a short while ago why I shed tears when I saw a few of those young men lying dead in the hilly Afghan soil. I don't mind saying we've discussed this a great deal lately at our gatherings. Not making much of apologies here. Let's say that perhaps we've seen the light. And I don't think it's too late at this point either. On with it, men!"

Phillip Redding maintained his huge presence in the front of the room and controlled the meeting as Jefferson had previously directed him.

"Well spoken, Lyle. I must advise all of you here that Al Sheldon of New Hartford, New York, and Mary Parker of Joliet, Illinois, have been assigned the task of recording the minutes of this meeting. We have a communications and printing facility up in the Mendocino National Forest. It is our intention to print and distribute these minutes to our key people in place all over the country. I think we shall prepare a special flyer on your remarks, Mr. Swansen."

"I have no objections, Mr. Redding."

"Mr. Redding, Mr. Redding, I demand the floor."

Ralph Walden was a resident of New York City. He was a computer programmer employed by Euro-Tech, once known as IBM. At age 43, he had a well-earned reputation as a genius in the high-tech field of computers and computer programming. There was nothing in modern, state-of-the-art computer design that escaped his attention. Born and raised in Long Island, New York, he attended MIT on scholarship and immediately upon graduation, was recruited by IBM and sent to work in its Computer and Planning Division in Armonk, New York. Still a very eligible bachelor, like so many others, he has tasted the so-called American good life. Blessed with natural good looks and endowed with a strong physique, he stood six feet two inches tall with blond hair and blue eyes. His plush penthouse on the forty-second floor of a very private condominium overlooking the Hudson River was the talk of his associates. As a very sexually active male he could count on, at the moment, more than one female acquaintance to enjoy the good life with him. With all the apparent good things going for him, he could never adequately explain or understand the personal loneliness he felt deep inside. He could hide it well, but it never truly left him. Marijuana, cocaine, and good whiskey often helped him through the rough nights, but as he neared age 44, he somehow knew he was missing something. Quite frankly, he had a strange fear that soon he might find it.

Ralph was always a nonpolitical person. He often boasted that he never voted for anything or anyone concerning politics in his entire life. It was unnecessary, and politicians and politics absolutely bored him. It was true that in 2036, he sweated it out for three months when Euro-Tech shut down after the banking collapse. However, nobody came looking for his condo payments, and his Mercedes seemed safe enough parked away in his condo complex garage. It was a godsend when two West German representatives from Euro-Tech came calling on him. Following a four-hour interview in his condo, they presented him with two bottles of bourbon and a month's supply of gas ration cards and told him not to worry about his job or the current political turmoil. That very night he hosted a small party at his place, and two days later his mobile phone service was restored, and he was told to report to his old office for work. Everything seemed back in place, and politics once again receded in its everyday importance. He just couldn't understand why politicians couldn't run governments in the same fashion as he did his computers.

However, on September 11, 2040, Ralph Walden came face-to-face with a new political reality when his taxicab became snarled in a traffic jam on New York's Fifth Avenue. He departed from his cab into the midst of an angry crowd of nearly thirty-five thousand New Yorkers who were bound and determined to verbally protest the latest European taxation transaction upon the residents and workers of the Big Apple (New York City) to help finance their recent government takeover of the internet. A new flat one-time fee of fifty-one American dollars had been assessed on each and every person over the age of eighteen who either resided or worked in New York. For many this was the last straw. The monies being collected were specifically earmarked for General Marcus Aurielle's European Defense Command. They were currently tasked with overseeing all communications and internet activities in America. Currently ten thousand of General Aurielle's military troops were presently deployed near the site of the old Fort Dix, New Jersey, army base conducting so-called American training exercises. Imagine, a crack French Army division sitting across the river from New York City in New Jersey. Some longtime residents of the historic Mount Vernon, Virginia, area near Alexandria along the banks of the Potomac River swore there were earth tremors felt there lately. Some folks were certain it was probably due to the ghost of George Washington about to burst from his nearby tomb over the thought of such foreign intrusion upon American soil.

Ralph never gave much concern about New York City gatherings. Usually for him they were amusing events that so often took on a party atmosphere. He actually once saw a crowd raise havoc and tie up traffic in Times Square one lunch hour as they gathered to protest horse manure droppings on the city streets, courtesy of the New York City Police Department Mounted Patrol. This event today, he immediately sensed, was different. One block north of him, he saw the line of helmeted police forming a human wedge in the middle of Fifth Avenue. The drawn weapons of some of the police alarmed him, but even more menacing was the armored personnel carriers sitting on the sidewalks on both sides of the street. Machine guns were mounted on them, and a police captain was stationed with a bullhorn a half block in front of the wedge. Police helicopters hovered amid the skyscrapers, and their presence became quite obvious. Ralph quickly moved off the street and pressed himself into the doorway of Gino's Italian Restaurant and Parlor. From there he had an excellent vantage point to survey the onrushing crowd. With the appearance of the drawn police weapons, the crowd took on a hostile nature. Ralph could see it was pretty much a blue-collar-type group, and the many hard hats in the crowd did not surprise him. He was not ignorant of the fact that so many Americans were becoming more upset over European taxation and control over American affairs. Those in the middle and lower class pay scales of American society were reeling from heavy taxation that left them virtually in debt beyond their ability to repay. The Europeans were generous in extending credit, but it was a system sinisterly designed to make slaves of men.

A great fear suddenly gripped Ralph. He sensed now he was about to witness something horrible. The vanguard of the crowd suddenly began hurling bottles and bricks in the direction of the wedge standing before them. He spotted three black men, one Hispanic man, and a white man all charge the police line. A sickening thought smashed against the inner recesses of his brain and left him gasping for breath. The melting pot of America represented in those charging angry men was about to taste the swift and sudden hatred of a world gone mad. A fusillade of machine gun bullets brought sudden death to the men as flesh and blood were torn asunder by hot lead. Ralph retched in disbelief as the fusillade continued and the machine guns atop the two armored carriers continued to fire. This was a calculated slaughter, designed to destroy. Two rooftops away, Ralph spotted the police command post. His worst fears suddenly wrenched his innards, and he almost defecated from horrifying fright. Ralph saw a police captain with radio in hand appearing to be giving instructions to his men. Standing next to him was a man wearing the hated blue-gray uniform of the European Defense Command. He was obviously an officer and gave the bearing of a man who was in complete charge. He was smiling, obviously enjoying the scene in front of and below him. Ralph had heard rumors about the New York Police Department taking orders from overseas. He had heard the stories about people disappearing and dismissed them as so much rabble-rousing gossip. It smacked too much of old war stories, Gestapo, and Russian KGB types, and foreign spies running loose in America. It was so much hogwash, a bunch of crap spread around by a bunch of malcontents. He remembered the stories, which at the time kind of pissed him off. Good lord, he was doing so well. Couldn't people just leave well enough alone? He was positive many people shared his views.

The sound of his knees knocking together helped bring Ralph out of his momentary daze. The crowd had gone berserk as thousands fled for their lives. He suddenly found himself running with the crowd. He headed south away from the gunfire as quickly as his legs would carry him. Immediately to Ralph's left, a young woman suddenly fell down into the street. A bullet had shattered the right side of her head, hitting her behind her right ear. The aortal stream of hot blood emitting from her once attractive face splashed along Ralph's left thigh, and a cry of anguish seemed to rise up out of the crowd. Ralph realized immediately it was his own voice uttering this sound, and he veered to his right, in panic, off the street onto the sidewalk. He found an alley. He never believed a garbage-strewn New York City alley would ever appear as the one place that he would want to be in. Indeed, at this moment, it was perhaps the only place he currently felt safe in. He wasn't alone. Six or seven other people raced ahead of him. The alley accessed other alleys, and Ralph quickly felt a sense of relief as he cut left down one alley and then again right down another. The sounds of gunfire and crowd hysteria began to recede. Ralph slowed to a fast walk, and he began to believe that he was going to survive this tragedy. He looked straight ahead and could not bring himself to look down on his blood-soaked trousers. He cut left, down another alley, and felt even more secure as he spotted a man sitting casually halfway down the alley. A smart man thought Ralph, sitting there, away from the crazy people out in the streets. As he neared the gentleman, Ralph sensed something was wrong. This was a man in his fifties, he thought, a businessman dressed in a sport coat and tie. As Ralph came upon him, the man cried out in pain.

"Please, please help me. I've been shot, and I think I'm dying."

A pool of blood was now noticeable beneath him. The left side of his shirt under his jacket was soaked crimson red. Ralph's first thought was to move him before a policeman came along. As he surveyed the alley, he spotted a door ten yards farther ahead. He quickly moved to it and tested the door handle. It was unlocked and opened out into the alley. Ralph quickly returned to the man and as gently as he could, lifted him to his feet. Together they staggered to the door. They entered and collapsed on the steps of the stairwell inside. Ralph closed the door and turned to face this poor wounded man.

"Please, sir, a cigarette, in my coat pocket."

Ralph reached in the man's left coat pocket and retrieved a pack of generic cigarettes and a Bic lighter He carefully lit one and then another for himself. Normally a nonsmoker, he felt he needed one now to help calm himself. The man sitting in front of him was bleeding profusely from his lower chest, and he felt helpless to act. The man sensed his own doom and began to speak very slowly and deliberately.

"My name is Vincent Grazadei. I am a buyer in the garment district. I live in Yonkers with my wife and two children. I have five, but only two are still home. I wasn't in the crowd, you know. I was watching from a block away. We just finished a big sale this morning, and I was just watching, minding my own business. I couldn't believe the police were really shooting. Been in the city for so many years now, and I've never seen anything like it. The next thing I knew, I was flat on my back. Something hit me, and my insides were on fire. I picked myself up, and I don't know how I got to where you found me. I remember vomiting as I got up, and I knew it was blood that was spewing from my mouth. I have been praying to God since then to save me from this terrible thing, but I feel that I'm a dead man soon. I don't want to die now. My wife, her name is Sarah, she won't take this easy. She's my second wife, you know. My boy Tony is sixteen, and Vinnie Junior will be eighteen next month. I'm only fifty-eight. I was born in Yonkers, you know, Riverside Hospital 1982. Live on Elm Street now."

Ralph remembered reading of accounts of a man's life flashing instantaneously in front of him in life-threatening situations as death came close to sucking life away. He stared in amazement at this man, a complete stranger, who began to recite his story. Ralph listened intently and slowly sat down beside him.

"I'm Italian, Roman Catholic, had a fine childhood. My dad fought in Vietnam, and when he retired from the service and came home for good, we all celebrated. I was a happy kid, went to school at Saint Mary's Elementary, and graduated high school at West Side Catholic in 2000. I went to New York University for two years and got married at the age of twenty. Maria Valentine was her name. We were just young kids, too smart for our own good. We wouldn't listen to anybody. We got married and had a daughter in 2004. Sonia is her name. She lives with her male friend out in Minnesota. No children though. She says too many complications. She lives for the joy of living. She tells me to go for the gusto—live for today. If you ask me, tomorrow she'll have nothing. Her mother and her left me in 2008. For six years, I worked hard to bring us financial success, a nice home, a nice neighborhood—the American dream, you know. I guess I worked too hard for it. I was never home. I worked two jobs and went back to college in the evenings. I didn't know better. I thought I was supposed to do that. One day I came home, and they were gone. Maria left me a three-page letter telling me of lonely nights and a need for love. I didn't know I was doing something wrong. Everybody that I knew was out there doing the same thing. But you know, all my friends ended up pretty much the same way. I can count on one hand the couples I know that are still together that got married back then. It's incredible, isn't it? We were most all of us doing it wrong, but somebody was telling us differently. You saw the movies, the television, the magazines. Go after the good life. We believed it and followed like cattle. It was all a big lie. Free enterprise out of control. It was just a few people who were making lots of money off of people who were buying too many material things. The more money spent, the more profit for the men who were selling. The more technologically advanced we became, the more erotic our methods of selling and merchandizing. There was too little thought given to spiritual values, love for one another, or the wear and tear on a person's body, mind, and family structure in order to achieve those material possessions. Success was measured in how many material possessions could one acquire. There we were trapped, unknowingly, victims of slick merchandizing with no fail-safe measures to handle the human emotional dilemmas that accompanied the pressure of everyday survival. Mental wards, AA groups, drug rehab centers, halfway houses, etc., etc., were after the fact attempts to deal with those of us who couldn't cope. I can see it now. It's much clearer now. Oh god, why could I not see it way back then?"

Vince Grazadei coughed and slumped further to the floor. Ralph thought he had lost him, but Vince recovered and rambling on continued his story.

"I met Sarah in 2009. She was working as an accountant down in the garment district. We were married in 2010, and soon there was Robert and Robin, and Vinnie and Tony. I toned down my aggressive drive for financial success, thanks to Sarah, and we struggled along. I found that I had less material things but a whole lot more love, and I've been a happier man ever since. Robert is out in San Diego. He's a fine son and a credit to his family. Sir, you must find my daughter Robin. She was out there in the crowd. Just twenty-five years old, she's taken up with one of the hard hats. She won't listen to me. You must call Sarah for me!"

Vince Grazadei shuddered, and his body convulsed and contorted in a last-ditch effort to remain alive. His battle was for naught, and he expired before Ralph had a chance to react or respond. Ralph, struck with grief, could only think and utter aloud, "Where the fuck have I been for the past thirty years?"

In a period of twenty minutes, he had met a man named Vince Grazadei and felt like he was his brother. Yesterday, if he had passed him in the street, he probably wouldn't have given him the time of day. He quickly searched Vince's clothing, found his wallet and personal effects, and gathered them up and set out on a mission to find a lady named Sarah and a rebel named Robin.

"Mr. Walden, you have the floor. Everyone, this man witnessed the great crime in the streets of New York, and I understand he is under a deadline to return to the city."

"Thank you, Mr. Redding. I will not stand here and take up your time to recite the horrors that occurred in New York. By now you are all well aware of what took place there. Because of my sensitive position with Euro-Tech, my movements are closely monitored. My employers believe I am visiting an ill relative in San Francisco, which I intend to do tomorrow. In two days, I am expected to be back at my desk. I'm here to relay to you that plans are now in the works to include all Americans in the same computer data banks that now govern the movements of all Europeans. Each American will be issued an ID card and virtually will not be able to conduct any legitimate business transactions without producing a current and up-to-date Euro-American ID card. I've seen the programs that are being prepared, and soon in the future you won't be able to make any purchases of any kind without producing your official card. I am saying to you now that we must make alternate plans to circumvent this system. Many Americans will be rejected. We must make plans that will enable us to feed and clothe ourselves and our family members. We probably won't be online with an alternate program for at least eight to twelve months. It will operate along with a clandestine black-market operation that is also now being put together. I will help in any way that I can. I will keep in close touch with your contacts in New York City. Thank you for your time, but I must leave immediately."

Mr. Redding quickly advised Al Sheldon and Mary Parker to mark Ralph Walden's remarks as confidential and to give him the updated list of names of key New York City contacts. As this was being accomplished, it was obvious the mood of the unusual members gathered to this meeting had changed. Unrest and an urgency to speak was replaced by the knowledge that all present would have their opportunity to speak and more deliberation and planning should be given to the serious discussion at hand. One by one Mr. Redding acknowledged each individual, and for the next six hours American patriots presented the many options available for constructive action to combat the present danger threatening the future existence of the United States of America. The consensus was that there was hope, but it was tempered with the caution that much blood would be shed, and the task ahead was at best difficult, beset with many obstacles.

At three in the morning of the twenty-second, the meeting was adjourned, with each individual dispatched to his hometown to continue organizing the efforts to save America. Tentative plans were made for a future meeting to be announced at a later date. Phil O'Dougherty, Phillip Redding, Al Sheldon, Anne Jones, and David John Jefferson remained behind to assess the accomplishments of what had just transpired. David Jefferson was ecstatic with the results, and all agreed that it was best perhaps to sleep on it and then critique the events more clearly after a good rest. With that, the five individuals departed in Mary Parker's van to a secluded tent village in the Mendocino National Forest.

Chapter 2

And the great dragon was cast out, that old serpent, called the Devil, and Satan, which deceiveth the whole world: he was cast out into the earth, and his angels were cast out with him.

—Revelation 12:9 KJV

On this same day, September 21, on Planet Earth, the newly appointed president of the European Republic declared for himself an official day of rest. At his home in Stuttgart, Germany, he was lounging in his study and had directed his aides to handle all affairs of the government and issued orders that absolutely no one contact him regarding official business. He had decided to heed the advice of his medical staff and take a stress-free day to simply stay at his private residence and relax. Even so, he was busy drafting an itinerary for his political confidants to follow for an upcoming clandestine meeting. Hans Rizarre, the brilliant West German politician, has captured the hearts and minds of the Western world as no other politician or world leader since the American John F. Kennedy of the last century in the 1960s. Indeed, he thought, John F. Kennedy would envy the following of Mr. Rizarre. He seemed to have the perfect blend of intellectual savoir faire combined with middle class and grassroots dialogue that appealed to the masses. His hawkish but attractive countenance sat well with his eloquent speaking style and those eyes of his. It was said he could hypnotize a European-wide television audience in the thick of a political campaign. He was an orator the scope of which no man or woman dare debate in public forum. No opponent could stand up to him. It was said by his peers that Mr. Rizarre single-handedly brought about the European Conference on

World Affairs (ECOWA), which paved the way for the establishment of the newly formed United Republic of Europe. He currently sat as a virtual dictator occupying one of the most powerful positions on the face of Planet Earth.

Sponsored by a majority of European nations, the European Republic, with Mr. Rizarre as its president, was now a political entity with more political clout and power than any other existing earthly government. Millions of Europeans watched on daily television as news accounts of Mr. Rizarre's appearances in Rome, Berlin, Paris, London, Athens, and Belfast stirred the imaginations and dreams of those who yearned for a strong and united Europe—one government, one army, one currency, one united people. His appeal to consolidate and in fact draw upon the vast resources and cultural advances of past Western civilization was awesome to behold. Not since the days of Holy Roman emperor Charlemagne had all of Europe acted so much as one. In point of fact, it was akin to Han's lifelong dream to bring about the restoration of the Holy Roman Empire, complete with a sitting Caesar who would command the world from a position of great power and prestige. Hans knew that history well. The coronation of Charlemagne (Charles the Great) in AD 800 marked the last great restoration of the western Roman Empire, the first revival of Roman Europe since Justinian's reign in AD 554. Hans Rizarre, a 1996 graduate from Berlin University, was a keen and zealous history buff. He possessed an eerie fixation with a certain event that occurred in the life of the great Charlemagne. His closest college confidants could recall Hans referencing this event on more than one occasion. As Hans would sometimes tell it (once disrupting a college history class to tell it), "December 25 AD 800—the great Charlemagne is kneeling in prayer. Where? St. Peter's Basilica All eyes are upon him as he quietly worships. Without warning, Pope Leo III suddenly places a golden crown upon Charles's head. Suddenly the church is filled with the cry—'Long life and victory to Charles Augustus crowned by God. Great peace-giving emperor of the of the Romans.' Imagine a Roman Emperor, imagine."

Born January 3, 1974, Hans Rizarre grew up in a somewhat comfortable middle-class environment, an only son, an only child.

His father, a lifelong German nationalist and proud supporter of the fatherland, earned a good wage as lead supervisor for Modena, a service and race preparation garage. His mother, nonpolitical and strictly a homemaker, worked hard to raise and educate her son. Studying the first twenty-one years of Han's life, one would be hard pressed to find anything unusual. He was a good student, a practicing Lutheran who attended church and church school programs weekly with his family and friends. He was active in sports and quite popular with his schoolmates because of his somewhat extroverted personality, and he communicated well with his peers. The only unusual thing that could be said about him was his fascination with reading the Bible, in particular, the book of Revelations. This was certainly somewhat unusual activity for a young man growing up in such a materialistic world, but of course, a positive oddity. His mother often spoke favorably of this activity.

A turning point in young Han's life occurred in his senior college year as he attended a theological seminar sponsored by the World Ecumenical Movement in the spring of 1996 in Venice, Italy. There he met a young Italian seminary student by the name of Tony Rondanelli (baptized in Roman Catholicism as Antonio Franciscus Rondanelli). The two young men developed an immediate friendship that one day would bring the planet Earth to the brink of despair and ruination. They felt they had possession of a secret and power that few men ever discussed and even fewer dared to utilize. It based its premise on the following biblical verse from Revelations:

> And the great dragon was cast out, that old serpent, called the Devil, and Satan, which deceiveth the whole world: he was cast out into the earth, and his angels were cast out with him. (Revelation 12:9 KJV)

As Hans would later explain it in simple terms to Tony, "Heaven and the rest of the universe may be ruled by God, but God cast Satan and his angels to earth. I am an earthling, and my loyalties lie with Satan. There is no other choice for me. Man has overlooked the obvious."

On March 24, 1996, Hans and Tony sealed a pact of trust as they sacrificially mixed their blood in an oath to Satan and vowed to work together to achieve political power and use their influence to ensure the power of Satan was firmly and forever established on earth despite whatever consequences their actions might bring. If they had to destroy all God-fearing and God-worshipping people to achieve this end, so be it. Their strategy was simple: work within the existing framework of established society, keep their secret to themselves, and rise to whatever heights of power they could. Hans would become active politically in Europe, and Tony would continue his priestly studies and attempt to rise through the political structure of the Roman Catholic Church. His Italian roots were ideal, and armed with his secret, he would attempt to rise through the ranks. And on this date, March 24, as their quest began, in a far distant city some four hundred light-years away, a great and powerful being cried out in anguish and seven faithful angelic spirits were ordered to the throne room and advised to ready their trumpets. Soon enough their blasts would echo across the universe, and the sound of their fury would be painfully felt on a planet whose inhabitants might expire from fright if they had even the slightest bit of knowledge of what was to soon befall them.

Chapter 3

*Therefore whosoever heareth these sayings of
mine, and doeth them, I will liken him unto a wise
man, which built his house upon a rock.*

—Matthew 7:24 KJV

September 23, 2040
Mendocino National Forest, California

Tucked away in an area of northern California known by some as the Redwood Empire, the Mendocino National Forest is located approximately sixty miles east of Laytonville, California. This is truly a land foreign to most Americans. Modern America has lived in relative ease and physical comfort. It was difficult to associate and identify with pioneer ancestors who had overcome and conquered the harshest of nature's experiences. However, in the Mendocino National Forest, one could experience quickly the reality of living and surviving amid nature's splendor. The Mendocino was in close proximity to the Eldorado National Forest, the Tahoe National Forest, the Plumas National Forest, the Lassen National Forest, and the Modoc National Forest. The very few who lived there, now off the grid, could find the spirit that long ago was alive and vibrant throughout the land. There still lived in America people living there among the splendor and wilderness of northern California's forests who represented the strength and character the country once knew and now so desperately needed.

David Jefferson awoke and slowly rubbed the sleep from his eyes. The exhaustion he felt from the previous day's meeting was overwhelming. He had attended a meeting two days previous in Johnston, Pennsylvania, drove to Harrisburg, Pennsylvania, and caught a plane to San Francisco, California. The long drive from there to Laytonville had taken its toll. He had very little sleep in two days, but the meeting at Laytonville's Health Center had exhilarated him. It wasn't until he settled in his tent in the forest that he realized how tired he was. At 5:00 a.m., he zipped up his sleeping bag, closed his eyes, and twelve hours later, he was slowly regaining his senses. He was now ready to undertake what was for him the most exciting part of his trip west, a tour of Camp Liberty.

Camp Liberty was the brainchild of Phil Redding and the vets of the Laytonville area, in conjunction with other veterans from Elk Creek and Paskenta. Located over toward the Sacramento Valley, a group of approximately 110 men and women over the past two and a half years had covertly erected this aboveground tent village just north of Snow Mountain. Stony Creek, the Eel River, and Lake Pillsbury provided a scenic and serene backdrop to what was a very serious project. Harold Baines was the chief ranger who supervised a contingent of five federal forest rangers who oversaw these six vast national forests for the United States federal government. No one in Washington knew that Ranger Baines had served with Phil Redding in the wars in Iraq and Afghanistan. Through the years they had kept in close touch with one another. It was no accident they worked hand in glove on the project they called Camp Liberty. Ranger Baines had carefully selected this contingent of federal rangers, and with their loyalty and devotion to concepts seemed lost by so many in America, they set about erecting their camps of refuge. Twenty-two tents of all shapes and sizes were now set in place. Carefully camouflaged and concealed, they formed a unique base throughout these forests that allowed for clandestine meetings and operational gatherings that were wholly unnoticed by the rest of California's citizens. Ranger Baines had four other rangers working in and controlling access to the five additional national forests of northern California in order to complete his Camp Liberty project. Hundreds of thousands of acres were available for all the clandestine and secretive projects he had put together. Both aboveground and underground units were carved out and put into place. David had heard rumors recently that some of the camps had gone underground. Secrecy and seclusion were of utmost importance, and all visitors were carefully screened. For the past fourteen months, armed guards had been in place to protect against intrusion from outsiders. As far as David knew, there had been no serious incidents to date that would jeopardize or compromise the secrecy of their operation.

Ranger Baines was most proud of the communications network he had help put in place at Camp Liberty. He had recruited a number of young people from the northwest states of California, Oregon, and Washington to work alongside the veterans. There was Thomas Lavendera, known as Two Hills to his friends. At age 23, he was a proud son of the Chico, California Mechoopda Indian Tribe. Along with his close friend, twenty-one-year-old Rebecca Claywell, known as Star Flower, from the state of Washington's Snoqualmie Indian Tribe, they developed an encryption code system for Ranger Baines that was similar to what the Navajo Indian code talkers had developed for the US Marines in World War II while fighting the Japanese in the Pacific Ocean theater of war. Thomas and Rebecca were responsible for this most unusual asset that Ranger Baines had put in place for all the Camp Liberty camp units throughout the multiforested region—the development of an encrypted communication code that would allow camp military personnel to communicate at a high level without fear of the government or others being able to understand what they were talking about if intercepted. Radio, internet, satellite, and mobile phone communication were kept to a strict minimum, and frequent drills were held between the different camps in order to bring about familiarization between the commo personnel that utilized the code in their sensitive daily discussions.

Thomas and Rebecca had met in San Francisco at an esports international gaming competition in 2029. For three straight years, they lived the gaming life of Xboxers, PlayStation, and PC competitions. They embraced their lifestyle of gaming on wargaming.net and battle.net. They were so proficient in their skills that for two years running, Two Hills and Starflower were both ranked in the top 40 worldwide list in their respective gaming divisions. In the first year of their respective competitions, they discovered their native American connection, and a friendship developed rapidly and soon there was a close connection between the Chico Mechoopda Tribe of California and the Snoqualmie Tribe of Washington.

Ranger Baines had first met Thomas "Two Hills" when he was a young teenager. Thomas loved to roam the Mendocino Forest with his young friends. They knew the forest intimately and frequently camped, hunted, and fished there. Ranger Baines gave them free rein in the forest as they were so respectful and knowledgeable about nature. Baines once rescued Thomas's friend, Jay, Rebecca's cousin, known as Swiftwater, after he was knocked unconscious when he hit his head on a sharp rock after diving off his canoe while fishing. Baines stayed with Two Hills and Swiftwater for seven hours while they waited for emergency crews to get into the forest and rescue them. He gave first aid to the young twelve-year-old and comforted him until help arrived. The Mechoopda and Snolqualmie tribes were forever grateful to Ranger Baines, and a long-term life bond was cemented between them. As he grew through his teenage years, young Thomas and his close friends became an integral part of the formation of Camp Liberty. They were fully involved in establishing the perimeter security of the camp. Thomas and Rebecca were responsible for the development of the encrypted communication code that would allow camp military personnel to communicate at a high level without fear of the government or any other outsiders being able to understand what they were talking about. Radio, internet, satellite, and mobile phone communication were essential to the efficient operation of the camps.

Another valuable addition to Camp Liberty was the addition of James (Jimmy) Wan. He was a computer geek programmer that Thomas Lavendera met in San Francisco during one of the gaming competitions. Not only was he a fierce competitor in the gaming competition, but he was employed by Xbox as a highly skilled computer programmer following his employment with the Capcom Pro Gaming Tour. Thomas and Jimmy battled against each other in practice sessions prior to the actual war gaming competition and became fast friends, resulting in Jimmy being invited to and spending a great deal of time at the Mechoopda tribe location in Chico, California. His computer expertise would be critical in the implementation of Camp Liberty's overall communications system and emblematic of the type of value young people were contributing to the camps. They had firmly developed a communication strategy that utilized joint operation planning, data collection, and assessments of all operational commands that were being established at camps throughout the forests and also other similar camps throughout the country. There was great synchronization among all top command personnel in a system that utilized standard operation military practices and strategy and was proactive in the utilization of all messages, images, and actions.

David, now fully awake, rose and slipped on a pair of blue jeans and a pullover sweater. He unpacked his generic sneakers, slipped them on, and headed out into the forest. Mary Parker was the first to notice him and immediately hailed him as he surveyed the area around him.

"David, David. Phil has scheduled a meeting for ten this evening. Prior to that, I'll be happy to show you around."

"This is the highlight of my trip, Mary. Please do."

"It will take us a good hour to walk around David and perhaps we can get you some food along the way if you like."

The communications tent was their first visit. Three desktop computers, ten mobile phone stations, a military radio transmitter-receiver, a CB base radio station and a large ham radio base were on-line and professionally maintained. A large gas-powered generator, professionally muffled, hummed somewhat noiselessly outside the tent giving power to the equipment inside. For the next forty-five minutes, David was astonished as he realized he was viewing a first-class military base of operation. Phil Redding and his veterans were well schooled in military tactics. Trip flares, laser sensors, underground weapons caches, and machine gun emplacement bunkers were in place, well concealed, and operational.

"David, this center is staffed twenty-four hours a day, seven days a week. In fact, this entire camp is operated in like fashion. We are all volunteers, and Phil's military expertise along with others has enabled us to perform in a very self-sufficient and efficient manner."

Phil Redding's arsenal included grenade launchers, antitank weapons, mortars, automatic weapons, and infrared devices for night vision. To his amazement, David was shown three missile-firing helicopters fully loaded and ready for action. Two mobile field kitchens were available and could handle two or three battalion-size military units in the field. David personally counted twenty-five military jeeps and three armored personnel carriers as he made his tour. America's very existence was at stake, and he thanked God there were groups such as this around the country who were ready to fight to save this great land. His country's leaders and politicians over the last number of years had been an embarrassment generally, and he could see here the real strength of America was to be found in the common man and woman. It was the average guy and gal who worked hard each day, the ones who never made the news headlines, the ones you never heard about, the "average American," as they were so often called. What a misnomer, David thought. Such a sick designation. Collectively, the average American represented a special greatness. The potential here was to fire once again some "shots" to be heard around the world as they were once before long ago at Lexington, Massachusetts.

Mary Parker advised David that it was about time for the meeting to be held. She led him off into the woods to a group of five young armed men who were casually resting under a huge California redwood tree. One of the young men quickly rose, and Mary introduced David to him. Jerry Parker, nineteen years old, was a lifelong resident of the Sacramento Valley. Ranger Baines knew his family well and had invited Jerry to the camp.

"Jerry, has the meeting started yet?"

"No, it hasn't. I know they are waiting for you, and they are waiting for General Williamson to arrive. We have been advised that he is in camp from South Carolina and should be here at the meeting place pretty soon now. I'll let you in."

Jerry led them a couple of steps behind the tree and reached down into the yellowed pine needles covering the ground and grabbed on to a wooden handle and deftly lifted up a camouflaged covering.

"I'll let you in the back way."

David smiled, and Mary quickly descended into the opening and climbed ten steps down a ladder. David was once again amazed, followed her, and found himself in a tunnel under the campgrounds. They traveled down a dimly lit passageway, and after three turns down adjoining passageways, they came into a well-lit large room that was staffed by five male and female veterans all clad in khaki clothing and seated behind respective desks. It reminded David of a typical office setting, and he paused for a moment to reflect if in fact he was seeing reality or instead still dreaming, fast asleep, in his tent above the ground.

"This way, David. We are here."

As Mary spoke, Phil Redding came through an adjacent doorway to greet them. They immediately entered an adjacent meeting room where a group of fourteen individuals had been assembled for this important meeting. David recognized Phil O'Dougherty, Al Sheldon, Anne Jones, Harold Baines, and Malcolm Hafid. As he carefully scrutinized the others, he could not recall any other familiar faces. Prior to the arrival of General Williamson, Phil made the proper introductions.

Monsignor Edmund McCarthy, a Catholic priest from Columbus, Ohio, had earned a reputation for being a rebel and was presently a priest without a parish. When the Catholic bishops had taken an active role in supporting the European monetary bailout, Monsignor McCarthy had grave reservations about it, and his church's continued support of European domination in America left a bitter taste in his mouth. When twelve months ago he began to voice his disapproval openly from the pulpit, he was quickly silenced by his bishop, and soon after he was removed from his parish responsibilities. He came to be a priest cut off from his church. Undaunted, he continued to voice his opposition whenever he could, and at this point in his life, he depended upon various Christians, whom he made members of his newly formed parish, for his existence. He was virtually penniless, and as far as the church was concerned, he was unemployed. Anne Jones had financed his trip west, and it was obvious his presence here held him in high esteem by those gathered here this evening.

Malcolm Hafid was introduced next. Born Jason Scott, at age 22, he became a member of the Muslim religion and changed his name to Malcolm Hafid. David knew him well and was pleased he was in attendance. At six feet seven inches tall, he had become one of the most prolific scorers in professional basketball sports history. He and David had become acquaintances during David's tenure as a congressman from Illinois.

Next was Roberta Blackwell from Dallas, Texas. She had earned quite a reputation in Texas politics. She was active in the Repub-Conservo Party and was well known for her organizational and fundraising skills. An attractive black woman, at age 49, she commanded respect and combined her natural Texas beauty with a keen political intelligence that kept her abreast of current events throughout the country as well as her home state of Texas. She was well acquainted with many of the movers and shakers in Washington, DC, and her influence was widespread.

John Walker was a successful businessman and political figure from Calgary, Canada. He helped lead the aggressive Canadian drive to remain independent from European controls over Canadian affairs. The Canadians had not survived unscathed following the American banking collapse. However, the tenacity to remain independent, due primarily to Mr. Walker and others, brought her through the trying times intact. It was not left unnoticed by the Europeans, and the British and French governments soon dissolved all their traditional ties with Canada.

"Fuck the rest of the world!" It was John Walker who'd hollered this openly in a publicly televised heated European Parliament discussion. Due to the efforts of Mr. Walker and several other of his colleagues, Canada passed through her crisis, and Hans Rizarre and Gustav Erikson decided to leave well enough alone. At this point, Canada presented no threat to Europe, and Europe had other more pressing matters at hand, especially the quiet takeover of America.

Following was John Lee and Davey Hardin from Detroit, Michigan. John Lee was a black leader in one of the economically depressed communities of Detroit. By the age of twenty-three, he had witnessed over eighteen murders in the tough ghetto environment. Streetwise and arrogant, he had somehow survived drug deals, street gang warfare, and a short stint as a high-rolling pimp. He finally saw the light after his two brothers and first cousin were murdered before his eyes in a blaze of gun fire in a drug deal that went bad. He was shot twice himself in the chest. Thanks to the miraculous work of three Detroit surgeons, he survived the massacre. It was while he lay in a hospital bed for four months that he turned his life around. Juanita Collas, a registered nurse, literally captured his soul and gave life new meaning for him. In fact, for the first time in his life, Johnny felt life was worth living, and Juanita convinced him that he still had time to live a quality life. Juanita had religious friends and through contacts, convinced Anne Jones to recruit Johnny for David Jefferson's movement. There was a great need for inner city leaders, and Johnny had fared extremely well in three previous interviews over the past six months.

Davey Hardin was a different story. Born and raised in the outer fringes of the big Detroit city, Davey was a twelve-year employee of Auto-Pro Motors Company. He had a reputation for being a star on the auto assembly line and being somewhat of a genius supervising the high-tech robotics running the production line. However, his great public notoriety stemmed from his activities in the bleacher section of professional baseball's Detroit Stadium. He was personally responsible for the closing of that section of the stadium on three different occasions. His outrageous public behavior was often on display at the ballpark. He thought nothing of throwing beer on ballplayers and fans and once was thrown out of the stadium for mooning everyone in general just to show his open disgust for a slumping Detroit baseball star. Although he was currently barred from the stadium, he was a hero of sorts to many Detroit sports spectators.

It was not difficult to see why America was in trouble. The signs were widespread. However, Jefferson's movement desperately needed help in the big cities. Despite being somewhat of an ass, Davey

Hardin wasn't all bad. He had been arrested twice in the last year for creating disturbances in the city but managed to avoid jail time and through good legal representation, was able to hold on to his job. He openly blasted the police and government officials in Detroit and told his coworkers they were producing automobiles and large profits for the "European Commies" and American elitists. He may not have been exactly on the mark, but he was a man who didn't hesitate to voice his convictions. His message was being heard, and just two weeks prior to this meeting, he barely escaped an assassination attempt upon his life when his prize automobile was blown to bits by an expertly placed car bomb. His girlfriend, Anita, turned the key and met her death that day. Davey went underground, and it took David Jefferson's contacts eight days to find him and secretly escort him west.

As the introductions were completed and seating for the meeting began, Jerry Parker entered the room with a military man of distinguished bearing, General Johnston Williamson, a South Carolinian by birth. He was presently commanding general of the Eighty-Second Airborne Division of the United Stated Army and was the highest-ranking recruiting effort of David Jefferson's long months of exhaustive and sometimes disappointing work.

Dressed in military khakis, at age 59, he was the epitome of military bearing. A 2002 graduate of West Point, an Iraq and Afghanistan distinguished veteran, a brilliant NATO tactician, he stood six feet three inches tall and was in the best of physical health. Although he was a major general and the commanding general of an airborne division, he knew he was on shaky ground if he considered directing troops in contradiction to orders from Washington, DC. No American military leader who had any sense at all had contemplated it in recent history. At least not since the American Civil War had any dared think it.

General Williamson was quickly introduced to all present, and Phil Redding started the meeting by asking Father McCarthy to lead them in prayer. With bowed heads, they listened to the monsignor beseech the Almighty to assist them in their great quest to keep

America a free land. The prayer was short and to the point, and Phil Redding once again stood at the rostrum in front of the group.

"Gentlemen and gentlewomen, the purpose of this meeting is to establish immediate plans and operational goals to actively rid the American continent of European domination. We have established the following obstacles that face us. First and foremost, our government in Washington is bound by signed agreements, incorporated and amended into our Constitution as emergency amendments that bind us to European control. The Europeans monitor all of our banking policies. They control and guarantee all of our federal loans and debts. They mandate all of our military expenditures and oversee the entire United States budget. They are now attempting to control all of our mobile, cell phone, and internet communications.

"Secondly, our president and Congress continue to rubber-stamp all types of legislation recommended by Hans Rizarre and Gustav Erikson. Most of this legislation is designed to control the movements of American citizens. For example, it is no longer legal for Americans to bear arms in public or private. It is no longer lawful for more than six citizens to gather for any kind of meeting without a local police permit. It is no longer lawful for newspaper editors to editorialize in their respective daily newspapers without first advising their local government leaders of the content of their editorials.

"The list goes on and on. It is also evident that many Americans are going along with these restrictions. Remember, the refusal to cooperate ultimately means the loss of one's job. We are going to have to combat the greed that helped get us in this mess to begin with. We are not talking of a fully united effort to overthrow a completely foreign element. We are at the least talking of what will be labeled by many as partaking in a second revolution, a second civil war. It will be primarily at first Americans against Americans and occupying foreign troops and personnel. General Williamson has offered to join us and will give us meaningful insights in regard to what we may expect in terms of resistance. It is imperative that we allow all of us here to speak and then listen to what the general has to say. Monsignor McCarthy, will you begin please?"

"Thank you, Mr. Redding. It is my desire to bring you as up to date as I possibly can on the activities of the church in America. There is now a widespread coalition of American church groups, in particular, Baptists, Lutherans, Catholics, and other Protestant Christian churches, who have joined together to assist the European effort. They base their support primarily on the decrees of the last Vatican and Ecumenical Council convened in Rome, Italy, just last year. Although Pope Veritatis I was an active participant, it has become obvious that the individual who was most instrumental behind the scenes was an Italian cardinal by the name of Antonio Rondanelli. It had been rumored and just lately verified that he is a close personal associate of Hans Rizarre, the present president of the Republic of Europe. During the Council, he was observed wining and dining the American church officials who were in attendance. I understand many promises were made, and it is easy to see why our current church leaders will resist our efforts. It will not be an easy task to convince all of America's church going worshippers to actively resist when they will hear some of their own priests and reverends counseling otherwise. But I can guarantee you this. I have had many discussions with my previous clergy colleagues, and many will be praying for us, and several have joined our efforts and are currently assisting us behind the scenes. I believe we have a lot of support there. That is all I wish to report for now. Just don't underestimate the power of the one called Cardinal Rondanelli. It is now rumored that he is actively seeking the papacy when Veritatis I steps down. However, the present pope is only sixty-three, and to all accounts he is in good health. Thank you."

David Jefferson was quick to respond.

"I believe the problem with the churches is the same as the one we have with our government. So many of our church leaders have failed us, and I believe that many people are beginning to realize this. There are a lot of fine clergies like Father McCarthy we need to turn to. It is apparent the church may be led by some people who could be said to be misguided, and misled themselves. It is my utmost belief that most Americans aspire to a better way for us, and that righteous moral conduct is not dead in the hearts and souls of most Americans.

"Phil, it won't be necessary for Johnny Lee and Davey Hardin to speak this evening. They both agreed to help us organize in the city of Detroit. They were invited here this evening to learn of the seriousness of our plans and will spend the next two weeks with the veterans and volunteers here before we return them to Detroit. We now have identified fourteen camps such as Camp Liberty in various parts of the country. None are as fine as this one we have here, but they are all located in rural areas, have connecting underground operations, and are as remote as possible. We need development such as this in the inner cities. Right now, we are going to start addressing this need."

As Phil thanked David for his remarks, he hastened to introduce Malcom Hafid next. At age 27, he was an athlete in prime condition. He had met David Jefferson when David was a congressman from Champaign, Illinois. Malcolm had been an All-American at the University of Illinois and on more than a couple of occasions, had attended fundraising affairs for the congressman when he held his seat there in Champaign. Upon graduation, he was drafted by the Washington High-Flyers of professional basketball. Playing pro ball in Washington, DC, gave Malcolm the opportunity to visit David often. Both "Fighting Illini," they developed a friendship and visited each other often whenever their busy schedules allowed.

"I'm well aware of and very familiar with the plans being discussed here. I've actually discussed them at length with Mr. Jefferson on various occasions. Because of the great popularity of pro sports in America, I have the opportunity to travel freely around the country. All of our sporting activities are in the major cities and urban areas, and I will spread the word whenever I can. There are others in the profession who are with me on this. We must be very careful. Due to the high salaries we receive, there are not too many of us ready to give that up at the moment. I am very interested in hearing what Mr. Walker from Canada and Ms. Blackwell from Texas have to say concerning this."

With this, John Walker addressed the group.

"Good evening, all. As you know, we Canadians have weathered our storm with the Europeans thus far. It has not been without great sacrifice. We have been excluded from trading in the world market, and if it were not for the Japanese and Chinese and the large American black-market underground trading with us, we would be in a desperate situation. I have been directed by our Canadian government to appear here officially to give you our support and to let you know where Canada stands. Our country has decided to place great emphasis in our country on agriculture and family farming. We encourage Americans to concentrate on family farming in as many areas as possible. As your revolution continues to grow in earnest, you will be cut off from the rest of the world. Your friends in Canada will be ready to supply you with seed and fertilizers. Believe me, there will be no problem getting back and forth across our borders. We feel we have complete control in this area, and we can move people, supplies, munitions, and whatever you need almost at will along several remote checkpoints we have established.

"One of the biggest disappointments for us Canadians has been the United States government's alliance with the Europeans. Your government has agreed with every sanction and every embargo placed upon us by the Europeans. We know we have many friends in America. You must know that the Canadians are your friends. We feel for you, we have shed tears for you, we bleed for you. My government has sent me here in an official capacity to let you know this. Our message to the American people is simple: North America must not fall. We are all brothers and sisters here, and we must stand together. Canada stands ready to assist our friends in America, and we will do all we possibly and humanly can to protect the very last bastions of freedom remaining on the planet. The concept of free men directing their governments shall not die. Have we returned to the Dark Ages, when men were at the mercy of their leaders? We simply cannot let it happen.

"I understand Ms. Blackwell can advise us on the latest feelings in Washington as to what the current line of thinking is among the congressional leaders there. Ms. Blackwell, can you enlighten us please?"

"Well, even though the situation is quite bleak, let me wish you all a good evening. The majority of our elected representatives are handpicked men who tow their party line. Since the European bailout, an individual can't even be nominated for any kind of public office unless he passes selective screening by the National Party Committees which sit in Washington. Ever since we allowed the Europeans to finance our election system, their people have virtually taken over the nominating and selection process. Those few who have slipped through the cracks, such as me, can't come close to achieving any kind of majority vote on anything that is vital to us. Quite honestly, the few good ones, such as David Jefferson, have left office and dropped out of the system. Those men and women presently in power will fight strongly to maintain their positions. They are nothing more than chief executives in the employ of a foreign government. I do have sympathetic friends scattered throughout the bureaucracy, but they fear for their positions and for the most part live in a closed Washington society cut off from the rest of the country.

"I will say that when I look at the state of Texas, the situation is more promising. Although there is apparent cooperation with the federal authorities, it is only for survival's sake. There is open criticism of what is going on, and when we get down to the local level, there is open hostility and a growing unrest over a bad situation. The slaughter in New York has not sat well with the local folks. You are on target when you point out that our hope lies in the rural areas, with the average citizens. I think it is safe to say that we may be close to rousing a sleeping giant there. However, we must be careful to protect our people. The wrath and fury of Washington will be quick and vengeful. I would say the police tactics that occurred in New York can be expected to be the normal response to any kind of resistance. We must plan our actions carefully and protect our people as best we can. However, we cannot sit and do nothing. It is obvious the time for action is now. Thank you."

As Ms. Blackwell. moved to her seat, General Johnston L. Williamson strode briskly to the rostrum. He gave the appearance of a man worried but also of one who could look trouble in the face and cope with it in a rational vein.

"I must say that I am overwhelmed by what I've been introduced to here at Camp Liberty. As a career soldier dedicated to the highest principles of conduct, I have spent a few weeks following my latest meeting with David Jefferson soul searching in an attempt to rationalize the decisions of our leaders in Washington. I've always tried to feel that they were acting in the best interests of this country. Quite honestly, I have had my doubts. But now I have seen firsthand the threat that is upon us. I thought it was too late to do anything about it. Then I met Mr. Jefferson through a mutual acquaintance, and although I still fear we may be too late, he has raised a new hope within me. My military intelligence sources advised me that the European military no longer considers us a viable military threat. In fact, they are concentrating their energies on new ways of competing against the Russians and the Chinese. The frightening information we have obtained is the European military's beliefs that it is in their best interest to completely neutralize America by the use of specially targeted nuclear devices if they have to engage in a warlike situation, rather than commit troops, time, and energy in America. They can better utilize those resources deployed on the European continent. This message has been conveyed to our congressional leaders, and this policy is clearly akin to nuclear blackmail. We have no retaliatory options. They have defused our missiles over twelve months ago. Of course, the American public is not aware of this, and the knowledge of this by only our top congressional leaders furthers their compliance with European directives. In their own minds now, by complying with the foreigners, they are protecting American citizens from a nuclear holocaust. It is a very complex situation that could clearly demoralize the entire North American continent if word of this should leak out. We are in one way existing in a very hopeless situation. In spite of this, in faith we must go on. I say 'in faith' because I don't believe there is anything else. Also I just learned earlier today on my way here another bit of depressing news. Next month, new coins are being issued from the United States Mints. The motto 'In God we trust' will no longer be stamped upon any of our coins. There is an overwhelming contradiction in a European Republic that literally spends millions of public relations dollars telling the world of its ties with Christianity, then in a very inconspicuous subtle political decision, decides to drop the name of God from newly minted coins. Something is rotten in Denmark, people—excuse me, in Stuttgart. I don't think we should wait any longer to find out exactly what that is. 'In God we trust' is all we have left. I believe it is our last option. Keeping that in mind, we must go forward—much in the same way as David when he slew Goliath, much in the same way as Moses when he parted the seas. It is in this faith and in this faith only that we shall be stirred to action and be saved."

Suddenly the meeting was interrupted as Jerry Parker came racing through the door.

"Colonel Redding, there has been a shooting. We just had an intrusion alarm in the northeast sector. Bluejay 1 Group and Bluejay 2 Group have advised they have neutralized the area, sir."

Phillip Redding bolted upright in his chair. He had never been eager to face crisis situations that he knew sooner or later would have to be met. He had faced enough death and destruction in Iraq and Afghanistan. It always sickened him. The men and woman of Camp Liberty were very special to him, and he dreaded the day when they would have to come face-to-face with evil to protect a right they were born with.

"General, please come with us. The rest of you will remain here. We have duplicated under the ground what we have topside. You will be very safe here. This is our most secure area. It is hopeful that this is an isolated incident and that the affected zone has been neutralized."

Colonel Redding, General Williamson, and Jerry Parker immediately headed out the door. David Jefferson was right behind them. Phil Redding quickly stopped him.

"David, you must stay here. We will not allow ourselves to expose you unnecessarily at this point."

As David began to object, Phillip gently turned him around stating there would be no further discussion. As three other armed men appeared and joined the colonel, it was obvious that the colonel would not be swayed, and David rejoined the others to await whatever news would arrive from above."

As the group gathered in the rear of the room to wait the return of their comrades, Phil O'Dougherty began to explain to them the current difficulty the media in his area of central and upstate New York were facing and the difficulty of getting the truth in print to the citizens. The only real truth was being distributed by outlawed underground newspapers. He and a group of ten others operating in upstate New York were doing their best to supply people with the realities of European influence in America. He spoke in glowing terms of Utica, New York, and the historic Mohawk Valley. It was in this area that some of our country's earliest patriots had shed their blood in the struggle for America's first battle for independence. He and his colleagues, with their Associated Press credentials, were able to travel around freely enough to find those who would assist them in getting information to the people. Their own editors couldn't print or publish the truth, so these men sought out those who would.

Mr. O'Dougherty spoke of Camp New York, much like Camp Liberty, that was located up in the Adirondack Mountains of New York State. He said it wasn't quite up to the same standards as here at Liberty, but it was close. He told a story of six off-duty Utica, New York, firemen and two off-duty Utica, New York, policemen who rescued him one night as he approached the camp. Two security personnel had followed him out of Syracuse, New York, on orders as he drove into the Adirondack foothills to deliver sensitive publications to one of their contacts at the camp. These men from Syracuse were now lying dead at the bottom of Raquette Lake. The off-duty Uticans swooped out of the hills, and the secret of the Adirondacks remained safe for the moment. This had happened just two months ago, and the seriousness of it sobered the listening group as they pondered the developments that were taking place at this very moment aboveground as they sat there talking.

Colonel Redding departed from his jeep as they arrived at Grindstone Creek in the northeast sector at exactly 12:20 a.m. He found John Ortiz and Harold Baines standing over the bullet-riddled body of a middle-aged man. Ranger Baines spoke first.

"Colonel, his papers and identification show him to be a detective from Sacramento."

He handed the fallen man's badge and ID to the colonel.

"Bob Callahan and Justin Wolcott challenged him when he came across Grindstone Creek. He showed his badge and said he was working a missing person case and had a lead that a certain Martha Schaffer might be found up in the Mendocino National Forest.

"Martha is one of our volunteers in camp and from Sacramento. She joined us about three months ago. I think someone got careless passing information, sir. Anyhow the boys told him they never heard of her and treated the man with respect. They showed no weapons, and the man seemed satisfied enough. For some reason, we don't know why, he pulled his service revolver. He didn't say anything, and we really don't know if he meant to do anything or not, but it was dark, and we had five men in the trees watching him. The men couldn't take any chances with the general in camp and the meeting going on. They opened up with automatic weapons and put him to rest. We found his car about a half mile east of the creek. His radio was off, so we don't think he was actively communicating with anyone. We have been monitoring the radio ever since, and there have been no unusual communications. We notified our communications center to monitor that frequency he was tuned to for the next couple of days and maintain a running log on it."

"Thank you, Major. I need you to bring up one of the semi-trailers and load up that car. I want it deposited as near Yuba City as possible by daylight. Use one of the federal trucks and then take his body and bury it back in the woods. I want him six feet deep if possible, and I want it done right. Have Father McCarthy picked up and brought over to say a prayer over the grave. He might have been okay, but the men were right, we can't afford to take any chances whatsoever."

"General Williamson, I don't know what to say, but this is it… the reality of where we are at."

"Colonel, you needn't say anything. There are no gray areas to our struggle. There is a clear-cut right way and a wrong way. We have no time to contemplate the gray zone. Mankind has spent centuries mired in assessing gray area. We have not the luxury nor the time to waste expending our energies in such fruitless meditation. All our little time left is valuable. I concur with your decisions here."

With that General Williamson and Colonel Redding were driven back to the campgrounds by Jerry Parker to report back to their assembled guests. As they arrived, the colonel advised Jerry to contact Major Baines and have him double the guards and put the entire camp on alert until further notice. Colonel Redding and General Williamson then had three armed volunteers escort them to the underground tunnel and rejoined their associates in the meeting room to fill them in all the details of what had just transpired.

The next two hours were spent in finishing up the meeting and allowing everyone to give input to the group. Shortly after 4:00 a.m. it was decided that it was time to end the discussions, and everyone retired to their respective areas to get some much-needed sleep. The morning would be a good time to reassemble and make sure everyone was up to date on what was going on.

Chapter 4

Do what you can, with what you have, where you are.

—Theodore Roosevelt

Dawn broke early on the twenty-fifth of September in the forest. David Jefferson rose early with the sun. Perhaps it was the excitement of the previous two days, or perhaps it was because he had to head back east this day, he wasn't sure, but he didn't sleep well, and as the sun rose in the east, he was up and about the camp. Anne Jones was leaving at 10:00 a.m., and he wished to meet with her prior to her departure.

A somewhat mysterious man known only as Mr. Jones had arrived in camp late last night, and he and Anne had disappeared into the night. He knew this Mr. and Mrs. Jones thing was a calculated ruse to protect identities. He knew Anne Jones was not married and had been working with Mr. Jones at the request of the US government. It frustrated him enormously over the last few months that whenever he was conversing with her, this mystery man would appear and rush her away. Anyhow, he needed to see her before she left. Her contacts with sympathetic followers throughout the country were as widespread as his. He felt it was necessary to coordinate between the various groups as much as possible. Now that he knew the Canadians were officially behind him and supported his plans, the possibilities for a successful movement were suddenly quite feasible. He was cautious with his optimism, but there appeared to be somewhat of a light at the end of this nightmare tunnel he felt trapped in.

With the camp still on an alert status, all major activities were being conducted underground, and David found Anne in the dining area having breakfast with General Williamson, Colonel Redding, Major Baines, and Mr. Jones. David went through the serving line and helped himself to generous portions of scrambled eggs, bacon, and toast. He accepted a cup of coffee from a young female posted at the end of the line. Surprised by her youth, he asked her name.

"Sally Watkins."

She replied with the exuberance of her youth. She could not have been more than seventeen years old, thought David.

"Mr. Baines is my uncle. As of last week, we have moved into camp permanently. We are sharing an underground bunker with two other families over at the Lassen Forest site. It's nothing like our home over in Red Bluff, but our whole family is committed to Colonel Redding in his fight to save the country. Red Bluff is a pretty quiet place, but we wanted to be here to help. We locked the house up and left. Mom is over in the kitchen area right now helping to cook and prepare meals. She gets off at 10:00 a.m., and then she is going on guard duty at 10:00 p.m. With the alert on, we are all working in twelve-hour shifts."

David thanked her and went to join his associates at their table.

"Anything new develop, Phil?"

"No, David. I did receive word back from the men that they were successful in delivering the detective's car just east of Yuba City early this morning. I am sure it will be found soon. His department may have known he was heading for the forest, but we want them to believe he never got this far. We have a few contacts on the Sacramento Police Department, so we will be pumping them for information as soon as possible. In the meantime, we are taking extra special precautions. John Walker has left already for Canada. He tells me I can have five more choppers down here in two weeks' time. We are going to use Interstate 5 north to Mount Shasta, then we'll utilize US 97 the rest of the way to the border."

David was not at all surprised by the quick cooperation of the Canadians. They had been slowly pushing for the past year for an American resistance movement. They knew America must save itself, but boy, were they ready to help.

"Well, Phil, in a couple of months, we'll all be hunted men. The important thing is that we strike out all over the country. We don't want any one group taking all the heat. Anne, I think it is important you get the word out to your people. I know some of your people believe in passive resistance and nonviolence for the most part. Just let them know we need their help. Hide us out, feed us, clothe us, whenever you can. I think it will sometimes possibly be brother against brother. We may not always know who the enemy really is. We have set November 19 as the date to begin. It will be the 177th anniversary of Abraham Lincoln's Gettysburg Address. Lincoln ended his address by stating that "government of the people, by the people, for the people shall not perish from the earth." Over the next six weeks, I'll be visiting as many of our camps around the country as I can to assist in preparing for that date. General Williamson will poll his airborne troops to see how many of them wish to join us and on the nineteenth will be with as many of them as possible along with Lyle Swansen somewhere just east of Gadsden, Alabama. If it is at all possible, we'll assassinate President Carlson that day as well. I intend to be up in the Adirondack Mountains that date helping to direct activities up there. We sincerely hope it will be a short-lived revolution. We will need a united effort when the Europeans strike back at us. There is no doubt that they will. I am hoping, Anne, that between now and then, you can travel around as much as you can and help put the word out."

At age 45, Anne Jones had matured into a breathtakingly beautiful woman. She was the kind of lady that caused heads to turn as she walked into a room. She combined her natural beauty with intelligence and charming wit. She possessed a quiet strength that earned her the respect and confidence of those who knew her. Her dedication to humanitarian causes allowed her to move in circles that were largely nonpolitical. Her secret to success in these endeavors had largely been the result of the earnestness of her convictions. She was personally responsible for organizing fundraising activities that brought much-needed relief to hard pressed areas throughout Third World countries where people were suffering from famine, drought, or some similar disaster. Not one to seek notoriety she somehow managed to stay pretty much in the background during these varied projects.

Primarily due to her low-key approach, Anne was able to accomplish much with those movers and shakers who preferred to operate in this same fashion. Because the motivations of her group transcended politics, her influence with politicians throughout the world was great because of the strong need of politicians to be associated with such powerful causes. Indeed, David Jefferson's own motives were guided by this very approach, and he only hoped that his cause was construed as being sufficient of merit so as to earn the respect and support of humankind everywhere. True he had opted for the sword, and if he had to die by it, then let it be. He believed in God, and the Ancient Bible book that he read was full of Old Testament men who hurled mighty swords with the blessing of God Almighty. If it was true "the meek shall inherit the earth," he was ready to sacrifice his own life to rid the planet of all the assholes on it so the meek could reside in peace. He could rest easy in his grave if he could help to achieve this.

Anne spoke to him quietly and firmly, "David, it will not be necessary to travel anywhere to put out the word. You underestimate the merits of your own cause and the people of this country you propose to represent. The day we strike will be the day you pick up the heavy yoke that burdens us all. Don't misinterpret passiveness to violent actions as a sign of weakness. It is filled with the strength of the ages, and if it is the Lord's work you are about, then get on with it. Everything else will fall into place. I think perhaps Mr. Jones could make a statement in regard to this. He has been anxious for some time to speak to the man called David Jefferson. The fact that General Williamson is with us this morning makes the occasion even more meaningful. Mr. Jones, please."

The so-called Mr. Jones struck a handsome figure. At first glance, he appeared younger than the forty-seven years he was thought to be. A close deep look, however, into his eyes found a man perhaps many years older than one dared to think. His slightly graying hair blended well into his still somewhat youthful dark brown mane. There was a certain wisdom in those eyes. You could see it clearly when you caught his gaze. When he spoke, it was as if he was otherworldly, opening his soul to communicate with you.

"David, my friend, believe me, it is not I who communicate this message to you. I have been directed to pass this message on to you. You sit now with a great General at your side. You have but a short time to work your plan. The time is right, and your friends are greater than you think. You are destined to lead a modern-day chosen people that is burdened by its own treachery. The Great One weeps tears over the folly of His children. There is only one path for you to take. All the souls of your ancestors past cry out for you to act. The road will surely be difficult, but how can you take any other path? Is your planet to be overrun by parasites and scum who believe to be bold and violent as wolves in the sheep pen?

"You need to be as a lion, David Jefferson. Take up your sword and cut a righteous path. Who can deny truth and virtuous action? Heated lead thrown by evil men can tear and rip flesh asunder. However, a powerful spirit as you can move mountains that will bury such dealers of death forever under the mighty will of a populous that merely wishes peace.

"Open your eyes, Jefferson. Do you not see Earth's young children, so innocent, living around you? How long will you allow them to be abused? The Great One hears your morning prayers. He hears the cries and pleadings. How often has He heard thusly, 'O God in heaven, how long will You let us suffer? When will we see Your vengeance wreaked upon our enemies?'

"Who among you has pondered the opposite? Perhaps our God utters the very same—'How long will you suffer yourselves to such misery? You can be as I. Take up your responsibility and seek My vengeance and deliver your own message of truth. You live in a land founded upon justice and solid foundation. Familiarize yourself with the document of your country's birth. It is the essence of a dream I still dream for you. Robots you are not. Take up your own burden and raise your brethren up. Rise up into the clouds, Jefferson, and take a look down from afar. The light-years that separate us are but a step when you perceive the right vision. Our universe can't tolerate or live when scum scarred hypocrites are allowed a free rein. Have faith, David. Let your lions loose.'"

The man called Mr. Jones signaled that he was finished for the moment. He reached over, shook David's hand, and quietly sat down next to Anne. The tone of his voice had been for the most part rather soft spoken but in an eerie way seemingly spoken as if from another world. The strength of the message was so loud that now a strange silence filled the room.

Phil Redding gathered himself together and quickly adjourned the group. As Mr. and Mrs. Jones bid their farewells and made preparations to depart Camp Liberty, David Jefferson and Johnston Williamson returned to their respective rooms to contemplate the breakfast discussion that had somehow reached into the deepest recesses of their souls. Mr. Jones somehow had cut through the informalities that usually accompany such gatherings. His message had somehow been directed toward each man personally. The awesomeness of their mission had been brought to light in a forthright fashion. It was as if some spirit being had just delivered to them a personal message. Each man thought his faith was strong. It was so easy to voice it, to express it to others. Now weak at the knees from the directed message, each man had to reinforce his great faith with sufficient action. Verbose expression was suddenly a thing of the past, supportive action to reinforce these words was a thing of the future. Each man hoped he was up to the task at hand.

Chapter 5

> As the end of the world approaches, the condition of
> human affairs must undergo a change and, through
> the prevalence of wickedness, become worse.
>
> —Book vii, the Divine Institutes, page 463

October 1, 2040
Venice, Italy

More than 150 canals take the place of streets on the islands of Venice, Italy and boats provide transportation. Black flat-bottomed boats called gondolas serve as Venice's chief means of transportation. Small wooden boats called topettas can be used in traveling about the canals on the 120 islands that make up the historic city. Today Cardinal Antonio Rondanelli beamed with delight as his ten-foot topetta driven by his chauffer, Roberto, pulled away from St. Mark's Cathedral. Adorned with a colorful St. Marks banner and bright red cardinal flags, the motorized topetta commanded attention as it traveled the canals of Venice. Cardinal Rondanelli had yearned for some time to come to Saint Mark's. Named for St. Mark the Evangelist, whose remains are kept there, it had remained to this date as one of the finest examples of Byzantine architecture in all of western Europe. Tony took great pride in having offered mass in such an historic place. The fact that just a few faithful were present didn't detract from the event. It was his desire to offer mass in as many holy places as possible. He was obsessed with it as a vile man who notches his wall following each woman he takes to bed. Tony Rondanelli faithfully recorded in his diary each holy place he desecrated. The joy of it was that only he knew what he was about. To fly in the face of God, he enjoyed it so. This was all in preparation for the day when he would offer mass in the Jewish temple in Jerusalem, if it ever be built in his lifetime. This would be the greatest coup. His body shivered as he contemplated the desired event.

"Your Eminence, if I'm correct, we are now in route to a 10:00 a.m. breakfast meeting at the Doge's Palace. His Eminence, Cardinal Reese from America, and Bishop Arcuri of Venice await your arrival."

"That is correct Roberto. I might remind you that you will also need to transport me to the private villa at 9:00 p.m. I will be on a holiday the following day, and you should pick me up at 10:00 a.m. the following day after that. I shall be waiting your arrival at the main portico."

"Most certainly, Your Eminence. I shall be prompt as always."

Tony was doubly ecstatic this day. His closest and dearest friend, Hans Adolph Rizarre was arriving from Stuttgart later in the evening to spend two nights and a day with him. The trip by Hans to Venice was extremely secretive in nature and known only by Tony and a few of Han's closest associates. As president of the republic, it was difficult for Hans to travel without the European Press being aware of his movements. However, when he so chose, Hans did anything he so desired, and his aides responded to his wishes or they weren't his aides anymore. Hans and Tony had much to discuss. The last few years had brought to fulfillment their greatest expectations. They both were close to achieving their long sought-after goals. Soon, they would rule the world. Tony thought of Jesus Christ's third temptation in the desert:

> Again, the devil taketh him up into an exceeding high mountain, and showeth him all the kingdoms of the world, and the glory of them; And saith unto Him, All these things will I give thee, if thou wilt fall down and worship me. Then saith Jesus unto him, Get thee hence, Satan: for it is written, Thou shalt worship the

Lord thy God, and Him only shalt thou serve.
(Matthew 4:8–10 KJV)

Tony was glad Jesus declined the offer. Now he and Hans were actively seeking the opportunity. Their private worship sessions to Satan were only known by the two of them. Success had followed them through the years, and Tony felt they were approaching the mountaintop.

"Your Eminence, the Doge's Palace. May God go with you."

"Bless you, Roberto. May His blessings be upon you and your family as well."

As the cardinal departed from his colorful topetta, a cadre of cassocked young priests bowed and greeted him, and Roberto was off to change out the topetta for the cardinal's official automobile. The young priests quickly escorted him into the majestic edifice. This Italian Gothic palace had served as the residence of the rulers of the Republic of Venice, Queen of the Adriatic, and the seat of the government. Its walls and ceilings were decorated with frescos by Tintoretto and Veronese. Masterpieces of the Italian Renaissance adorned the walls throughout its hallowed chambers.

Cardinal Reese and Bishop Arcuri greeted Cardinal Rondanelli in a private area of the visiting section of the Doge Apartments. They had reserved three tables in the southeast corner to ensure privacy, and two young priests sat nearby sipping coffee to make sure there would be no unnecessary interruptions. As a master of many languages, in fluent English Tony Rondanelli began to speak.

"And how is my dear friend from America? Bishop Arcuri has spoken of you with the utmost respect and praise. We are most pleased to have you as a guest here in Europe."

"I am most grateful for your generous hospitality, Your Eminence. It has been a very positive trip so far. I love your Italy so much. I wish I could stay longer, but I will be returning to America in a couple of days."

"Yes, the good bishop here has informed me that you visited for the past two days with our Holy Father, Veritatis I. I expect all went well."

Cardinal Rondanelli knew very well from his papal sources of the two-day secret sessions between Cardinal Reese and Veritatis I. The secrecy surrounding the meetings was unusual, and Tony was intent on finding out what went on. The primary purpose for his attending this breakfast meeting was to attempt to learn what had transpired if he could.

"As a matter of fact, things really couldn't have gone any better than they did. His Holiness has made a commitment to the American church. He will make a public statement tomorrow for release to the American press. Primarily I am here to ask you to intercede on our behalf. I know of your close association with President Rizarre, and we need his support if we expect our program to succeed."

Tony calmly hid his alarm over Cardinal Reese's remarks. He had met the man once only briefly during the last Ecumenical Council meeting held in Rome. He had been supportive of measures favoring the European situation. He was largely an unknown bishop then, and Tony was surprised Veritatis I elevated him to the rank of cardinal six months ago. He was based in Chicago, Illinois, and had been a most uncontroversial figure since assuming his new duties.

"Certainly, you exaggerate my influence with the great president of the European Republic. It is true we have had dealings through the years. Of course, they were of political necessity, and it is also true we have always successfully worked things out. The church has benefitted from these ventures through God's intercession, I am sure."

Cardinal Reese overlooked Cardinal Rondanelli's apparent modesty and pursued his case.

"God surely does work in mysterious ways, my dear cardinal. Your humble attitude speaks well for you. It is just this attitude that we need to present America's case right now. As you know, our country is greatly troubled at the moment. Surely you are aware of the recent murder of so many of our people in New York City. We have received quite an outcry from our church members at home. At first, of course, the reaction was that the police were very justified in silencing an unruly mob. The American clergy dutifully voiced this opinion from thousands of pulpits immediately following this episode. The problem now is that the sheep are not following the shepherds.

Each week that passes brings us news of other different episodes. Although they don't compare to New York, the unrest of our people is becoming obvious. The purpose of my meetings with His Holiness has been to express these concerns and to see if the church in Rome can assist to help ease the current situation. His Holiness has agreed to publicly state that perhaps Europe should take another look at the American situation. Perhaps it would be to everyone's benefit if certain restrictions were eased and certain taxes cut back."

Tony hid his alarm at what he was hearing but knew the American cardinal was treading on dangerous ground. This prelate was obviously taking his job way too seriously.

"Cardinal Rondanelli, we were hoping that you might be able to reach out to President Rizarre. Perhaps you could convince him to initiate some type of compromise or at the least give some public consideration to the proposal Veritatis I will offer. It is imperative we calm the unrest in America. We feel it will be beneficial to both our countries."

Cardinal Rondanelli paused and breathed deeply before he spoke.

"My dear Cardinal Reese, your proposal merits praise. You are surely about the work of God. The courage of Veritatis I bespeaks of a man truly inspired. I am in awe of your efforts."

Cardinal Reese and Bishop Arcuri smiled approvingly. The reaction of Cardinal Rondanelli was more than they had hoped for. Despite Tony's modesty in regard to his association with President Rizarre, rumors in church circles indicated quite the contrary. A favorable response by Cardinal Rondanelli could spell success to almost any project. Cardinal Rondanelli picked up his coffee and eyed the two churchmen opposite him as he slowly sipped some of the finest espresso in all of Venice. He would have to deal with this development quickly.

"Gentlemen, I am pleased to be of such service. Rest assured that I will use my contacts to further the goals of the church. Of course, I can make no promises. Just keep me in your prayers, and I will do my part. I am sorry I must cut this meeting short. I have rather urgent matters to take care of."

Cardinal Reese squeezed Bishop Arcuri by the arm in an affectionate manner.

"God be with you, Your Eminence. The saints in heaven shall sing your praise."

"You are much too kind, Father. However, I must ask you both to make a certain commitment to me. I wish no one to know of our meeting here today. It is imperative that you maintain complete silence on any part I might play in this. I insist upon it. Any mention of it could damage my credibility with President Rizarre. These politicians are very sensitive people and many times difficult to deal with. Also, Bishop Arcuri, I wish the names of the two young prelates who are sitting guard for us over there. I also expect their secrecy with respect to this meeting."

"Certainly, Your Eminence. They are part of my staff, and I will telephone their names into your office today. You can fully expect our cooperation in regards to anything you ask."

Satisfied with the response, Tony stood up and made preparations to leave.

"Your Eminence, I trust that Bishop Arcuri will host you properly on your last day in Venice. I must return to my humble duties, and I pray that God goes with you on your journey back to America."

Cardinal Reese beamed with gratitude as he bid farewell.

"Bishop Arcuri will be staying with me at the Airport Sheraton, and we will be giving praise for your assistance. May God go with you."

The two churchmen stared in awe as Cardinal Rondanelli departed escorted by the two young priests who were dutifully assigned this task by Bishop Arcuri. If only all the members of the church hierarchy acted as such, thought Cardinal Reese, the world would be so much better. He hoped that one day he could cast on an affirmative vote to help elevate this great man to the papacy.

Cardinal Rondanelli hurriedly made his way to the lobby of the Doge's and hailed his loyal chauffer. Roberto quickly laid down his newspaper and dashed off to retrieve the cardinal's rental car. As Tony awaited, he pondered the significance of the meeting that just took place. His Holiness Veritatis I was venturing into the realm of politics. The pope could very well bump heads with the president of the European Republic over this. The formation of the European Republic had been the most recent attempt in history to restore what was known as the Holy Roman Empire. The idea of a pope interfering in the affairs of state was nothing new to the Empire. Since Pope Gregory VII came to the papal throne in 1703 the struggle for dominant power and influence had been a struggle that caused great friction between the Roman Catholic Church and European states throughout the enduring centuries. Pope Gregory had once declared, "The pope is the master of emperors."

This concept of church and state has been carried to the present day. The struggle has evolved into a clear-cut compromise between the two with well-defined areas and parameters established. A most important concept had been passed on throughout history. The theme and ultimate realization of European unity is well founded and rests upon the basis of common religious heritage. Since 1945, every sitting Catholic pope has given his endorsement to political moves that called for a supranational European community. Early on in his papacy. Pope Veritatis I uttered the following in regard to European unity when he emphasized the, "Values which are sacred to all Europe."

It is sufficient to say this history was long and varied. Cardinal Antonio Franciscus Rondanelli was on record as being against any kind of new schism between church and state. It was his personal ambition that one day soon that he be the one to place an emperor's crown upon the head of Hans Rizarre and permanently establish the link between the church in Rome and the Empire once again. Nothing would stand in his way to achieve this—nothing.

"Your Eminence."

Roberto was heard hollering and waving from the Doge's doorway. Cardinal Rondanelli departed the ancient edifice and as the sleek rented Mercedes automobile pulled away the two young black cassocks bowed in reverence.

"Roberto, take me straight to the villa. Drop me off there, and you will pick me up as I have previously instructed two days from now."

"Yes, Your Eminence, as you have instructed."

As the villa was located approximately thirty miles northwest of the city near Cazzaro, the rural setting was ideal for Tony's somewhat bizarre activities that he conducted there. His nearest neighbor was a mile and a half away, and he maintained a staff of two very devoted followers to oversee the premises. The surrounding thirty acres of land was fenced with chain link topped with barbed wire. Six trained Doberman dogs roamed the grounds, and there were never any problems with intruders. The villa itself was a three-story, twenty-room edifice constructed in the 1930s. It somehow survived World War II sustaining only minor damage and had undergone extensive rehabilitation. At one time, it was a favorite haunt for German and Italian military generals who thought it was best suited to their needs. Tony had purchased the property in 2025 utilizing church funds that were earmarked for other projects. Using an assumed name, he transacted a private deal and purchased the property with cash. It had served since then as a private hideaway for Hans Rizarre and himself. His faithful chauffeur was the only one involved in the employ of the church that knew anything about this place along with two caretakers.

The two caretakers who managed the villa were discovered totally by accident. In his official duties as a cardinal, Tony traveled to a small town on the outskirts of Turin, Italy, to investigate a scandal that had made the local newspaper concerning some Benedictine monks at Saint Alessandro's Abbey up in the mountains east of Turin. Apparently, some local vendors who supplied dairy products to the abbey had complained to the regional bishop of homosexual activity that was observed by them during some of their visits to the abbey. The bishop had ignored the complaint, and one of the vendors then told the story to the local newspaper reporter. The story broke when the reporter himself was propositioned inside the abbey grounds. Cardinal Rondanelli conducted a ruthless investigation and squelched the scandal. Fourteen of the one hundred and twenty monks abiding at Saint Alessandro's were dismissed. The two prime instigators, Brother Arizzmo and Brother Alfredo, were secretly removed from the premises not to be seen there ever again. Their outrageous behavior could only be hinted at in the press. Their unashamed attraction for each other was obvious to only those that were present when they unabashedly clung to each other as they departed the abbey. Cardinal Rondanelli had the abbey cleaned out and any trace of the scandal completely out of the press and public eye within a two-week period. He had a reputation for complete thoroughness in everything he did.

It was forty-five minutes before the Mercedes arrived at the front of the villa. Roberto had docked the topetta on the outskirts of Venice. There, the Mercedes was ready and waiting for the trip to the villa. It was a sun-filled late summer day, and Tony had asked Roberto to drive slowly through the hills so he could enjoy the view. He thought of his youth during the slow drive, of the days when his father used to enjoy so much driving through the countryside. Occasionally Tony had a deep yearning to return to those days. Whenever he found himself feeling so, he quickly fought to regain his composure and chased away the dreams that once distracted his soul.

"Remember, Roberto, two days and not a minute before 10:00 a.m."

"Yes, Your Eminence. God go with you. I shall be prompt as always."

As Tony watched him drive away, the two overseers came out to greet him.

"Alfredo, I need you to set up my phone bank in the study. I will be working for the next three to four hours."

"Yes, dear master, I shall do it right away."

"Arizzmo, our dear friend Hans will arrive this evening. Please make preparations for us. I want the same young ladies we had the last time, and remind them we take care of them well."

"Yes, dear master, I will see to it that everything is in order."

Tony wasted no time in shedding his cardinal robes. Soon he was in the study clad in his leisure wear and smoking jacket.

"Alfredo, I thought parachute pants went out of style last century. You never cease to amaze me."

"It is true, dear one, but I have always been behind the times."

"Fair enough, Alfredo. Please leave me alone now. I have much work to do. Also, I think you and Arizzmo should be ready to put on a little show for Hans tonight."

"Yes, dear one, we shall be pleased to give such pleasure to the great one. Excuse me, I shall go ahead about my duties."

As Alfredo departed the room, Tony wondered how Hans could get such pleasure from seeing two men make love to each other, especially these two. They were both ugly and grotesque when viewed with their clothes off. Tony worried about Hans sometimes. If the people of Europe, whom he led, knew of his personal sexual appetites, they would retch in disbelief. Tony chuckled as he thought of this and set himself down at his desk to begin working. He quickly turned to the combination lock on the front of his desk and soon had the sliding doors on his attached wall cabinet open. He reached in and removed his address book. He immediately opened the book to the letter *D* and set the book down next to his private phone and started dialing. The phone rang three times, and a husky voice answered.

"Dominick here."

"Dominick, this is your good friend Tony. I need you to deliver some wine to the villa."

"How soon do you need this wine, Tony?"

"I need it right now. There is no time to waste. Will you deliver it right now?"

"Okay. Tony, I'll be there in two hours. Bye."

Tony then picked up his overseas telephone and opened his book to the letter *G*. He knew it should be about 6:00 a.m. in New York City. Certainly, Bishop Grimes should be in. He headed one of the largest Catholic archdioceses in New York City and was Tony's closest confidant in America. The phone rang a good ten times before a sleepy voice answered.

"Hello…hello?"

"Andrew, wake up. Life is passing you by, my son. This is Tony."

"Oh, Tony. What's going on? What did I do?"

"Nothing, Andrew, nothing. I just wanted you to wake up and talk to me. Sit up and tell me what the latest news is. I understand the people over there are getting a little restless. What can we expect next?"

Bishop Grimes, somewhat startled by the early morning call, lifted himself up and sat on the end of his bed. He reached for his doctor prescribed breathalyzer and breathed deeply to clear his senses. One had to be sharp when he spoke to Cardinal Rondanelli.

"Well, Tony…Well, Cardinal, it's pretty hard to put one finger on it really. Six months ago we didn't have this problem. Now since the shootings, there seems to be a real growing unrest. There is talk of underground movements, formation of resistance groups, and so on. I have not seen any tangible evidence of it yet. But there has been a number of little things. Three police officers got beat up here yesterday, just down the street from the church. Somebody put some bricks through some car windows over by the European embassy this past week. Just things like that, Tony."

"Well, Andrew, it is the little things that lead to big things. I understand it's not just confined to New York City, and by the way, what is Cardinal Reese doing over here talking to Veritatis I? I thought we had a handle on the American church."

"I don't understand it, Tony. I knew Cardinal Reese was in Rome visiting. Believe me, there has been no movement here in the church. I would have heard about it. I have contacts all over the country. We are vigorously telling the people to remain calm. We have no desire to upset the applecart. Your generous funding to the American Church has kept us alive and healthy. I don't know of any poor parishes in my diocese."

"Calm down, Andrew. Look, forget what I said about Cardinal Reese. I was just fishing. Get those priests and clergymen out into the pulpits. I want a stop put to this nonsense. You advise the Ecumenical Council that I shall dent their funding real significantly if they don't produce. Get up and get with it."

"Okay, okay, I'll see to it. I'll call a meeting later today. We'll get right on it."

"I know you will, Andrew. Goodbye."

Tony pretty much heard what he expected. Cardinal Reese was apparently operating alone. If there were any others involved, Bishop

Grimes would have picked up something. The unrest that Cardinal Reese talked about appeared to be authentic. Tony didn't appreciate the fact that this news was so slow to reach him. Obviously, his underlings in America did not want to upset him. Anyhow, he found out what he wanted to know. He put his phones away and relocked his cabinet. It was now time to prepare for the arrival of Dominick. Tony rang the alarm buzzer on his study intercom and proceeded to the liquor cabinet.

"Yes, Your Eminence."

"Alfredo, could you please watch the front gate? Dominick will be arriving shortly. Also, tell Arizzmo that Hans will be bringing an additional two or three bodyguards. Please prepare some extra rooms."

"It will be done, Your Eminence."

Fifty-five minutes later, Dominick Forducci braked his Ferrari at the front portico and entered the Villa grounds. A Sicilian by birth, he was presently at age 49, the undisputed leader of Italy's largest underworld mob family. The two Benedictine monks always made themselves scarce when he was around. Death seemed to hang over him like a cloud, and as repugnant as their particular social behavior was, they were about living.

At five feet nine inches tall and weighing a one hundred and eighty pounds around a big boned frame, Dominick was in robust health. He was methodical and ruthless in his business affairs. Everything in life to him was business. He took nothing, outside of family matters, personal. However, Tony Rondanelli was personal to him. He ensured his family members were baptized, went to confession, received first communion, were confirmed, wedded, and buried in a righteous manner. In return, Dominick ensured that Tony's dedication to him be rewarded by swift response to occasional favors. It was true that Tony's sometime arrogance and demanding attitude irked Dominick. But after all he was a Roman cardinal, a man of the cloth. Good God! He might even be pope one day. Dominick, on more than one occasion, envisioned one of his grandchildren being baptized by who he hoped to be the future pope Rondanelli. He could see a future Sicilian parade that would honor him, and yes, he could retire in peace as a legend in his own time.

The meeting between Cardinal Rondanelli and Dominick lasted only thirty minutes. Over a Scotch and a glass of wine, they toasted the future, and soon the jet-black Ferrari was seen departing the villa grounds soaring through the front gates into the Italian countryside much like an Italian golden eagle as it swoops down upon its prey. Tony then walked over to his very comfortable sofa, kicked off his shoes, and lay down to get some rest before the arrival of his partner, Hans.

Hans arrived shortly after 9:00 p.m. with his typical dramatic flair on display. Five private limousines pulled up to the front entrance, and twenty armed men quickly positioned themselves in and about the villa grounds. Fifteen minutes later, two helicopters landed just east of the front portico, and Hans was greeted by Tony as he came up the front steps. Tony mocked as he jovially greeted his dear friend.

"Hail Caesar!"

"Fuck you, Brutus."

Tony's retort was short as Hans and he embraced each other vigorously. They immediately disappeared into the study, poured each other a drink, and sat down to brief each other on the most current events in each other's lives.

Since Han's reaffirmation as president in June of last year in 2039, Tony and Hans had only been able to get together on one occasion. They had spent four hours together in a very private café in Brussels at the end of August while both were attending the final ECOWA meetings. Since then Hans had made it a point to call Tony almost every other day. Hans, of late, had been suffering from a very serious ego problem. He was feeling very insecure about himself. Tony spent most of his time on the phone reassuring him that he was indeed a great man. Did not ECOWA just broaden his powers stopping just short of providing him dictatorial-type authority? Tony knew the power of Satan was enveloping the man as they had both opted for his assistance. Until now there had been no adverse effects upon either of them, with the exception of a few troubling dreams. Han's behavior troubled Tony, and he consistently bolstered the man's ego whenever he called.

"Hans, how is your health of late? You do have a troubled look about you."

This was not necessarily so, but Tony was curious to probe a bit.

"Actually, Tony, I am fine. Your advice has been a great strength to me. I think I have figured out some of my problems. I believe that God is upset with me. The closer we get to our goal by asking for Lucifer's assistance, the angrier He becomes. I am going to increase my satanic sessions, and I think I shall be all right."

"Your perception is acute, Hans. I think you may be right. I was thinking that myself. And in fact, the great pressures of your office alone would rattle most men. By the way, thinking about pressures of office, we have problems in America. Are you aware of how serious they may be?"

"Quite frankly, I am not very aware of what is happening over there. I am really not too concerned about it though. Remember back in 2036 when we formed the EECB to bail the Americans out. At that time, we Europeans were feeling the true benefits of our economic freedom after sabotaging the American economy. I'll never forget the meetings we had with General Aurielle. He was delighted at the great fall America took. We were immediately set free from that crippling world economic competition, and soon the American missile power threat was no more. We suddenly were the great power on earth. The Russians had no choice but to regroup, and yet still they seem preoccupied with the Americans. I was the one right about the Americans anyway. I knew they would fall in line once we waved that wonderous large money bailout in their face. They still have that juvenile cowboy attitude over there, don't they? They watched way too much television. They never knew if they should be the good guy or the bad guy. I do not like them. I always thought they were the true assholes of the world."

"Well, Hans, they can't take that title all by themselves. I think the Russians are right there with them."

"The ironic thing, Tony, is that the Americans and the Russians never knew how much they have in common. Their people are really very much alike. They never reached and never will reach the cultural heights of us Europeans. It is heartening to know we could destroy them both. Anyhow, back in 2038, we decided to economically rape America. For two years now, we have been tearing them apart. I really think if they want to start killing each other, so much the better. Let them destroy themselves. When they get done, we simply pick up the pieces. If it gets too bad, I'll simply have General Aurielle nuke them a bit, and that will be the end of it. After that, we will concentrate on the rest of the world."

"Hans, it is very positive to hear you speak this way. It reaffirms my faith in you. We must put an end to our long separations and spend more real time with each other."

"You took the words right out of my mouth. I plan to advise Pope Veritatis that I wish an official of the church hierarchy be appointed to my executive staff. My choice will be you. And I won't take no for an answer."

"Well, Hans, I had an unusual breakfast meeting this morning that involved a discussion concerning Veritatis. You will be surprised at what he is up to."

Tony explained in depth the unusual conversations he had this day as Hans listened attentively. As Tony explained how he would resolve the situation, Hans smiled and agreed with the cardinal's plan of action. They refilled their drinks and toasted their bond with each other. Tired from the day's events, they decided to call it an evening. Hans wandered off with Arizzmo and Alfredo with an obvious leer akin to lust, and Tony went to his bedroom to entertain three young ladies who were more than eager to please the great cardinal.

Chapter 6

When you reach the end of your rope, tie a knot in it and hang on.

—Franklin D. Roosevelt

October 2, 2040, broke with a dazzling sunrise in Venice. It promised to be another beautiful autumn day. It promised also to be the kind of day that it was just a joy to be alive, a bright sparkling sun, a slightly chill breeze in the air, a sensual awakening by Mother Nature. However, at 7:00 a.m., the residents of Venice were startled by early morning radio broadcasts.

"At 6:45 a.m. today, a huge explosion ripped through the Sheraton-Venice Hotel. Located adjacent to the airport terminal, the hotel was full of sleeping guests. Police and fire officials are now at the scene, and it appears that loss of life will be great. The only confirmation from the scene has come from eyewitnesses that stated the explosion emanated from the east wing about the third floor level. Portions of the building have collapsed, and the scene is one of chaos. More details will be broadcast as this tragedy unfolds. Venice police are also investigating the shooting deaths of two young priests assigned to the local archdiocese. Early reports indicate they were murdered as they slept at the rectory located adjacent to Bishop Arcuri's residence. Police believe the motive may have been robbery as their quarters were ransacked and valuables taken. Despite this terrible news, Venetians can expect a beautiful late autumn day weatherwise."

Dominick Forducci turned off his radio, smiled, rolled over, and went back to sleep. He was proud of his efficient organization, and he would tell his men that personally later that day he thought as he dozed off.

October 2, 2040
Belgium

"Major, can you bring me the most current reports on that bombing in Venice? I wish to be home by 9:00 p.m., so please hurry."

"Yes, General, it is 7:30 p.m. right now. I will have it for you in fifteen minutes. As a matter of fact, Lieutenant Duier is working on it over in intelligence right now."

General Aurielle was deep in thought over this latest terrorist incident. As commanding general of the entire European Defense Command, he made it his business to keep abreast of most everything that was going on in the world. Born Marcus Jean Aurielle in a small village south of Paris, France, Marcus was a career soldier who was noted for having attended more military schools during his distinguished career than any other officer in the Western world. Following his graduation from cadet training in France, he subsequently attended in depth training seminars and a variety of varied strategy planning courses and military schools in Germany, Italy, Spain, America, Australia, Israel, South Africa, and Central America. After France left NATO, he was instrumental in the preparation planning for the deployment of French troops in defiance of American pressure to adhere to Western alliance plans for the defense of Europe.

Marcus's great strength found its roots in his great love and admiration of the military concept of swift, sudden massive military attacks by air and land forces. He was a student, a sleeping protégé so to speak, of the deceased American general of World War II fame, George Patton. In point of fact, there was probably no living American who could tell you more about General Patton than General Aurielle. He even once jokingly remarked to a close aide that he could become actively aroused reading about and studying the military exploits of the world-famous general. Heaven on earth for Marcus was modern military communications, swift motorized military vehicles traveling the expressways of Europe, combined with speed and modern air cover and thousands of troops in the field. He was adamant in the belief that Europe mobilized under his command could destroy any Russian, American, or Chinese army. Just give him the chance, nuclear weapons be damned, he could swiftly neutralize any opponent. One of the wisest moves on the part of the general was to express these views through the years only in confidential gatherings. The individuals who were privy to his personal views were few and confined to the highest levels of the European Defense Command. The world would soon discover him in a blitzkrieg-type fashion, and he would become entrenched in a position of power long before those who should have known would.

More than fifteen minutes had passed since Major Roland had left to get his report. The general was beginning to get irritated as the major rushed into his office at 8:00 p.m.

"I have it here, General. The incident appears somewhat obvious."

"Look, Major, I don't have time to read this right now. Please brief me orally. What happened?"

"Well, sir, our intelligence sources tell us that it may point to a Shiite Muslim connection of some kind. It was definitely indicative of an Iranian Muslim connection. They are still studying it closely. There was an Israeli Cabinet Minister staying on the third floor of that hotel. We believe he was there to meet an American cardinal by the name of Reese. The strength of the explosion coincides with the way the Middle Easterners work. They obliterated the entire northeast section of that building. Eighty-two people have been confirmed killed, including the Israeli government official as well as the American cardinal. There was a message phoned into the authorities by someone identifying himself as a spokesperson for the radical Warriors for Allah group proclaiming, 'Death to all infidels.' We have since had vehement denials from their known contacts. However, there are so many splinter groups it appears that they certainly could be responsible. Nobody blows things up with as much flair as they do."

"What about this American cardinal? What's the connection? What was he doing there?"

"Well, we know he visited with Pope Veritatis for two days and then went straight to Venice. It's possible he may have been paying a social call to Cardinal Rondanelli. We understand he is in Venice somewhere. There was news out of Rome today concerning Veritatis. He canceled a scheduled twelve noon press conference and appeared before the press for a five-minute statement attacking the terrorists who murdered his cardinal. Apparently, there was an Italian bishop who was with the American, and he perished also. We don't know what the content of his press conference was going to be. It was unplanned and announced just yesterday. Anyhow the murder of all those people left the good pope in no mood to hold a press conference. That, briefly, is what we have to report to you right now."

"Thank you, Major. It appears somewhat clear as you say. Let's stay on it and see if there is any more there than what we have got. I shall see you in the morning. I have a meeting tomorrow with Gustav Erikson. Please set up the conference study room by 9:00 a.m."

"Yes, sir, we'll have everything ready and in order."

"Good night, Major."

"Good night, General."

Major Roland snapped to attention and saluted as the general departed.

General Aurielle tried hard to not let the major see that he was visibly upset regarding his report. As he stepped out into the brisk evening air, the contents of the report troubled him. An American carinal dead in Venice, a mysterious canceled papal press conference, and Cardinal Rondanelli in Venice—all did not sit well with him. He felt sure that Cardinal Rondanelli might in some way be connected with this episode. His intelligence sources kept him well advised of the cardinal's activities. It was no secret that he was very influential with the president of the European Republic, and certainly most Europeans were ecstatic over the creation of such a strong European government. It was an ancient dream starting to come true, the resurrection of the Holy Roman Empire. Sure enough, the church was playing its role as always. Through the centuries, the church and the

European governments did not always see eye to eye on everything, and there had been some major conflicts sometimes involving displays of power politics causing disruption and chaos between the two entities. General Aurielle certainly did not wish to see any such conflict between church and state happen again, especially now. As he was driven off into the night, he knew he would have to bring the matter up with Gustav Erikson in the morning.

CHAPTER 7

The supreme art of war is to subdue the enemy without fighting.

—Sun Tzu

October 3, 2040

    Gustav Erikson arrived at European Defense Command Headquarters at 7:45 a.m. It was his routine to be early for meetings. It allowed him time to relax and review whatever was on the agenda. In his sixties agewise, he was extremely energetic and routinely put in a twelve-hour workday. In the field of financial planning, he was considered one of the top professionals in his field. His reputation was worldwide, and his influence second only to Hans Rizarre himself. For almost thirty years, he helped shape the economic policies of the European Common Market. Due to his leadership, the new European Republic represented the wealthiest block of nations on the entire planet Earth. Europe was in control of the world market, and Gustav worked hard to ensure things would stay that way. His greatest piece of work had been the bail out following the conspiratorial action against America. He had been studying the world situation very closely back then and knew quite well the Americans were so very vulnerable. For fourteen years in a row, they had run huge record budget deficits, and the mighty country was beginning to reel from its effects. The only thing he wasn't prepared for was how easy the Americans came to terms and accepted his plan following their collapse.

    Gustav knew of the so-called American good life and their materialistic values. But to see firsthand the disgusting greed of their leaders was shocking to him. Gustav had a reputation as a hard bargainer, but usually he knew he had to compromise to be successful. The American leaders didn't even suggest it. In order to reestablish their status quo, they agreed to every deal Gustav offered them. The more money he waved in front of them, the more they quickly signed off and agreed to each measure he offered. Gustav walked away with America virtually in Europe's hip pocket. Now, just a few later, he knew trouble was brewing. The purpose of his meeting today with General Aurielle was to discuss this very topic. Americans historically had been slow to react, but two seemingly long years of having their pockets emptied out and new Euro taxes imposed on them was apparently beginning to stir the masses. Gustav hoped the good general might have some answers. As much as he publicly wouldn't admit it, he counted a great deal on the natural resources of America. It was still a land of plenty, and right now it was being used to fill up the treasure vaults of the new republic. He did not want anything to upset his financial empire at this point. As he meditated on all this, 9:00 a.m. was suddenly upon him.

"Good morning, Gustav. You're hard at work already I see."

"Marcus, Marcus, it's always a pleasure to see you. How goes the war these days?"

"Well, Gustav, if we were at war, it would be much simpler for me. Of course, I prepare for it every day. No one will fight us. Who can stand up to us? No one, no one at all. I wish someone would try."

"General, the reason for our meeting is along these lines. I know you have defused the American military and their machinations. I am worried about their civilian population now. They could really disrupt things if we let them get out of hand."

"I certainly don't wish them to get out of hand either. I'll tell you right now I will not advise to committing any great amount of troops to such a foreign adventure. The republic cannot be threatened by such over extensions of troops and supplies that history has shown to be folly. If they get too far out of hand, I'll have to consider nuclear options. I've previously discussed this in detail with President Rizarre. We, fortunately are in agreement on that point. We'll use limited troops and lots of specially targeted nuclear clout. Surely their people will respect that."

"Yes, General, anyone would respect that kind of power. The republic must be protected at all costs. However, I must warn you against any large scale destruction of their resources. They are very important to us. It seems sometimes the Americans forget they are descendants of our own forefathers. They left us to go to America, and we've had to fend for ourselves. We have survived and owe it to our forefathers, as well as theirs, to make whatever sacrifice possible to preserve European integrity and civilization. We are presently blessed with a powerful and charismatic leader who so far has exceeded our expectations of uniting all of Europe. If he doesn't make the same kinds of mistakes attributed to the likes of Napoleon and Hitler, then we may see ourselves launching the greatest civilization ever created on this earth."

"So far, so good, Gustav. Right now the only thing I worry about is Han's close association with Cardinal Rondanelli. What are your thoughts about that?"

"General, up to this point, I think it is good. The church in Rome has always presented a valuable link with European governments. I believe it enhances our cultural existence. It provides a valuable control over the masses of people that support our government. As long as there is no large conflict between the two, the concept of church and state working in harmony is something we should strive for."

"I agree. What bothers me, I guess, is Rondanelli's influence. He'll be the next pope, I am pretty sure of it. His influence in the church is worldwide. He controls the purse strings that flow out of the Vatican. Too many cardinals owe him favors at this point. He'll collect on all his debts when the time comes. The problem I foresee is his unusual closeness to the president. Do you know Hans talks to him on the phone every other day?"

"No, I wasn't aware of it. You are one of the few who would be privy to that kind of information. Look, through the years, I've heard nothing but good things about this cardinal. I have met him ten or more times at meetings and social events. He is a positively charming individual. I am sure if he wasn't a cardinal, he would be a strong political figure of some sort. Exactly what are you getting at, General?"

"I can't seem to put my finger on it exactly, and perhaps I'm overreacting. My utmost concern is for the preservation of the republic. I don't wish to see some power-hungry cardinal unduly influence our president. History repeats itself much too often. I think we need to be on our guard to prevent any undue influence or disruptions, that's all."

"I agree with you wholeheartedly. I commend your alertness to detail. Please continue monitoring this situation and keep me advised. In the meantime, we shall have to keep a close eye on America. If you want to look at history, look at them. Who would have thought they would bring Britain to her knees in the 1770s. Their military strengths were worse at that time than they are now. Yet they survived. Look what they did in World War I. They sat around for two or three years and talked about entering the conflict. Yet when they did, the Germans were done. Look at World War II. They sat around and talked about it again. Yet when the Japanese gave them a knockout punch, they rose off the canvas and saved the world. In 1945 even the mighty German storm troopers were in dread of facing American military men. General, their history shows them to rise to the occasions, and I'm worried."

"I'll blow them up, Gustav. Nobody will get off the canvas when I'm finished."

"Listen closely to what I am saying, General. It's not the leaders or politicians that bother me. It's their people and their ideas. President Rizarre calls them cowboys and cowgirls. I think he oversimplifies his disgust for them. The truth of the matter is that they founded that country on principles which defy the use of the sword. Their founding fathers talked about 'trust in God,' 'Divine Providence,' 'All men are created equal.' It's like an Ancient Book rendition of the chosen people. Sometimes I think they are the true Israelites. You talk about a land of plenty, a country flowing with milk and honey. That is the promised land if you ask me.

"Excuse me, General, if you think I am delving in unknown areas here., but I have thought about this a great deal lately. Primarily because I don't want to lose that source of revenue, and I need you to be careful when blowing them up is discussed. I think the American people lost sight of their heritage in the decades of the 1970s, 1980s, and 1990s. Now they are a suffering people. I hear of these so-called resistance groups they are forming that no one seems able to find. That, I guess, is to be expected. But what bothers me more is what these people are saying. Your Major Roland was kind enough to supply me with one of their underground leaflets your people managed to get their hands on. Did you understand the significance of the words?"

"Quite frankly, I am not sure what you are getting at. I have reviewed it and filed it away as typical rabble-rousing."

"Gustav, just let me read a few excerpts from this. If I may?"

Gustav pulled the leaflet from his folder and reached for a yellow highlight marker from his briefcase.

"I will highlight as I go. Look, General: 'As for the support of our cause, we rely heavily on the protection of *Divine Providence*,' 'We request the gracious favor of *Almighty God*,' 'the great eye of *Providence* be upon us,' and 'one nation under *God*.'

"Just look at this, a one-page leaflet and they call upon God four times. I'll grant you there is a lot of scum in America—that's one reason they fell. Let's face it, the masses of people let them get away with it. What I don't like now is the sudden appearance of the kind of Americans who are now calling upon Divine Providence. They believe in what they are saying. They believe He'll really save them."

"Gustav, the only thing I can say to you is this. When I get done with them, they'll need God to save them. My first concern is to preserve and protect the republic, then I may worry about God."

"I believe our meeting here has been quite successful, Marcus. What say we follow it up with lunch? I think we deserve a drink."

"Exactly right. Gustav, your insight has been beneficial this morning. I shall keep a closer ear attuned to America."

The two gentlemen called their respective aides into the meeting room, made arrangements for an afternoon conference session with intelligence specialists, and together strode off to the VIP dining area for some food, drink, and relaxation.

Chapter 8

Righteous art thou, O Lord, when I plead with thee: yet let me talk with thee of thy judgments: Wherefore doth the way of the wicked prosper? wherefore are all they happy that deal very treacherously?

—Jeremiah 12:1 KJV

Issac Pelensky was deep in thought as he parked his 2037 Z-Cutlass automobile behind the Westside Pleasure Emporium. It was one of his duties as a Los Angeles city inspector to make weekly rounds of those establishments on the west side that brought large amounts of revenue into the city coffers. The city of Los Angeles had earned a reputation for being the city in America that contributed the largest amount of funds to the European cause. The city fathers in Los Angeles had devised several schemes which were so profitable in nature they allowed the city to remain solvent even after doling out their required amounts to Washington, DC.

Issac personally was pretty disgusted with the operation. As a city employee, he saw firsthand the corruption that engulfed him. Born in 1994 in Newark, New Jersey, of proud Polish parents, he was very familiar with a big-city environment. His grandparents, John and Vera Pelensky, had raised him in a rather strict family-oriented style that embraced a typical Polish Christian upbringing. His great-grandparents, Joseph and Eva Pelensky, could trace his family roots back to the terror days of Joseph Stalin and Russian communist involvement in Poland following World War II. They fled to America and arrived in Newark, New Jersey, in 1955 and survived together with faith only in God whom they truly believed spared them. They found what they believed to be the American dream settling in

Newark. His mother still kept the picture of the Statue of Liberty that was a favorite of his grandfather. It was now in a glass-enclosed frame with the proper inscriptions:

> Keep, ancient lands, your storied pomp! Cries the silent lips. Give me your tired, your poor, your huddled masses yearning to breathe free, the wretched refuse of your teeming shore. Send these, the homeless, tempest-tost to me, I lift my lamp beside the golden door! (Emma Lazarus)

For the first eighteen years of his life, Issac heard the tragic stories of life in Europe as they were experienced by his great-grandparents. It was difficult for a young boy residing in comfort to envision a refugee's dilemma. He could not even begin to feel the pain of a people so vigorously oppressed. He was well fed, well clothed, and had a spacious house to dwell in. He couldn't feel the tears that ran down his great-grandfather's cheek as he told of his own father loading his brother and sister into a carcass cart back in the Ukraine. The cart ran daily through his village to pick up dead bodies, the victims of a communist starvation program designed to starve to death as many Poles as possible. Somehow, Issac felt a stranger among his elders. He knew that his generation lived in a different world. At age 46, he was just beginning to feel guilty at how he felt at age 18. Back in 2011, following his high school graduation, Issac joined the US Army just to get away from his hometown. He was sick of hearing about all the woes his ancestors had to face. Why did they continually dwell on it? It was really no concern of his. He lived in America; he was an American. Forget the past. Live the good life in America and forget it. Now somehow, the good life had turned sour. He could see it firsthand. In his daily duties, he witnessed the worst part of what was going on in America. The city of Los Angeles, like other cities in America, had zoned certain sections of its city as areas legal for so-called adult entertainment to exist. The city fathers of Los Angeles went a step further than most and decided to cash in on the decadence of some of its citizens by sharing in the ownership and profits of the now legalized establishments. His best friend, Roger Wallace, managed the Westside Pleasure Emporium. Here, the latest first-class pornography was made available to the public. The interior design displayed a first-class environment. The upstairs and lower level bar areas and lounges were available for those who did not wish to sit in the theater area. The films were broadcast and portrayed on the latest life-size video screens available, and combined within an alcohol and lounge environment, were quite an attraction for the working public. Fourteen such establishments were operated by the city of Los Angeles. Five were located in Issac's area of responsibility. It was his duty to ensure that correct body counts were being taken of patrons attending, and he routinely audited the books of the establishments assigned to him. Everything was computerized and linked with city hall anyway, so his checks were more a double-check to attempt to spot any irregularities that might exist. The decadence of the films was so blatant that sex was construed more as a sport than anything else. They certainly did not resemble anything that portrayed any act of love. In fact, twice a week live shows were highlighted by legalized wagering on whether certain sexual exploits could be accomplished or not. Of course, the lounges stacked the decks with drugged-up sexual deviates whose drug habits were fed according to the monies they brought in. If they didn't perform, they were quickly replaced. Issac was not totally immune to this. He was torn and emotionally distraught over such an insensitive public program. However, he needed his job badly. Part of his wages were used to help take care of his sick mother back east. Jobs were extremely difficult to get, and if he lost this one, he would soon be at the mercy of whomever would want to help support him, indeed if anyone would.

As Issac continued to sit in his parked car, he began to ponder over the past six months about things that had recently occurred in his life which reached deep down into the roots of his soul. He witnessed tragic events on the streets of Los Angeles which smacked of stories once told him by his great-grandfather that occurred in Poland. Callous, cold-blooded murder in the streets of Los Angeles by smiling cold men in blue chilled him to the bone. Public relief and welfare were long gone since the economic crisis, and thousands were left to fend for themselves, wandering the fringes of America's big cities. Tent cities and shanty towns sprung up quickly and soon added a new subculture to the American society. It didn't take long for them to become scapegoats of the cities' public officials. Retribution against acts of crime was swift and deadly. The news media in most cases weren't even allowed to report on events in these areas. In June of 2040, while on a routine inspection tour, Issac witnessed a public execution of a man accused of stealing a loaf of bread and two cans of corn. Two hulking men in uniforms assigned to the Los Angeles PD Motorcycle Division had caught the man red-handed. Three bullets to the brain rid this supposed menace from the earth's grasp. The bread and corn were soon traded for sex in an alleyway, and a sixteen-year-old waif ran off to help feed her malnourished, starving family.

One month following this episode, Issac's good friend Roger Wallace was nearly killed as he drove home after closing the Emporium for the night. As he rounded a curve on the outskirts of one of the tent cities, a bullet smashed through his windshield. He immediately stopped his car, and a Los Angeles PD squad car pulled alongside him. A quick apology was proffered. The two officers inside the squad car were engaged in target practice to keep their shooting eyes sharp, and the resultant broken windshield was merely an accident. One of the officers wrote down a phone number of where the window could be fixed with no questions asked. A shaky Roger quickly drove away and counted at least three bleeding bodies lying in the road as he accelerated to a safer area of Los Angeles proper. He had heard similar stories from others, and it seemed these incidents were happening much too often. You never read about them in the newspaper or viewed them on the TV news. It was always whispered conversation with friends who heard about them from other friends. If you did your job and went about your business, nobody bothered you. But if you even gave the appearance of questioning city police, you soon found yourself being monitored. You might even be called down to city hall for an interview. It was like being called to a school principal's office as a kid. The main intent was to inspire a certain fear and respect for the powers to be.

PLANET EARTH

On the seventh of August 2040, Issac Pelensky's life was dramatically altered when he decided to use his allotted ten days of vacation owed to him by the city. He packed his camping gear and casually traveled north for two days until he reached the Mendocino National Forest. It was by coincidence he ended up there. His main purpose was to drive as far away from Los Angeles as he could. As the long drive started to weigh on him and he finally got to the forest, exhaustion overtook him, and he entered what he thought would be a haven from the storm of life he was living in. He parked his car off a side road ignoring the posted No Trespassing sign. He removed his camping gear, locked the vehicle, and wandered into the woods with his gear attached firmly to his back. About a mile into the woods, he came upon a small clearing, pitched his tent, unrolled his sleeping bag, and fell fast asleep.

On the morning of August 10, Issac awoke as a slight mist engulfed his tent. It appeared to be an ideal day to test his fishing prowess. He retrieved his California map and surveyed the area he wandered into. Being a city employee down in Los Angeles had given him certain advantages, and prior to leaving, he made sure he had in his possession the best maps of California the city had. He had gotten off Interstate 5 just south of Sacramento and headed west. As he perused the map, he knew he wasn't far from Stoney Creek. He donned his rain jacket, packed his gear, and wandered deeper into the forest. He found the hike to be exhilarating and the peace of the forest an inner calm to his soul.

After an hour's trek, Issac came upon what must be Stoney Creek. A clear, fast-running creek suddenly barred his way. It was about fifteen to twenty yards wide and appeared to be deep enough to prevent one from wading across. The setting was picture postcard material, thought Issac, as he set up camp. If the fish were biting, he might just spend the next seven days right here. By the time his two fishing poles were in position, the mist had cleared, and it promised to be a pleasant day.

Issac smiled as he tied a line to one of the six-packs of beer he had stashed in the bottom of his tote bag. He couldn't envision himself roughing it without being able to occasionally sip some brew.

He dropped it into the cool water and tied it securely to a small tree on the bank. Now he would just sit and watch his lines and hope he would get a bite or two.

It was about forty-five minutes later when Issac discovered he was not alone in his idyllic setting. Upriver, about a quarter of a mile away, a jeep suddenly appeared and stopped at the edge of the creek. Looking through his binoculars, it appeared to have some official markings, and it didn't alarm him that the two men in the jeep appeared to be scrutinizing him. One had a pair of field glasses to his eyes, and Issac waved in their direction. Both men waved back and appeared to be not too concerned with the man fishing in Stoney Creek. Issac had failed to purchase fishing licenses, and he was hoping these gentlemen were not park officials who would begin to spoil his well-earned vacation. He was confident his credentials as a Los Angeles city employee might ease him out of any type of official hassle. He was wise to the games of trading favors and was prepared to use his skills if the occasion arose. The two men in the jeep suddenly propelled their vehicle forward and crossed the creek just north of his camp. They couldn't maneuver their vehicle to his campsite and stopped about one hundred and fifty yards short of his location. One was a middle-aged man wearing what appeared to be a park ranger's uniform. The other man was young and dressed in jeans and a western-style long-sleeved shirt. Issac rose and strode along the bank to greet them. There was no use concealing his fishing lines as it was obvious to the two men what he was doing.

"Hello, my name is Issac Pelensky. I'm a city inspector from Los Angeles. I'm presently enjoying my vacation. I hope nothing is wrong with my camping here."

"Not at all, Mr. Pelensky. I'm United States Forest Ranger Richard Whitley, and this is my young friend Jerry Parker. If you don't mind, I need to see some type of identification please, sir."

"Certainly, Officer Whitley. My wallet is with my gear. I'm sure you will see everything is in order."

Issac hated identification cards. Everywhere one went in this country, he had to show ID of some kind. Every time he stopped on Interstate 5, whether it was to get gas or something to eat or drink, out came the ID. It was a demeaning and time-consuming exercise. As he retrieved his wallet and papers from his vehicle, he was not aware armed men were watching him closely from the forest. He had no idea that his presence along Stoney Creek was looked upon with concern by the residents of Camp Liberty. He would have been greatly alarmed if he had known three men watched him all night long as he had slept the previous evening. He handed his papers to Ranger Whitley and wondered if he should offer to share one of his beers. Perhaps he should wait to see if the ranger questioned his licensing status.

"Everything appears to be in order as you say, Mr. Pelensky." Ranger Whitley felt he should query Mr. Pelensky to get any information he could without appearing to be overly aggressive or demanding.

"What would the city officials say if you exceeded your vacation time limitations and got lost in the forest?"

"Quite frankly, sir, I'd be in some kind of trouble. I'm sure that they wouldn't let me back to work unless I reported to city hall and explained what happened. I don't intend to have to sit through that kind of drama. I'll be back on time. I'm sure it's similar to what you would have to go through on the federal level."

"That's most certainly the case. My superiors wouldn't allow or stand for that kind of mistake without making a major fuss."

Ranger Whitley responded to Issac as Chief Ranger Baines had instructed all his men to. The fact of the matter was, Chief Ranger Baines personally detested the ID procedures initiated by the Europeans. They were un-American and a threat to personal freedoms previously guaranteed by the US Constitution. Regardless, the present system called for this procedure, and anyone who wished to hold down a wage-earning job complied with the present law of the land or he would not have a wage-earning job.

"Mr. Pelensky, I should advise you that no one is allowed on the other side of Stoney Creek. You are welcome to stay here where you are for as long as you like."

"I understand. Look, forget the Mr. Pelensky stuff. It's Issac. I can't hardly believe we are standing out here in the middle of God's country being so darn formal."

"Issac it is then. I would just as soon be called Richard myself."

"Hey, Issac, Look! You've got some action on one of your lines."

The three men rushed back to the campsite, and Issac yanked his pole out of the ground and began to do battle with the game fish on the end of his line. In five minutes' time, he had reeled in a seven-pound salmon. The next two hours were as magical moments for the three men. They were as young boys again, fishing in the woods without a thought to the cares of the world. Three more salmon were reeled in, skinned, and fried over Issac's skillet. As the six-pack was retrieved from the creek, there was nothing in the world that prevented these three souls from playing hooky temporarily from the rest of the planet.

This was Issac's introduction to the residents of Camp Liberty. By the time his vacation had ended, he had been personally invited into the inner sanctum. Indeed his last night was spent on a cot underneath the ground adjacent to Phil Redding's command cubicle. He had started his vacation as a man seeking solace from a lonely, cruel world. He had finished it as a man reborn, with a new purpose and a vengeance in his heart. He had been given a vision of hope for the future, and he was willing to take an active role. When he returned to Laytonville for the September 21st meeting, he was filled with exhilaration as the meeting offered hope and promised positive action for the dreams he and his new friends now shared.

Now as he sat in his car outside the West Side Emporium, Issac wondered if he could take his friend Roger into his confidence before things started to happen. In about three weeks' time, Americans around the country would begin a vigorous battle against injustices that could no longer be tolerated. On November 19, it was not to be tea that would be dumped into Boston Harbor. If things went right, a clear message would be delivered to Europe that America was a land that was no longer theirs for the taking. The era of raping America would officially be over.

Issac got out of his car, locked it up, and went inside the Emporium to begin his inspection. It was still early in the day, and Roger didn't get too many patrons prior to 4:00 p.m. Tim Kessler was behind the bar readying things for the evening's business.

"Where's Roger, Timmy?"

"He's upstairs in his office. He came in about 10:00 a.m. and I haven't seen him for the last hour. He looked as though he was upset about something, so I haven't bothered him. Do you want to see the books?"

"I'll do that when I come back down. I want to talk to Roger first."

Issac took the two flights of stairs up to Roger's office easily, knocked, and entered the manager's office.

"What's going on today, Roger? Timmy tells me you were upset about something this morning."

Roger did not answer as he appeared to be sleeping at his desk. His head was on the table, and Issac thought this was rather unusual behavior for him.

"C'mon, Roger, wake up. Things aren't so bad. Get with it."

There was no response, and Issac began to get concerned. He suddenly realized his friend was not breathing. He quickly grabbed his friend by the shoulders and shook him. Roger did not budge, and the stiffness in his body confirmed there was no more life stirring within him. Issac noticed an envelope underneath his left forearm. He pulled it out and read the writing scribbled across the front: "To Whom It May Concern." Issac stuffed the envelope neatly under his shirt and raced downstairs.

"Tim, call the paramedics, right now. I think Roger is dead."

As Tim attempted to grasp the reality of what was just told him, Issac tried to put into perspective what Roger's death meant to him. He knew that as soon as the incident was called in to the police, he would receive instructions to perform a complete audit of the Emporium. It would be an exhaustive two- to three-day affair with other inspectors called in to assist. The powers to be always considered the worst when something like this happened. They automatically assumed foul play was involved, and it probably had something to do with theft of their monies. If the facts of the audit proved otherwise, then they didn't really care. Someone else was assigned the position, and life went on. Issac suspected it was suicide, and he decided that his friend's last words would not be sullied by uncaring, insensitive men who would relegate his message of distress to the trash barrel as soon as they discovered their money was safe.

"Tim, for crying out loud, haven't you got through yet?"

Tim was obviously upset and was having a difficult time calling the emergency number. Issac wished to return upstairs to his friend, but common sense cautioned him to stay where he was at. Police questioning Tim would certainly make note of the fact that he returned upstairs. At the moment, he thought it best not to cast any undue suspicion his way. City hall always looked for scapegoats and would lock anyone up on a whim. It was an easy way to eliminate people. He knew he couldn't help his friend now and would follow department policy in handling such matters. He couldn't afford to jeopardize his partaking in upcoming events and would have to maintain a low profile for a while. Tim finally got his message through to the paramedics. It would be just a few minutes before you could pick up the wail of their sirens.

"What happened, Issac? How did it happen?"

"Your guess is as good as mine, Tim. You'd better stay behind the bar and conduct business as usual. City hall wouldn't stand for any disruption in business. They would expect you to capitalize on this event. When the curiosity seekers follow the medics and police through the door, you better start plying them with the drinks."

"Hey, Pelensky, I intend to. I know what time of day it is. You don't have to remind me of my duties. If I play this right, I should be able to step right into Roger's job. You know the books are fine here. Roger didn't rip anybody off. You conduct your audit. You'll see. I want his job when you're through."

Issac could hear the sirens of the emergency vehicles in the distance, and soon the Emporium would be crawling with people.

"Okay, Tim. As a matter of fact, I think I'll start my checks right now. Don't call city hall yet. The police are supposed to do that. Just remain calm and you will come out on top when this is over."

Issac excused himself and immediately went to Roger's downstairs office located down the hall from the lounge area. He closed the door behind him and breathed a sigh of relief when he found the copy machine was turned on. He immediately retrieved the envelope stuffed underneath his shirt and quickly removed the two-page letter and placed the first sheet on the copier. In two minutes' time, he had run off four copies. The two pages were written on both sides, and Issac double-checked his copies and replaced the pages in their original envelope. He then placed the envelope in the center drawer of Roger's desk, where it would be easily found. Suicides most always were accompanied by notes, which were always of great interest to the authorities. Issac realized he had about a minute or two left before the medics came crashing through the front door. He took his four copies, folded them up, stuck them neatly under his shirt, and quietly slipped out the back door. No one was around anywhere. He casually walked to his car, unlocked it, and slipped in behind the steering wheel. In thirty seconds' time, he had his copies secured in a hidden compartment underneath his dashboard. He relocked his car and returned inside. As he walked down the hall toward the lounge, three medics came charging through the front door. Tim pointed the stairway to them, and Issac followed them to the upstairs office.

There was nothing the medics could do for Roger Whitley. Five minutes after greeting Tim in the lounge, he sat behind his desk and swallowed three cyanide pills. One had been enough dosage to do the job, but he wasn't going to take any chances. He wanted out of this world, and no one was going to bring him back. Police Sergeant Robert Washburn arrived within a half hour. The paramedics had the body bag laid out, but they could not remove the body without official police permission.

Sergeant Robert Washburn was a twelve-year veteran of the police department. He had seen the Los Angeles Police Department go through many changes in his time. It took him almost twelve years to make sergeant. He remembered well the sensitivity of the department with regard to the public and the press. The sudden turn of events of the last three years was difficult for him to fathom. Now they could stop and detain anyone they pleased, anytime they wanted. Many officers on the force were overjoyed at this change in policy. But he and a few of the old-timers had serious reservations about this new and current policy. They had held their tongues about policy in the previous years, and they did now also. They were just good policemen, and they would do their job regardless of the policy-making idiots who sat behind their office desks from 8:00 a.m. to 5:00 p.m. every day. As a policeman on the street, Washburn never could relate very well to the administrators who set policy and dictated how his day-to-day duties were to be performed. A good cop had no use for the headquarters' prima donnas. All the politics and name-dropping by the so-called brass at HQ was considered so much bullshit. An administrator was nobody unless he had worked the streets. There were far too few of those kind around now, and the Los Angeles Police Department was currently top-heavy with officers who were nothing more than friends of friends who rewarded their acquaintances by granting high-ranking police positions through the political patronage system.

Despite a great animosity between the top police hierarchy and the street cops, the department managed to function quite well. This was in large measure thanks to the middle management line officers and support staff who for the most part handled their positions in a very responsible manner. They formed the buffer between the administrators and the street cops. The captains, lieutenants, and sergeants formed the backbone of the operation. Most knew how to tactfully ignore the memorandums that daily floated down from their superiors and just as tactfully soothe the ruffled feathers of the troops in the field as they fired their own memos upward. Fortunately, most of the frivolous paperwork never got to where they were supposed to due to the skill of the professionals caught in between.

Sergeant Washburn questioned the medics about the victim, and the body was ordered removed for an autopsy. Two uniformed officers arrived and were assigned to taking statements from Issac and Tim. Three other employees who were due to report for work were contacted at home to come in for questioning. Sergeant Washburn relegated to himself the duty of checking Roger's offices out. Issac hoped he would discover the suicide note soon. Tim and he were a little uptight, and the downstairs was beginning to fill up with patrons.

When the officers discovered Issac was a city employee after checking ID papers, they treated him with noticeable respect. They were in effect employees of the city together, and it was good practice to work together whenever possible. Life on the streets was tough enough as it was. This case appeared to be not too much of a problem to resolve. In fact, within the hour, Sergeant Washburn discovered Roger's note. He thought it strange it was in his downstairs office and his body found upstairs. But he had seen much stranger things than this throughout the years, and the note told the story. Roger popped the cyanide pills to end a life filled with fear and no meaning. He apologized to his good friend Issac for not confiding in him and stated that he was the only one in his miserable life that he loved and respected. Of course, Sergeant Washburn could not give Issac the suicide note. It was against departmental policy. If the autopsy reports verified the death due to drug poisoning, Sergeant Washburn, in confidence, told Issac that he would destroy the note. It was the sergeant's policy not to cast undue suspicion on an innocent person. He would not ruin someone's life or career just to make himself look good, and in this case, it would put him in good standing with a city inspector who he might be able to seek a favor from in the future.

The fact that Issac's name was mentioned in the note could cause him trouble. Washburn knew this was so much crap. He always tried to close up his cases as they taught him when he went to the academy. Today they were teaching police cadets things that caused his bones to shake and rattle a bit. Issac thanked the good sergeant profusely and contemplated his good fortune in not mentioning Camp Liberty to Roger before this. Any mention of that in the suicide note could have spelled out big trouble for Issac and his friends up north. Perhaps he himself should carry some cyanide capsules also. He preferred a quick death as opposed to forcibly revealing by torture the whereabouts and activities of his friends.

Sergeant Washburn quickly finished up his investigation, promptly notified city hall of his findings, and left the premises with the two uniformed officers, traveling on to and preparing for the next crisis that would come their way. Issac had Tim pour him a beer, and he relaxed in the lounge awaiting the call he knew was soon to come. Within twenty minutes, his supervisor called him and ordered a special audit of the West Side Emporium. Two other inspectors had been dispatched to the site, and Issac was to have a complete report back to city hall within forty-eight hours. Issac knew full well the results would be positive, and he sat down to finish his beer and wait patiently for the other two men to arrive. Roger's death was a real loss to Issac personally, but all things considered, it could have turned out much, much worse than it did. Issac decided that now would be a good time to read Roger's note. He went to his car, retrieved the concealed envelope, and returned to the lounge. He found a secluded corner booth away from the crowded bar area that was rapidly filling up, slid into a comfortable seat, and opened up his friend's suicide note, his last will and testament so to speak. It read as follows:

To Whom It May Concern

Today I bid this bitter life farewell. Hope is gone, and my love is lost. This city has stolen my self-respect, and my hard-earned wages are used to support sinful men. I can no longer work in a place that offers up lies every day. When I was young, I dreamed great dreams for the future. Now the future holds nothing but nightmares and frightening dread. The tent cities grow larger, and the rich live in armed suburbia surrounded by alarmed chain link fences. I'm caught in the middle, and the big squeeze is on. I regret with disgust this all suffocating pressure. Issac, my friend, I'm sorry for leaving you. Don't mourn my death, just run…run as fast as you can. I can't take it anymore. My love is lost. When they murdered my Susan, they murdered me. Just because her mom stood up to them, the whole family is gone. When a sixty-eight-year-old woman has more courage than I, when they gun down my dearest love and I tremble with fear, unable to react, then it is time for me to leave this world. I go quietly with no fanfare. I put an end to this farce the only way I know how. God, please save me.

Roger Wallace

    Issac wiped a tear and wished his friend could hear him so he could properly express his grief. He had known Roger was distraught over losing his girlfriend, Susan. Her mother had defied the police on several occasions. She repeatedly refused to show her ID papers when passing through different sections of the city. By doing this, she became a neighborhood hero. The Fifteenth Precinct police commander thought a lesson was in order. A passing squad car gunned down Susan, her sister, and her mother as they waited at a bus stop two blocks from their home. Death left its message in the neighborhood, and Roger was left a devastated man. It seemed strange he never talked much about it to Issac. But then, as life in America was full of so much that didn't make sense, one was often left numb and speechless. In a few short years, America had been turned upside down. It was very difficult to adjust. For many, the changes had proven too much to take, and each day new stories unfolded as a desperate people sometimes took desperate measures to express a growing hatred and rejection of policies and rules that directed their lives in such an arbitrary fashion.

Chapter 9

> Blow ye the trumpet in Zion, and sound an alarm in my holy mountain: let all the inhabitants of the land tremble: for the day of the Lord cometh, for it is nigh at hand.
>
> —Joel 2:1 KJV

November 20, 2040
Europe and America

It was in the early morning hours of the twentieth of November when the European world first learned in dramatic fashion of the shocking news from America that had occurred the day before. European newspapers headlined their morning dailies in large bold print:

REBELLION ROCKS AMERICA—PRESIDENT RIZARRE CALLS EMERGENCY MEETING (*UPI United Press International*, Brussels)

TERRORISM STRIKES THE AMERICAN CONTINENT. THOUSANDS LIE DEAD AS ASSASSINS PROWL THE STREETS (*Associated Press*, Paris)

AMERICAN PRESIDENT CARLSON IN HIDING. TWO US SENATORS MURDERED IN US CAPITOL (*Associated Press*, London)

NEW YORK CITY STAGGERS AS ARMED REBELS RUN RAMPANT (*United Press International*, Stuttgart)

PLANET EARTH

Pope Veritatis I Denounces American Rebels as Pagan Insurrectionists (*Vatican News Service*, Rome)

Television and radio stations were giving exclusive news coverage to an event that caught the world unawares.

The British Broadcasting Company (BBC) was running uninterrupted coverage receiving live reports from correspondents on the scene in New York city and Washington, DC. Initial reports appeared to be erratic and confusing. It was first reported that the American president had been assassinated. However, it was later confirmed that Senator Hugh Everett from New Jersey was the one actually murdered. The president and senator had been breakfasting in private senate chambers and had just left the building when a fusillade of bullets greeted them. President Carlson had miraculously escaped while the senator died instantly. The exact whereabouts of the president was not presently known, but it was confirmed by the German press that he had since been in personal contact with European president Rizarre. The true enormity of the American situation was not known until late that same evening. By then it was with grim realization that President Rizarre and his advisors were aware that a massive well-organized movement was in full operation. Thirty-seven American cities had reported armed assaults against political and public authorities. Each and every one was of the hit-and-run type. At exactly 7:00 a.m. in each one of these cities, large explosions ripped through public buildings. Police station headquarters, offices, and precinct command posts were the primary targets. Thirteen chiefs of police were murdered before they made it to work, and in some cases police departments were effectively shut down for the day. A large number of European government consultants and advisors were injured as well. It was known that at least three of them perished in the attack. In the large metropolitan areas, the police were able to maintain at least a semblance of order but were in true disarray. This was especially true in New York City, Chicago, Philadelphia, Detroit, and Washington, DC. The explosions in these cities were staggered to detonate at various times throughout the morning. The actual armed assaults were all hit-and-run affairs and ceased immediately at 11:30 a.m. The armed invaders vanished as quickly as they had appeared, and police departments were put on full alert, bracing for further attacks that might occur. In Los Angeles, Major Robinson Jones and his two top aides were blown up as they entered their city-owned limousine. Altogether, ten city mayors were assassinated, and forty-two councilpersons from various cities were systematically eliminated.

Thousands of leaflets were distributed throughout the cities calling for all Americans to recall their heritage and reject the present American government. An individual by the name of David J. Jefferson had signed the leaflet and called for the resurrection of the Sons of Liberty and the overthrowing of all foreign bonds. All over the world, people read, watched, and listened to the story of America erupting and exploding in violence and open revolt. It would be interesting to see what the reaction of the European government would be. Certainly, this would be a dramatic test of President Rizarre's leadership and action in a period of grave crises.

At Camp Liberty, Colonel Redding and his followers rested from the day's events. Their various raiding parties had successfully fulfilled their mission and returned to their home bases. They had succeeded in eliminating almost entirely all the key targeted police and government leaders that they were after in Sacramento, San Francisco, and Oakland. San Diego and San Jose were also successful ventures undertaken in southern California. Los Angeles was a different matter. The LAPD was a disciplined paramilitary force that reacted efficiently to turmoil. Despite the loss of their mayor and five key police officials, they had managed to close their ranks and maintain control of the city. Within four hours of the initial attacks, they had imposed a strict curfew on all the city's residents and closed off all main roads surrounding the city limits. A twenty-man force sent at the direction of Camp Liberty radioed that they barely left the city limits as police units erected barricades that would have greatly hindered their escape and possibly caused their demise.

The initial blow by the American rebels was so successful that few casualties were reported. However, David Jefferson and the revolutionary leadership were wise enough to realize that it was a mere token first step. They would now sit back and monitor the reaction of the American government and the American people. Without continuous and widespread support from the people, the cause would be sufficiently jeopardized. The initial plan was to strike a realistic blow and then slink away into the woodwork. It was too early to actually secure and hold military targets. That would expose them to military operations and possible losses they cared not to receive. Guerilla warfare–type tactics were the order of the day for now. It was obvious the revolutionaries could easily secure the small and rural areas of the country. Methodical planning and patience would be the tactics in the bigger cities. One of the major concerns to the movement was how the military would react to government instructions to suppress the insurrection. Jefferson had followed General Williamson's plan of action to the letter. By staging attacks all over the country, the military would be initially slow to react not knowing exactly where to strike back at. Also, it was possible to assassinate twelve leading generals as dawn broke on November 19. That, in fact, combined with General Williamson's secretly activating his airborne division and successfully moving them into the Alabama countryside, resulted in the US military not acting at all. Although military alerts were issued at bases all over the country, military commanders ignored orders to react until a full assessment of what was going on could be determined. After issuing weapons and securing their own particular base perimeters, they sat and waited. General Williamson issued an official communication advising other military commanders around the country of his action and inviting them, indeed imploring them, in the names of George Washington, Andrew Jackson, Douglas MacArthur, and Omar Bradley to join his troops in a cause of righteousness and action that obligated men of fortitude and great virtue to save the country from the brink of ruination.

 The enormity of that bold message rocked the upper echelon of the military community. No commander would make a hasty decision to do battle with General Williamson and his airborne troops. It made good sense to sit back and closely analyze this situation before any troops would be committed. Jefferson and General Williamson also utilized their military connections to assist with the distribution of thousands of leaflets all over America urging citizens to strike out and support the overthrow of their oppressive leaders. Jefferson personally got the Canadians to promise publicly their support and to offer refuge to any Americans who wished to flee. The Canadian premier advised that Canadian troops were now patrolling the northern border areas to assist Americans in any way they could.

In contrast, the mood in Europe was very different. General Aurielle was furious over the turn of events and ordered the European military forces to be put on full alert status. Gustav Erikson was seen throwing his attaché case against the wall of a meeting room in the ornate office of the Bank of Belgium in Brussels. However, President Rizarre appeared briefly before television cameras in Stuttgart, Germany, and reassured the European community that the situation would be dealt with and it represented no real concern for the average European citizen. His public demeanor and oratory brilliance always left his viewing public with a sense of confidence in his leadership. The vast majority of people in Europe idolized him, and if Hans Rizarre said everything would be okay, then as far as they were concerned, it would be.

Privately, Hans was as upset as the rest of his colleagues. He did not take the idea of an American revolution lightly. The republic needed the natural resources of America, and no insurrectionists would be allowed to take that away so easily. A series of meetings was planned to establish a plan of action.

Upon hearing of the news in America for the first time, Hans felt a sudden urge to utilize the so-called nuclear option. Voices deep within him counseled sudden retaliation and slaughter. Unleash the powers at hand and show the world your wonders, he thought. He envisioned with delight Americans waking to see mushroom clouds hovering over their large cities. Surely that would bring them to their knees. He couldn't wait to convene his meetings and somehow allow others to suggest the horrors that he was now contemplating.

Young Jeremy Cox of Athens, Georgia, lay in his bed contemplating the day's events. He was a bona fide member of the Athens, Georgia, Thirteenth Regular Militia. At age 18, he had been an ardent supporter of the militia group since its inception seven months prior.

They had been formed due to the leadership of Caleb Clark. He was a local pharmacist who told the local Klansmen about a man named David Jefferson. At their very secret meetings, he advised that Southerners should start preparing for the day they could rise up and help save the nation. There was something to be said for the Southerners' pride. Their heritage demanded a certain dedication to duty when honor and righteousness were at stake. There were still deep wounds left from the long ago Civil War, and Southern pride never seemed to rationalize the treatment they received following President Abraham Lincoln's death. If he had lived, they might have known his compassion and kindness. Yet he died, and to this day for some Southerners, their wounds had not fully healed.

Perhaps one could say that it is the design of the Great One, that in the South in 2040 laid the seeds of America's salvation. As the Northern cities of America declined in population and industrial might in the 1970s, 1980s, and 1990s, the South expanded and grew. Despite growing industrial and economic might, they held on to their Southern culture. The Bible Belt simply rejected the fast-paced Northern mode of life. Respect for rural affairs was maintained and as a general rule, reigned supreme in this part of the country. It was true the South had its share of gin mills and porno houses, but for the most part, the city fathers of the Southern communities kept these establishments in their place, and on Saturdays and Sundays, the name of the Great One could be heard loud and clear emanating from the church pulpits. A young boy or girl could still grow up in the hills of Georgia and get lost in a Huckleberry Finn–type of existence. They could still believe in America and the life it promised and know not the wickedness of its ways.

In 2040, such was Jeremy Cox, an innocent lad, standing six feet one inch tall. His slim body looked all skin and bones. To look at his often-smiling face, you might think him a naive and weak-kneed lad. But if you saw him in the Georgia backwoods stalking a black bear for hours on end, he would conjure up thoughts of David Crockett and Daniel Boone. He was a fearless lad, and the South was full of many young men and women just like him. Jeremy had participated in the very early morning raid in Atlanta. For over a month, his group had prepared for the assault. He had been fearful of how he would react in an actual combat situation. It was easy enough to sit in the backwoods and talk of how courageous their actions were going to be. It was another thing to pick up a weapon, face another man in the eye, and follow through on a plan of action. Jeremy had read the book *The Red Badge of Courage*, and he personally felt the fear and inner dread that urges one to run and hide.

Jeremy had prepared well for the day of the raid. The men had practiced their routines over and over again. They even made two trips to Atlanta to observe the police stations and federal buildings they were going to attack. The highlight of their last trip was when they viewed two European generals descending the steps of the federal courthouse escorted by an Atlanta police captain. But now as Jeremy lay in his bed thinking of the previous day's raid, he felt that he had performed well after all. He thanked the Great One for giving him the courage to stand up and do what he thought was right. He was personally responsible for saving the lives of two of his comrades. They had just destroyed an ID checkpoint on Peach Street when an Atlanta policeman who survived the assault picked up a service revolver and prepared to open fire on the two men. Jeremy had not hesitated as he ended the man's life. Indeed, he was troubled at how quickly and efficiently he had performed the task. General Williamson, in a prior visit to the camp, had explained the various ways a man could and would react in a combat situation. If he had faith in his abilities and the courage of his convictions, he would survive any encounter intact. Jeremy fell asleep longing for the peace of the backwoods and hoping the conflict that lay ahead would not be a long one.

David Jefferson sat around the Adirondack Mountain campfire sharing hot coffee and companionship with the men of Camp Mohawk. The members of this group had led successful raids in Albany and Syracuse, New York. For the past three years, David had dreamed of leading Americans in the field of battle and winning great victories. Now that the moment was at hand, he felt somewhat frustrated. The men he led and gave inspiration to would not allow him to lead troops in the field. He was considered too valuable to lose, and the consensus of the Americans that supported him was that he stay well hidden and away from areas of armed conflict. Jefferson was furious over this and would not be consoled. A compromise was reached this day, and it was agreed he would travel with the men at least to the staging area just north of the New York State Thruway halfway between Albany and Syracuse, New York.

David had tears in his eyes as he bid farewell to the two hundred-plus man force that departed three hours before dawn. He was like a doting parent as he paced the upstate central New York foothills awaiting their return. But then he was as a schoolboy again when nine hours later, they returned victorious. The day was one of exhilaration and emotional exhaustion. He ran the full gamut of emotions that one man could feel in a day's time. Now as he sat around the campfire with his comrades, he felt a deep personal satisfaction. He had traveled a long hard lonely road. He had watched his fellow Americans through the years fall victim to their own greed and foolish ways. So many people had sat idly by and let others run and direct their lives. So many people had watched silently as their country and heritage was being sold away. It wasn't until enough people had these things affect them personally that he finally was able to get people to really listen to him. Now not only were so many willing to listen, they were ready to fight and die for a righteous cause.

So what was at the root of the problem that anyone had to die because of the mistakes of so many? It was both saddening and sobering to contemplate the sins of the past. Yet it was joyous and intoxicating to envision a people so eager to atone for those very sins. Human beings, thought David, were a complex and frustrating creature to figure out. He was just thankful that he believed the Great One was out there somewhere and would control the ultimate destiny of them all. The strategy now was to wait and see how the rest of America was going to react to the day's events and then see what measures Hans Rizarre and the Europeans would take against America.

Chapter 10

And I will bring distress upon men, that they shall walk like blind men, because they have sinned against the Lord: and their blood shall be poured out as dust, and their flesh as the dung.

—Zephaniah 1:17 KJV

November 21, 2040
European headquarters
Stuttgart, West Germany

All of Europe was astir with excitement of the news from America. Hundreds of newsmen gathered to observe the special meeting in Stuttgart. President Hans Rizarre ordered both the Upper House and the Lower House of Parliament to convene to discuss the American situation. In addition, his top aides had been meeting since the crises began. The fact that the attacks in America were only defined as raids by the military and no cities had actually been taken over meant that the European leadership had time to discuss the available options of response. Indeed, it was thought by some that perhaps this is what the rebels intended. It was known that a personal message had been delivered to President Rizarre by the Revolutionary group. The contents of the message had not been released to the news media as yet. It was hoped that perhaps before the day was over, it would be available for broadcast. The city of Stuttgart now took on a holiday-like atmosphere. Many citizens were out on the streets in full force so as to catch a firsthand glimpse of their leaders in action. The politicians and government leaders responded in kind with outward displays of pompous and stern facial expressions, government limousines, attaché cases filled to overflowing, and articulate responses to hastily called press conferences that announced to the waiting world such deep and profound statements as:

> I think we will soon get to the bottom of this. (Carlos Perez, Upper House, Spain)

> If Churchill were alive today, we would have a better grasp of this. (Jeano Amondos, Upper House, Italy)

> I think the Americans are angry with us. (Rohami Jahilo, Lower House, Sierra Leone)

> In essence, we can assume the crises may perhaps be premature, but on the other hand the powers that be will react in accordance. (Horst Von Riesen, Upper House, Germany)

It was a field day for media professionals who historically have been able to achieve such dramatic responses from such a willing political segment of our planet's government leaders. Whenever you would find a cameraman and a microphone, you could find an eager official ready to trade meaningless verbalization for a precious few minutes of air time. Usually it wasn't so important what you said; many people would forget it anyhow. But come election time, they might remember they saw your name and face in front of the camera. It was a true art form developed by some professional politicians. Don't say anything important or controversial but say something, say anything relevant to the topic. The more exposure, the better. In 2040 especially, it was dangerous to say anything in public that might be considered controversial. Politicians made it a point to espouse their own party and government positions, and public statements were carefully watered down to avoid criticism from anyone.

The entire morning of the twenty-first was spent seating upper and lower members of Parliament in their respective chambers. Party leaders busily made their rounds instructing colleagues on the format of the meeting. The afternoon was to be spent in public debate and open forum to allow each sitting member the opportunity to express his or her opinions concerning the American crises. It was expected that President Rizarre would address the full assembly sometime in the evening hours. His day was to be taken up meeting with his economic and military advisors to bring him totally up to date on the latest breaking developments.

As the dawn broke this same day in America, all appeared to be calm. David Jefferson's strategy was to draw back into the hills and carefully analyze the impact of the various raids. Further attacks were scheduled for the near future, but it was important to assess the initial impact.

Positive reactions were flowing in from all over the country. It was obvious government and police officials felt they were in a very precarious position. The United States military was stunned by General Williamson's defection, and it was rumored that the armored divisions under General Colson encamped at Fort Knox, Kentucky, had mobilized to join forces with him in Alabama. Radio communication into Camp Mohawk confirmed that, in fact, they were advised that the entire division had vacated Fort Knox during the evening. Mr. Jefferson was particularly ecstatic over this news although it was not surprising. Major General Cranston S. Colson was a thirty-year close associate of General Williamson. They held the same views on tactics and policy as well as having grave concerns over the future of America. This action would certainly cause the executive branch of government in Washington, DC, to be very alarmed and concerned. Not only were their citizens rebelling but also the military strength they needed to put down any such rebellion.

The rebels quickly had put themselves in a position of strength. They could not afford to relinquish their momentum, and Jefferson hurriedly drafted a letter to be dispatched to President Carlson. He would call for a meeting and suggest to negotiate a solution. The Europeans, of course, would not allow it, but at the least it could reduce the amount of bloodshed between American brethren on opposite sides of the fence.

No one in either country was prepared for what was to happen in New York City this day. It had seemed that all across America people were content to let this day rest in peace. It was after all an emotional experience that demanded some rest from a terrible public trauma. Not so in New York City. At approximately 10:00 a.m., about twenty-five thousand New Yorkers converged on Times Square. It started off as a quiet crowd. Instead of reporting to work this day, these New Yorkers converged on the streets, and soon signs appeared throughout the square and adjacent streets.

> Sons of Liberty Forever—Death to Foreigners
> David Jefferson for President—Now
> God Bless America—God Bless This Revolution
> Death to the Police Goon Squads
> Hans Rizarre Is No Friend of Ours
> Remember the New York 2000
> Death-Vengeance to Their Murderers

The crowd moved slowly through the streets. Weapons were spotted everywhere. There was no question more blood was to be spilled this day. Police units initially responded, and just as quickly withdrew to protect their respective precinct stations. At 11:15 a.m. in the center of Times Square, a makeshift podium was erected, and three khaki-garbed men appeared with a bullhorn. Three quick short speeches were made that sent the crowd into a frenzy. The men spoke of the New Yorkers who were ruthlessly murdered and the three years of humiliation they had all experienced. The last man to speak was Oliver Lee, a nineteen-year-old black man from East Harlem. His brother and sister both had been murdered by police hit squads since the murders had occurred. When he lifted his military M-16 rifle into the air and cried, "True New Yorkers, let's retake our city right now," the crowd went berserk, and their rage was fully vented. Over 550 citizens would lie dead, and thousands more would be hurt before this day was over. The initial crowd of people soon turned into a raging river of humanity that attracted thousands more that swelled the crowd into nearly 250,000 souls. Public buildings and foreign consulate offices were a main target of attack. Three police precincts were overrun and their offices ransacked. It took a personal televised appeal by David Jefferson himself to finally calm this storm. Fires had been set all along the docks, and several explosive devices so effectively rocked the waterfronts that the port authority closed down its operation. On Wall Street in Manhattan, there seemed to be not a building standing that did not have its ground floor windows smashed and offices in disarray. The fury of the crowd was as a violent storm unleashed. No bullets or police response would stop the wrath of this hurricane of human madness. The police withdrew to the outer perimeter of this chaos and let it take its course. After millions of dollars of damage had been done, the crowd disappeared into the concrete jungle that is New York City, and the police authorities took control of the streets. Hundreds of New Yorkers were detained, but less than fifty were actually arrested and charged with the crime of disorderly conduct.

The news of the riot in New York City reached Europe approximately three hours prior to President Rizarre's address to the assembled Parliament. It caused such a stir among the sitting members that they immediately recessed to await the president's address. The riotous actions of the New Yorkers gave rise to the need for a quick European response. Hans was under the gun, and the world held its breath, awaiting the words of his wisdom they so desperately wished to hear. It was 8:00 p.m. when President Rizarre stepped up to the podium.

"My dear members of Parliament and honored guests, I ask you for your attention please. My fellow Europeans who are listening and watching, please take heed. I have a message in my hands from American Revolutionaries across the sea. They tell me of the present horrors their own government imposes upon them. They list several misdeeds sanctioned by their president, Mr. Carlson, and the executive leadership in Washington, DC. For example, and I quote their spokesman, Mr. David John Jefferson, 'Police death squads are an ever-present threat to the citizens of our large cities. Our graveyards are filling to capacity, and we are helpless to react.' He goes on to say, 'Our checkpoint ID's smack of the worst of Gestapo and

Stormtrooper terror and control tactics. We are humiliated each and every day that we live. The yoke of Europe lies heavy across our necks. You over tax us and rape and ravage our land.'

"Yes, these are strong accusations to render against us. We, my fellow men and women of Europe, who have nurtured a sick giant America back to health, are so terribly accused. Yet as I speak, our accusers are as barbarians as they riot in the streets of New York City and elsewhere, as we have since learned. We have reports of a city out of control, under attack by ruthless rampaging mobs. Are we then to listen to such pleas for amends? Are we not given a moment to discuss such grievances? It appears not."

Hans held the podium for one hour and twenty minutes. He was at his best in oratorical skills, and when he was finished, all of Europe was as one with him It was obvious the Americans were ungrateful and not appreciative of the European efforts on their behalf. He demanded Parliament to draft a plan of action to deal with the outlaws in America. Within forty-eight hours, he wanted constructive options on his desk to allow him unlimited powers to respond and crush this revolution. There would be no negotiating with rebel outlaws, and Europe simply would not put up with any malcontents who would stand in the way of the Europeans' struggle and goal to become the ultimate civilization that planet Earth had ever known.

The following morning, as sporadic rioting continued to plague New York City, tens of thousands of Europeans demonstrated in support of President Rizarre. In all of Europe, there seemed not a single voice of support for the American revolution. It represented a far cry from the 1770s so long ago when many Europeans expressed outspoken support for the then American colonies. On November 22, 2040, there was not heard or not seen in public view one single opinion that could be construed as positive toward America. In the midst of its darkest hour, its gravest crisis to date, America could count on but a few friends anywhere in the world.

Chapter 11

The great day of the Lord is near; it is near and hasteneth greatly, even the voice of the day of the Lord; the mighty man shall cry there bitterly. That day is a day of wrath, a day of trouble and distress, a day of waste and desolation, a day of darkness and gloominess, a day of clouds and thick darkness, a day of the trumpet and alarm against the fortified cities and against the high towers.

—Zephaniah 1:14–16 KJV

November 23, 2040
Vatican City, Italy

Frost covered the Italian countryside as dawn broke in Vatican City, Italy. Large numbers of people were expected to gather in Saint Peter's Square as Pope Veritatis I was scheduled to give a major address concerning the chaos in America. He had spent the past two days communicating with the American church leaders via the complex communications network that was in place inside the Vatican. Every diocese in the world fed information into the Vatican computer. It was possible for the Vatican staff to access their computers and receive printouts from almost any parish in the world. The printouts could list every bit of information concerning an individual parish. It would include the pastor, the assistants, the complete and current financial status, and the names and current addresses of each registered parishioner. It was the pope's intention to utilize the television satellite hookup to communicate with America. He had issued an urgent plea to the Americans to show restraint and withhold from any further violence. He promised his personal efforts on their behalf to attempt to address their grievances in a diplomatic and nonviolent arena. Several American bishops had received personal phone calls from His Holiness urging them to get personally involved with their congregations: "Take to the streets and walk among the people. Preach the love and restraint of Jesus. Tell them the Holy Father in Rome weeps over their troubles."

Veritatis I's associates in the Vatican were duly impressed by his sincere efforts to reach the flock across the sea. He also talked about flying to Boston to make a personal appeal to America. He placed personal phone calls to President Rizarre, Gustav Erikson, and General Marcus Aurielle to caution restraint in their public rhetoric and action. Associates who knew him personally marveled at his aggressive approach to a terrible tragedy. He was a human dynamo in the amount of human effort and personal energy he was exerting. At twelve noon, he would address the crowds in Saint Peter's Square and make a public statement that would be carried live throughout the world.

At 10:00 a.m. he received a call from Cardinal Antonio Rondanelli that greatly encouraged him. The cardinal was en route to Rome and voiced his dedication and support to whatever His Holiness felt was the appropriate action for the church to take at this time. Aware of the cardinal's close relationship with President Rizarre, Pope Veritatis was elated to receive this type of call. He planned to meet with Cardinal Rondanelli after he arrived in Rome and possibly together they could develop plans that would allow the church to ease the strife that was causing so much grief. Perhaps they could set the church up as an intermediary and assist in negotiating a peaceful resolution to the conflict.

At 10:30 a.m., Pope Veritatis sat down in his private quarters to have a light breakfast prior to his speech. Cardinal Luciano Gazilli, his American language interpreter, joined him. The half-hour breakfast was spent reviewing the text of His Holiness's speech. Veritatis personally dictated it the evening before, and there seemed little to change as they reviewed together the final draft to be delivered to the news media. At exactly 11:00 a.m., Cardinal Gazilli let the kitchen staff know that he would like another cup of tea brought up to their quarters. Five minutes later, a newly hired young aide promptly arrived with the tea. Veritatis was not concerned over viewing a new face on his staff. He knew all his household staff personally. However, because of the constant stir of activity over the past few days, it was not unusual to see faces that were not familiar. In fact, Cardinal Rondanelli had told him earlier during their phone conversation that he had personally assigned some of his Italian staff to the Vatican to assist in the various activities that needed attention. Other cardinals had done the same, and it was heartening to see the church in Rome pulling together as a real family. It inspired hope when it was needed most.

Pope Veritatis I and Cardinal Gazilli never saw the young man pull a silencer attached nine-millimeter automatic pistol out from underneath his cassock. They were too busy discussing their work and sipping their tea. Three rounds each entered the back of the heads of the two clergymen. Death converged upon them instantaneously, and the young man exited as swiftly as he arrived nodding to the two Swiss Guards as they stood guard outside the door. The over one hundred thousand people who had stood waiting outside in the cold of Saint Peter's Square had no inkling that the man they so faithfully waited for would never appear before them. Ninety minutes later, when word finally leaked out to them, there was a public wailing and outburst of grief that shocked the world as television cameras viewed the scene at Saint Peter's. Teary-eyed and grief-stricken newscasters would give on the scene news updates that would leave the entire world with a shocking view of an unstable world gone mad.

It was fifteen minutes following the shooting that a Vatican aide entered the private quarters of His Holiness, was stunned by what he saw, and shrieked out in agonized grief his terrible discovery. In the early evening hours later, Cardinal Antonio Rondanelli held a Vatican press conference and stated to the world his offices had received an anonymous phone call from a male identifying himself as an American Minuteman. He advised that they took claim for the papal assassination and warned that more would be forthcoming.

It is difficult to describe how this news was received by the European Parliament sitting in Stuttgart, West Germany. For over six hours, the lions of Europe roared death to the American rebels. At 9:30 p.m., they delivered a document to President Rizarre, urging him to take quick and powerful measures to respond to this rebellious insurrection. He was given full powers through unanimous vote of Parliament to utilize whatever options he chose in order to crush the rebellion. Parliament would ask no questions and pose no obstacles in his path. Vengeance would not be the Lord's but President Rizarre's. It represented a turn of events that spelled out terrible gloom for the American continent. Forces were gathering in strength around the world that left America a land alone and isolated. A consensus of world opinion was forming that indicated even more restrictions would be imposed than previously. In its past of more than two hundred and sixty-some years of existence, Americans had known some very difficult moments. Many were moments that tested the character and inner strength of its people. Late in the year of our Lord 2040, one of the toughest tests that ever faced this young nation lay at its doorstep.

Chapter 12

> The only thing necessary for the triumph of
> evil is for good men to do nothing.
>
> —Edmund Burke

November 25, 2040
Sioux City, Iowa, USA

    The riots in New York and the shock of a papal assassination left the American revolutionary movement with a major unnerving crises. The events were unexpected, and following so soon upon the heels of the well-planned coordinated rebel attacks, the revolutionary movement felt the need for high-level meetings of its leadership to plan carefully its future actions. Sioux City, Iowa, was chosen as the site to meet for two reasons. It was located centrally in the continental United States, and it was one of quite a few small American cities completely in the hands of the revolutionary movement. David Jefferson, Generals Williamson and Colson, Colonel Redding, and ninety-two other rebel leaders hastened to this city of some eighty-five thousand residents. Although secrecy was of great importance in establishing a meeting place, word spread quickly among the Iowans that their city was hosting the current heroes of the revolution. The leadership of the city hurriedly secured the main access roads and sealed off Sioux City to all outsiders. The campus of Western Iowa Technical Community College was selected as the staging area for the meeting. The students and faculty here had played a major role in the taking of the city. For over a year, the campus had been a haven for those who had espoused a better way of life for America.

Underground newspapers were brought to life there and freely distributed to the residents of Sioux City. Although the city officials did not condone the openness of the activities, they chose not to attempt to prevent it from existing. Clearly the students were voicing the inner feeling of so many Midwesterners, and when the actual day of the revolution raids arrived, the citizens of Sioux City quickly capitulated and joined the movement. The entire city police force arrived to work on November 19 dressed in rebel khaki green, and not a shot or explosion of any kind was heard there that day.

Now, six days later, with a winter chill in the air and a light snow falling, the students' auditorium at Western Tech was established as a meeting hall for the revolutionary leadership. At 8:00 p.m., Phillip Redding, who had arrived from California, called the meeting to order. An adjacent room was set up for the news media. It was clear that following the meeting, official statements would be made available for distribution throughout the country. It was important to advise all Americans of the latest news and developments. In fact, David Jefferson was scheduled to appear at a local television station at 11:00 p.m. and broadcast a message that would be transmitted to as many Americans as possible. David Jefferson stepped up to the podium amid a great round of applause. There was no doubt that the assembled leaders had felt a certain pride with regard to their initial successes. Only their eagerness to hear his words this evening prevented the small crowd from rushing to the stage with plaudits for their champion.

"Thank you, all. I am so honored by your support. Thank you. Your confidence and support help ease the burden of an overwhelming task. In approximately three hours, I will be making a television address that I hope many Americans will have the opportunity to view. We must deny the vicious story that our people assassinated the pope. We have no people of ours operating anywhere outside of the continental United States, with the exception of a small group that is presently up in Canada, on the border, assisting Americans who wish to cross over into Canada. I implore each of you to get the word back to your people. It appears that the masses of Americans are with us. We don't need these types of lies perpetrated to divide us. We have decided that within the next two weeks, we must make a concerted effort to take control of as much of America as we can and attempt to establish a new government. Right now we feel that it is safe to say that the rural population of this country is solidly behind us. General Williamson and his troops will soon converge on the Washington, DC, area. New York City, Chicago, Detroit, and Los Angeles will follow. There is a possibility we can achieve victory with very little bloodshed. If we are successful in these cities, the entire country will be ours. At this point, we must move swiftly. It is possible General Aurielle could well dispatch troops to this country. At this point, we believe we will be unable to prevent them from doing this. If they do, then all bets are off regarding our ability to take over the entire country. We must take as much ground as possible now as soon as possible. Right now, I am going to turn this meeting over to the general and his staff. Listen closely, they will be providing the specific details of our planned attacks next week. We wish them to be as coordinated as our first effort. Success is achieved by swift and decisive action. May the Lord be with us as we march to victory."

Again a great shout went up as Jefferson strode off the stage. America had some genuine heroes assembled in this college auditorium, and it was heartwarming and emotional to see these men and women of such high character giving praise and applause to the man that inspired them. For the next five hours, the general and his staff went over the specifics of the upcoming military actions. The plan called for the threat of invasions rather than for any actual real battles. The revolutionary leadership did not feel that government and police authorities still in power had any real desire to wage any kind of extensive warfare. There was still the issue of the ten thousand French troops sitting near the old Fort Dix area in New Jersey. So far, no one had made any attempt to harm them. They would be left alone entirely for right now. It was hoped they would stay where they were. So far, they had. Even during the height of the New York City riots, they had not budged from their current staging area.

The meetings at Sioux City lasted for three days before the leadership dispersed to their various hometowns throughout the country. A consensus was reached that a victory of sorts could be achieved quickly and quietly. If it could be done prior to any European mobilization of military resources, then perhaps President Rizarre would not pursue it. He let the Canadians off the hook three years prior, so why not the Americans now. David Jefferson was not so sure that it was going to be that easy. He cautioned the leadership in his final address that they should be prepared for a long hard struggle. An effective blockade and trade embargo by the Europeans would place extreme economic hardships upon all Americans. There was no question that Europe could respond with an awesome display of military force. It depended upon just how badly they wished to punish the Americans and retaliate against such a large-scale revolt. In his television address to America, Jefferson urged everyone to start the process of rebuilding their society. It would take long years of hard work to reestablish the United States as any type of viable world power. He urged Americans to get back into the fields and regain the agricultural flavor this country once knew. He urged the businessmen and businesswoman of the cities to reestablish their factories and once again turn out products made solely in the United States of America—"We would have to do it. The markets of the world would suddenly be closed to us. The sooner we got started with these projects, the better off we would all be." Jefferson finished up by pleading with all Americans that they call upon God to oversee this great effort. America's motto was going to continue to be "In God we trust." These words could not just be mouthed, they must be totally believed and accepted. This is the one thing that would ensure total victory. Faith in God would reap the reward of the toil.

Hans Rizarre retched in pain when he viewed the latest American newsreel. Gustav Erikson retired in silence to his private study, and General Marcus Aurielle called his generals together for a major briefing session. The rest of the world waited in breathtaking silence as the awful calm began to set in before the real storm raged. It was obvious to all the storm clouds were gathering, and it was just a question of how they would dissipate that was on everyone's minds. Mankind had once again worked itself into a dilemma of huge proportions. Matters of national pride on both sides of the

Atlantic Ocean demanded actions be taken. The year 2040 was an age of nuclear weaponry.

The most intelligent of planet Earth's leaders had stated through the years that such awesome weapons of destruction would never be used. How could they be? For shame, for shame, such foolish thinking. When at any time in the history of mortal man on this planet Earth have men refrained from using devices they have made? The answer is simply never. If, in fact, a country founded upon a firm belief in God and His Divine Providence, dropped two nuclear devices upon a civilian population in Japan in 1945, who then could expect in his right mind that others believing in their own righteous principles will not do the same? Who then can expect such foolish thought to be acceptable sane thinking? How long shall such delusions prevail? When will the children of men cast all such weapons of death into the sea, to be buried forever?

Chapter 13

And he said, Take heed that ye be not deceived: for many shall come in my name, saying, I am Christ; and the time draweth near: go ye not therefore after them.

—Luke 21:8 KJV

December 1, 2040,
Saint Peter's Square, Vatican City, Italy

The dark clouds of late autumn hovered over the huge crowd standing vigil in the large square at Saint Peter's in Vatican City. The Italians were well versed in papal elections. Although it was 5:00 a.m. on a rather frigid December day, the people assembled in the square warmed to the idea that the new pope would be chosen on the first ballot. In fact, the whole world was quite sure that Antonio Franciscus Rondanelli would be chosen the next man to follow the line of Saint Peter. Even though this view was widespread and many seemed to have the whole papal succession process figured out, no one seemed to know when the announcements would exactly be made. The cardinals were all locked up together at twelve midnight the previous evening. The results of the first ballot should be forthcoming soon.

At 5:20 a.m., a small murmur began to run through the crowd of almost one-half million faithful souls. It was evident smoke was rising from the special papal chimney. White smoke meant a new successor had been chosen. Black smoke meant the ballot was unsuccessful and another vote had to be taken. Against the somewhat black morning sky, it was very evident that white smoke was spewing upward. However, the crowd had been fooled in prior years and waited a good twenty seconds to ensure that it was white smoke that continued to rise. Finally convinced, the crowd's initial murmur rose to a roar, and soon the chant "Viva il Papa" (Long live the pope) was begun. As the crowd came to life, so too the news media appeared as if from out of the cracks of the walls of the great basilica that rose above them. Television stations around the world interrupted their present programming and switched live to Saint Peter's Square. At exactly 6:00 a.m., it was officially announced, a new pope had been chosen. The powerful school of Roman cardinals had selected on the very first ballot the man that most everyone throughout the world thought would be chosen.

At 6:05 a.m. Cardinal Antonio Franciscus Rondanelli, clothed in papal white, stepped out onto the balcony overlooking Saint Peter's Square. He addressed the assembled throng gathered below him. To show the waiting world his sincerity, he brought two American cardinals out onto the balcony with him. This gesture was to show the world his earnest desire to bring peace wherever he could do so on the planet. He publicly appealed for all Americans to throw down their arms and come to terms peacefully with the European Republic. He was sure he could mediate a peaceful solution.

"America, trust me," he declared.

To those who listened on television or watched on their live internet feeds on their computers, laptops, or smartphones, it was quite a convincing appeal. The new pope seemed sincere, and it was difficult not to accept him on good faith terms as he spoke for the first time as the chief shepherd of an enormous flock of faithful souls spread throughout the four corners of the world. It was very difficult for even the Americans not to be affected by his words. Some news commentators mentioned they thought they detected tears running down his cheeks as he spoke of the troubled world they all lived in and the great need to come together as brothers and sisters. For a few moments following his short address, public commentators were actually mentioning the possibility that perhaps this new world leader could have a positive impact upon the world scene and perhaps even negotiate a settlement with the rebel faction in America.

At 6:30 a.m. the new pope gave a final blessing to the crowd and left the balcony. As he reentered the safety of his quarters, he was given a telephone by one of his staff. President Rizarre was on the other end. His Holiness advised everyone to leave the room, and he spoke in private to the most powerful man on the planet.

"Tony, that was one hell of a fine show you just put on. This phone is clean. You can say anything you want to."

"Thanks, Hans. I hope I was convincing enough. I don't want those bastards to know what we are up to."

"I can appreciate that all right. I've got a real surprise in store for everyone real soon. I'm so excited about it I can't hardly stand it. In fact, whenever I think about it, I break up laughing. Some of these clowns around me here think I'm cracking up."

"Well, clue me in, Hans. It would be nice to know what you are planning. I need to know what position to take from this end."

"Tony, I can't tell you now. It would spoil the surprise. You'll love it. We talked about it before. I'm not giving you any more clues than that. It'll spoil it for you. Let's say we get together for a week at your place outside Venice beginning December 8."

"It sounds great to me, Hans. Do I have to wait that long to find out what you're up to?"

"You'll learn of it by then, believe me. We'll be able to celebrate properly."

"It sounds good to me, Hans. I'll call and have the boys make the proper arrangements."

"Good, Tony. I'll see you then. In the meantime, say a few prayers for me."

The laughter was loud and hard as Hans put down the phone. Tony was pleased that he was in such fine spirits.

CHAPTER 14

Think not that I am come to send peace upon the earth: I came not to send peace, but a sword. For I am come to set a man at variance against his father, and the daughter against her mother, and the daughter-in-law against mother-in-law. And a man's foes shall be they of his own household.

—Matthew 10:34–36 KJV

December 6, 2040
New York City

Ralph Walden was disturbed by the turn of events that were occurring in New York City. Although the majority of workers and citizens overall were supportive of David Jefferson's goals of the revolution, an unusual number of varying groups suddenly surfaced to lay claim as the chief spokesperson for what was right for all New Yorkers. Groups such as the Flatbush Friends of Freedom and the Rockaway Renegades supported Jefferson fanatically. They believed negotiating from a position of strength and limited violence was the proper course of action. On the other hand, the Flushing Meadows Marauders and the Cross Island Crusaders believed in massive forces of arms and fanatical guerilla tactics as quick means to victory. They actively participated in the three-day riot and outspokenly urged it on. Their intention was to riot until the city was completely destroyed. Although David Jefferson's personal appeals calmed them down for the moment, it was apparent they would not be held in check for long. In the Bronx, the Bronx Bombers were living up to their name. They were bombing two or three public buildings on an almost daily basis. The Van Cortland Park Rangers were vicious and ruthless. They publicly executed seven city council persons and European sympathizers and vowed that this was just the beginning. Such a wide divergence of groups and tactics made it quite difficult to present an organized effort, and it would take strong action by these various group leaders to bring direction and unity to the apparent chaos that presently existed.

Ralph Walden had reluctantly joined Jefferson's group. He had witnessed firsthand the need for a dramatic change in America. However, the price that was being paid was a real horror to him. The everyday violence, bloodshed, and dead bodies appearing on the streets of what he felt was the greatest American city was appalling to him. It was necessary to carry a concealed weapon with you wherever you traveled. Each day was filled with explaining your group affiliations and what group you belonged to. Tension was high, and the sound of gunfire was heard much too often. To make matters worse, the New York City Police Department still represented a major obstacle to the success of the revolution. They had withdrawn from their various precincts and consolidated their forces in the southern part of the city. They held Brooklyn to the southwest and the entire city south of Atlantic Avenue including John F. Kennedy Airport. Also, there were thousands of New Yorkers who still clung to the Europeans as their only hope for the future. They flocked behind the police lines and in many cases, took up arms to join their cause. It was true that there were some defections to the revolutionary cause, but for the most part, the New York Police Department was holding together. They had too much to lose. They had achieved such a position of power throughout the city, they weren't about to give it up easily. Walden, through his intelligence-gathering efforts, had advised Jefferson that the police force as it was presently deployed, could inflict great damage on the rebels if they chose to strike out at selected targets within the city. It would take a well-organized, cohesive military operation to defeat them.

At the present time, David Jefferson was now encamped near West Point, New York, assembling a small army that could move into New York City and command a takeover of the city. JFK Airport and

Newark Airports were key targets of the revolutionary group's focus as European troops could be flown in here and the city could be lost to them for a long time.

At approximately 8:00 p.m. on December 6, 2040, Ralph Walden descended into a manhole cover somewhere in the vicinity of Central Park in Manhattan. He was staying with twenty-five members of the Flatbush Friends of Freedom. They were utilizing an abandoned section of the city sewer system as their present meeting area. Located beneath the city streets. it was spacious enough and ideal for carrying out clandestine operations. Every entrance was properly alarmed. and very few people knew all the ways one could get in and out. The Flatbush Friends of Freedom had easy access to more than eighteen blocks of Manhattan and could move freely and rapidly underground. Ralph had helped assemble the group in a bunker-like staging area. The group talked of ways they could best assist Jefferson in his proposed military assault against the city. A consensus was reached that it was best just to sit it out and wait for Jefferson to arrive with his army. It was decided there was no point in trying to bring together all the various New York City factions at this point. Any sizeable army would absorb them collectively, and their individual personalities and claims to fame would suddenly become negligible at best.

Kelly O'Brien, an ex-city school teacher and new Flatbush member, was responsible for radio communications with the various revolutionary factions. Flatbush had their own transmitter and receiver underground with them. They had just installed new antennae earlier in the day. One was sitting atop a building two and a half blocks away from the main entrance to their underground facility. It had taken three different raids to get all the antennae cable they needed. Kelly was attempting to hook Ralph up with radio communication with David Jefferson, who was up north in the mountains along the Hudson River. She knew how important it was for the inner-city groups to have communication with the soon-approaching army that was now gathering upriver in the Catskill Mountains. At 10:00 p.m., she made her first contact.

"Flatbush Friends of Freedom calling Mr. Jefferson. Flatbush Friends of Freedom calling Mr. Jefferson, over."

"Roger, Flatbush, we know of the man you are seeking, over."

"Roger. We are awaiting his arrival. Please identify yourself. Over."

"Roger, this is Bluebird Alpha base one. We are an advance unit of the Thirty-Second Militia out of Albany, New York. We have many friends assembled here who are assisting your Mr. Jefferson. Over."

"10-4, Bluebird. Advise Mr. Jefferson that Mr. Walden and his friends in Flatbush eagerly await his arrival. God bless and Godspeed. Over."

"Roger, Flatbush. We will advise. Keep your radio waves open. We will be talking to you real soon. Bluebird Alpha, base one, out."

Kelly had been quick to record this message and had it hurriedly sent to Ralph with the news. The small group was ecstatic and elated over the communication. They knew help was on the way, and the best plan of action was to continue to sit tight and wait until they arrived. The Flatbush Friends of Freedom lay their heads in contented sleep this evening, and Ralph thanked god that David Jefferson and his friends were close by.

Chapter 15

Therefore have I poured out mine indignation upon them; I have consumed them with the fire of my wrath: their own way have I recompensed upon their heads, saith the Lord God.

—Ezekiel 22:31 KJV

December 7, 2040
Stuttgart, Germany

It took the European Press Corps just thirty minutes to assemble in the lobby of President Rizarre's quarters. At 9:00 a.m., his press secretary had announced that a presidential appearance was forthcoming concerning the American situation. President Rizarre would appear and give a brief statement at 10:00 a.m. There would be no question-and-answer period following the statement, and President Rizarre was expected to leave immediately for a brief vacation at an undisclosed location. Europeans were anxiously awaiting a presidential response to the American revolution. Reports had been flowing in all week concerning large buildups of men and materials around the major cities of America. It was obvious New York City, Washington, DC, Chicago, Detroit, and Los Angeles were being targeted by the rebels. In a surprise development, on December 1, in a major military movement, the ten thousand French troops encamped in New Jersey were transported to John F. Kennedy Airport and flown to Paris, France. Within four days, they were gone. It was extremely baffling because the world was expecting more European troops to be dispatched to America shortly, not European troops leaving America and coming home to France. The tremendous amount of activity around European Defense Headquarters of late gave much support to this belief. Ninety thousand European troops were already put on alert and moved to staging areas around airfields in France, Germany, and Great Britain. Sending troops in the opposite direction gave rise to all sorts of new speculation. It was difficult to believe that the European leadership would abandon their holdings in America so easily.

President Rizarre arrived promptly at 10:00 a.m. and began his address immediately.

"My fellow Europeans and to all citizens of the world that may be listening, I ask you all to pay strict attention and listen closely to my message this morning. After much thought and deliberation, I have reached a decision with regards to the American situation. I have grieved as a father does over an errant favorite son. As I speak to you now, our American brethren are receiving my message. No longer will we tolerate blatant disregard for our authority. History has shown what weakness in the face of adversity can mean to world stability. Our planet has grown too small to ignore open defiance regardless of how far removed from us in miles it may be. Let the world know what has befallen the rebels in New York City. As I speak, this wicked city lays like a wounded animal. Years ago our medical doctors discovered that radiation treatments quickly applied can eliminate body cancer rapidly and thoroughly. I have applied the same type of treatment to the cancer festering in New York City, which will serve as a warning to America that we will bring ruination upon them if they fail to yield to our direction. The very distinguished general Marcus Aurielle has delivered from me this fine December morning low-yield ten-kiloton nuclear bombs from our high-tech missiles that should help eliminate that particular cancer that has spread so in New York City. Our planet, seen as a living body, needs to be rid of this terrible menace. To allow it to grow any further threatens the whole planet body. A second missile delivered a low-yield ten-kiloton bomb to the city of Philadelphia, Pennsylvania. We sympathize with our American brethren deeply. I find it a difficult task to chastise them so. There is no malice in the message I deliver. I have also responded to their complaints that their own government has abused them. Let it be known that I will not tolerate such injustices against them. I have also unleashed a low-yield ten-kiloton nuclear bomb on Washington, DC, the heart of their government and their troubles. The present government in Washington, DC, hopefully will step down to exist no more. I am sure the world will applaud me for this particular action. Let the world know the power and might of the Europeans. We shall not be deterred from our goals. We exist solely to protect the quality of life for our citizens here. No one shall threaten or defy us. Next week I shall dispatch members of our Parliament to Chicago, Illinois, in America to help the citizens of the United States reestablish their government. It has been our intention all along to assist them. I am confident that following my message of today, there will no longer be any problems with America working together with us. I thank you all for your time and attention this morning. Long live the republic. Fear not tomorrow for we are working hard today to ensure that our citizens shall lead the world to new heights and a future full of promise. Thank you."

The three hundred and eighty-three people that were summoned to listen to the presidential announcement were left speechless. The enormity of what they just heard was overwhelming. A very large number of television crews and major news network reporters were present at the event, and it was all captured on live TV. All news reports were now being released to a worldwide audience that was mostly stunned by what they had just heard. Nuclear devices used against the United States was shocking and difficult to comprehend. European Republic Parliamentarians in attendance seemed taken aback and somewhat subdued. They were observed slowly coming back to life, conversing and comparing notes to make sure they had all heard the same thing. The event was both shocking and stunning. They must all now sit and wait to see how the rest of the world responds to this most awful news they have just shared with the rest of the planet.

Chapter 16

Where there is love, there is life.

—Mahatma Gandhi

December 7, 2040
United States of America

In America, the citizens of Washington, DC, Philadelphia, and New York City had not the luxury of time to reflect. It was true. The president of the European Republic, Mr. Hans Rizarre, had unleashed nuclear missiles and delivered devastation upon a country whose previous troubles paled terribly in comparison to what it found on its doorstep today. Throughout history, mankind has applied varied definitions to the word *hell*. Many humans are often apt to describe their individual versions of hell through their own real-life experiences. Before this day was over, a new hell version could be found in America: approximately 200,000 souls perished in each city, and another 350,000 were injured in each city. Within a couple of minutes' time, New York City, Philadelphia, and Washington, DC, were reduced to zones of chaos and terror. Five-hundred-mile-per-hour winds and an enormous shock wave raged throughout these cities, hurling buildings, bodies, bricks, and debris in all directions. Power blackouts and communication power failures adversely affected the entire Eastern Seaboard in most all areas east of Harrisburg, Pennsylvania; Baltimore, Maryland; Knoxville, Tennessee; and extending as far south as Charlotte, North Carolina. Those who lived on the periphery of the blasts knew full well what had happened. However, many Americans did not learn what had transpired until early evening. The entire country was left aghast and reeling with disbelief over the reality of what had befallen America. It was Captain Ronald (Rainbow) Rivers who was responsible for reporting quickly the eyewitness account of the explosion as it actually occurred. An American Airlines pilot, Rivers earned the nickname Rainbow for his uncanny ability through the years to be able to maneuver through the harshest of storms and air turbulence conditions made worse by glaring climate changes that were negatively affecting planet earth. Through twelve years of flying, he had ridden many a thunderhead amid great turbulence and always poked through to calming skies and never once failed to bring his passengers home safely. This shivering cold and windy Friday December morning, cruising at almost thirty thousand feet, Captain Rivers was bringing one hundred and eighty residents of the Los Angeles area to the airport at Newark, New Jersey, on a specially chartered flight. Despite the unrest throughout the country, sick as it may seem, this was considered prime time in the professional football season, and the Giants of New Jersey were hosting the Rams from the West Coast in a 7:00 p.m. Saturday major matchup. Now at predawn, Captain Rivers was nearing Wilkes-Barre, Pennsylvania, contemplating on beginning his descent into Newark when the New York air traffic controllers began a dialogue about an unknown blip that suddenly appeared on their screen.

"JFK, this is Newark Air Traffic Operations. Are you expecting a visitor?"

"Negative, Newark. It's nothing we know about. I'll contact ground security to alert them of a possible arrival."

"Well, JFK, it's moving too fast to be a commercial flight. Could be a military jet. You ought to check it out, my friend."

"Roger, Newark. If we could we would. It might be an unexpected visitor from Europe. We've been expecting troops, but this appears to be just one aircraft."

Captain Rivers listened with interest. He certainly didn't want to bring his aircraft into an area that might possibly be involved in some type of military strife. Although he was still a good thirty-five minutes from pulling up to the landing gate, he would keep some other options open. His copilot, Dick Evans, was excellent whenever situations arose like this that demanded quick thinking.

"Mr. Evans, I think you should chart us a couple of alternate landing spots just in case. I don't want to bring this down in the middle of a bombing run or firefight. Use the alternate channel and contact Philadelphia or Allentown. They can still bus them over to the game from either one of those places."

"Sure thing, Captain. If need be, we can wait it out up here for a while. We've got enough fuel."

"'Thanks, Dick. Maybe we'll just do that. I'll continue to listen in on this."

As copilot, Evans adjusted his headphones and began to call Allentown. Captain Rivers was interrupted by a frantic voice coming out of air traffic control at Newark.

"This is Air Traffic, Newark Operations, to all listening stations. We have a Mayday. I repeat we have a Mayday. United States Air Force has just advised that the unknown blip on the screen is an incoming missile. Target is unknown, but missile is approaching fast. I repeat, we have a—"

At this moment, the transmission ended, and Captain Rivers suddenly saw the eastern horizon light up. It was as if the sun had suddenly popped up like a jack-in-the-box. Rainbow Rivers was no fool. He knew exactly what had happened. The use of nuclear weaponry by the Europeans had been spoken of as a viable option of late, but few people on the planet ever thought it would happen. He immediately grabbed the headphones of his copilot and screamed, "Evans, we've been nuked. We're turning this baby around and quick."

Instinctively both men flew into action, and in a matter of twenty seconds or so, the big jet was turned around and with full power, heading back west.

"Where to, Captain?"

"We sure as hell aren't going to Chicago. They may have targeted that as well. Let's make it Cincinnati. I can't imagine them thinking to drop one there."

"Good grief, Captain! Look to your left behind you. It looks like they dropped another one further south along the coast."

"It appears in the direction of Baltimore or DC. It's hard to know how many they are going to drop. I don't believe this is happening. Look, I'm going to announce to the passengers what I think has happened. You get on the radio and see if we can't raise somebody. We may have to land this on our own."

It was one and one-half hours later when Captain Rivers landed his aircraft safely in Cincinnati, Ohio. It was just twenty-nine minutes prior to touchdown when he finally made radio contact with Cincinnati Air Traffic Control and reported what they had all witnessed. The passengers on board had wished to attend a spirited sporting event but instead witnessed a couple of the deadliest passes that any man could have ever thrown.

At 3:50 a.m. on December 7, David Jefferson received an urgent call from General Williamson. He was told to seek shelter immediately. The United States military had confirmed that at least two missiles were approaching the United States continent and in less than fifteen minutes, would hit their targets. Early target projections were the New York City area and possibly Baltimore or Washington, DC.

The role of the United States military had been altered a great deal within the last two weeks. Because of large-scale defections to the rebel cause, it was decided the military would remain neutral for now. As a matter of policy, it was decided by the Joint Chiefs of Staff that open lines of communication would be maintained with President Carlson, in hiding somewhere in Virginia, and General Williamson, representing David Jefferson. At the right moment, it was hoped that sufficient pressure could be brought on both of these leaders to affect a peaceful settlement. In the meantime, United States troops were kept on alert status and prepared to move out as directed. The plan was to keep the military prepared and on alert status but to refrain from actual combat. The military was divided in its loyalties and wisely decided not to destroy itself by taking sides. Although the United States had lost its nuclear capability, it still represented a formidable conventional force of arms. There was no doubt that a unified effort by the United States Army, Navy, Air Force, Coast Guard, and Marine personnel could eke out some type of victory or stalemate in a prolonged American Civil War. The problem was that the troops who were to do the fighting had more sympathy with the American rebels rather than with the American government. Field commanders were working overtime to prevent their troops from defecting to the rebel cause. A commitment to fight on behalf of or to defend the existing government might have caused the immediate loss of any viable kind of an American military force, and the United States would immediately be without any kind of professional military capability.

On the very early morning of December 7, United States military radar stations detected the presence of two missiles on defense radar screens. An alarm was sounded, and ten US Air Force jets were in the air within five minutes' time. Both President Carlson and General Williamson were advised to seek shelter. The jets fired a full complement of missiles in a vigorous and aggressive attempt to knock out the incoming arrows of death. They soon learned there was a third missile. It became obvious the nuclear warhead missiles were armed with sophisticated electronic gear that caused the US antimissile missiles to veer away from their targets on every occasion. Two of the pilots courageously attempted to place their aircraft in front of the incoming New York missile but found out that all efforts to halt it were futile. This entire episode took place in less than twenty minutes. There was little time to let anyone know of what was going on. Of the close to seven hundred and fifty thousand souls that perished this day, less than one hundred had any foreknowledge at all of what had caused their sudden demise.

Chapter 17

Yesterday, December 7, 1941—a date which will live in infamy—the United States of America was suddenly and deliberately attacked by naval and air forces of the Empire of Japan.

—Franklin D. Roosevelt

David Jefferson was beside himself with grief. His worst fears had suddenly come to life. Helpless to react against such awesome violence, he wondered now what would become of the great struggle to free America. Was it worth the price they were all paying? The euphoria he felt with his small army ready to approach and win New York city was now replaced with crushing depression. Only the outrageous injustice of such a dastardly act kept him from losing control of his senses and human emotions. The inner anger that arose within him jolted him out of a temporary stupor and moved him to action. He quickly passed word through his field commanders that they should immediately prepare to move out. There was much danger from the fallout, and the farther north they moved up the Hudson River, the better chance for survival. It was fortunate this day that strong winds were blowing east along a cold front positioned just west of the States of New York and Pennsylvania. The immediate effect resulted in a life-threatening fallout over the New York City, Philadelphia, and Washington, DC, metropolitan areas to be swiftly blown out over the Atlantic Ocean. Thousands more American citizens could have been contaminated and killed if the winds had been blowing differently.

Despite the existence of the cold front, the detonation of the three nuclear warheads caused an immediate and massive exodus of those people who lived and survived on the outer peripheries of the blast. Americans, for the first time in many years, truly came together. Families and individuals who fled their homes in terror had no problems finding refuge. The traumatic psychological impact of everyone being in the same predicament tore down any barriers that previously existed. Adjacent towns and communities rallied to help and support. They knew immediately that a life-and-death struggle was in progress, and everyone must reach out to act as brothers and sisters united to ensure any kind of hope for their future.

On December 10, David Jefferson, now camped just east of Albany, New York, received an urgent request via the military from President Carlson, hiding still in Northern Virginia, to meet as soon as possible at any city Jefferson chose to designate. They must discuss uniting in some fashion in order to save America. Jefferson felt it imperative that they get together quickly.

It was just two days later that Jefferson and Carlson met in Cincinnati, Ohio. The hatchet between them was buried, and the American Civil War ceased to exist. President Carlson resigned his presidency and joined a government group of three men comprised of David Jefferson, General Williamson, and himself. A simple one-page letter was drafted that stated,

> America rejects Europe's raping of her resources, her slave state approach to world government, and most of all, her outrageous, irresponsible use of nuclear weapons with wanton disregard of the human suffering, loss of life, and personal misery that accompanies them. President Rizarre can use all the missiles that Europe possesses, but he can also rest assured that as long as there is one American left alive, that same one American would respond in similar fashion. We reject your negative, materialistic, inhumane policies that shall surely doom you to hell. We have stood at the edge of a dreadful precipice for much too long. We indeed can see that we have reaped

what we have sown. The immoral and irresponsible policies we have allowed to be caused here in America are now reeling and impacting us with their awful reality and affecting us obviously in painful ways. The God of Abraham in His mercy has allowed us yet to survive. We have faith that He shall shield us and deliver us from future evils and terrors. As Americans, we shall stand together and with the assistance of Divine Providence, rebuild this land, and learning, in such a dramatic and firsthand way, from our mistakes of the past, build toward a future that will provide for all Americans equally and fairly, with trust and kindness utilized as the motto of our living endeavors.

The quickness with which the American leaders made peace with each other was instrumental in solidifying American unity. Most Americans knew the country could not long withstand a nuclear onslaught, but there was irony in Hans Rizarre's caveman approach. He often laughed at Americans as juvenile-type cowboys and failed to go beyond his superficial attitude concerning the United States of America. He failed to realize the true essence of old American cowboy heroes. Made-for-television heroes such as the Lone Ranger, Hopalong Cassidy, Roy Rogers, John Wayne, Gene Autry, etc., etc., etc., struck at the very heart of what America had hoped to stand for—law and order, above all justice for all. The good guys surviving against the bad guys. The underlying theme was that goodness and adhering to following good moral principles were essential and honorable ideals to strive for. Although over the past years, so many Americans had let these ideals slip away and become low-priority items, they never were totally lost sight of. This was primarily due to their essential importance when discussing concepts concerning the American dream. Events of the past few years, culminating with the nuclear attack against America, suddenly brought these lost ideals to the surface in a rush. Americans could immediately relate to their ancestors of centuries past, the thousands of people who fled European oppression, came to America, and built a land and country based on solid principles and rules of life. There arose a realization that rules and regulations were initially laid out to protect everyone. To massage and amend rules of living for material expediency resulted in ruinous destruction. In order for society to survive in a stable and harmonious environment, principles and laws forged with wisdom and careful planning should not fall prey to the profit-hungry wolves of the marketplace. David Jefferson and his associates espoused true American ideals and gave voice to the inner feelings of a majority of their countrymen. Hans Rizarre had no idea or clear grasp of the unity that was now solidifying the American people into a strong cohesive unit. He truly believed they were a crushed and beaten people that soon would be once again catering and begging for his favors no matter what the cost. He was soon to learn he was grossly mistaken.

Chapter 18

> But they that wait upon the Lord shall renew their strength;
> they shall mount up with wings as eagles; they shall run,
> and not be weary; and they shall walk, and not faint.
>
> —Isaiah 40:31 KJV

December 16, 2040
O'Hare Airport
Chicago, Illinois, America

It was nine days since the European attack against America. At approximately 10:00 a.m., a delegation of European parliamentarians were scheduled to arrive at O'Hare Airport to begin a new era of European direction concerning American affairs. Europeans supported President Rizarre's strong measures toward America. The rest of the world pretty much kept its silence about the matter. Following the blatant December 7th Pearl Harbor Day–type attack against the United States, no one really cared to incur the wrath of Mr. Rizarre. After all, he had enough decency to clear out all the foreign embassies in Washington, DC, prior to dropping his nuclear devices. It was a fairly easy process especially since most people knew that American General Williamson was marching on DC with his airborne and armored troops. Most all the American politicians and American dignitaries had already fled the city and were in hiding. It was clear Mr. Rizarre's problem was solely with the Americans. If he so ordered all foreigners to depart quickly, then so be it.

On December 13th, following the nuclear attack, American leadership officially reestablished communications with the European leadership. This was done through the Mexican government via diplomatic courier in Mexico City. A message was delivered to Hans Rizarre and simply stated,

> America looks with disgust at your pitiful attempts to subjugate her citizens. We will meet your delegation in Chicago but openly reject any attempts to influence our future destiny. We call upon Divine Providence to rend you asunder.
>
> Signed,
> D. J. Jefferson

The American leadership fully expected thousands of European troops to land at O'Hare Airport along with the European delegation dispatched by Hans Rizarre. The press was out in full force to report to the world the dramatic unfolding of events as they occurred. The American triumvirate of Jefferson, Williamson, and Carlson were determined to try to forcibly remove any foreign troops that attempted to occupy any part of United States soil. The mood in Chicago was one of open hostility toward the arrival of such unwanted guests. Americans were outraged and in a mood to vent their anger. Thousands of demonstrators had intended to converge at the airport to openly protest their dissatisfaction to the Europeans as they arrived. Instead, they were met by United States military troops who had sealed off the entire airport area. A high percentage of the United States citizenry were now armed, and it presented an extremely dangerous situation for any foreigner who chose to land on United States soil regardless of whatever his mission might be. It was an extremely tense environment that had everyone on edge as all America worried about what new crises would face them each day.

The sleek Lufthansa jet set down on the runway at exactly 10:04 a.m. A light snow was falling, but visibility presented no problems. Military radar tracking the commercial jetliner confirmed that no additional aircraft were escorting the plane, and none at all had been sighted anywhere over the Atlantic Ocean. Major General Jacob

Reiner had been assigned by General Williamson to greet the delegation. His instructions were to advise the Europeans on board "that the newly formed United States government appreciates Europe's interest in assisting all Americans, but we really wish to be on our own again and it is our express desire that you return home immediately."

Air traffic controllers on duty immediately advised the Lufthansa pilot that the jet would not be allowed normal unloading procedures and that an American general would greet them as they neared the Lufthansa terminal. A special unloading platform was set up a hundred yards away from the normal deplaning gate. The giant aircraft slowly taxied into position, and the terminal maintenance crew quickly rolled the unloading platform into position as the plane's powerful engines ceased to operate. General Reiner and an aide quickly moved up the steps as the aircraft's door was readied for opening.

Born and raised in west central Odessa, Texas, Jacob Reiner was a no-nonsense Texan instilled with a great amount of military fervor. A 2008 graduate of the West Point Academy, he had very limited combat experience. However, having graduated second in his class at West Point and endowed with a keen sense of military bearing and unswerving loyalty to his superiors, he quickly rose through the ranks and was responsible for several key commands. Presently he was General Williamson's chief field commander. He was personally responsible for overseeing all operational matters concerning the movement and field tactics of General Williamson's army.

Major General Reiner was very eager to perform his urgent mission this day, and he was at the top of the platform, with his aide trailing behind him, as the rear door to the aircraft opened. A young flight attendant greeted him and stepped aside to allow the general to enter. He was immediately greeted by a middle-aged Spaniard who identified himself as Gregorio T. Robles, senior senator from Madrid, Spain, and chief delegation spokesperson so designated by Hans Rizarre.

"Good morning, Mr. Robles. I am Major General Jacob Reiner. May I ask what your business is here?"

"Yes, my good man. I have been dispatched by our great leader, Hans Rizarre, to implement immediately new standing orders of operation for governing your country. I have brought along with me two hundred and forty-two individuals representing various departments of our government that shall assist you in more effectively interacting with the republic."

"Well, my dear Mr. Robles, I have sad news for you. I must advise you that your great interest in our country is greatly appreciated, but we intend to be on our own, and we ask you now very nicely to return home."

"I'm afraid that's impossible, General. We have our orders, and we intend to deplane and carry them out."

General Reiner was sometimes deceiving with his laid-back Southern drawl. One soon learned that behind that Texas cordiality was an ironclad determination to stick to his mission.

"Well, Mr. Robles, I wouldn't recommend doing that. Anyone other than my young lieutenant here, and myself of course, who attempts to leave this airplane will be shot. My men on the ground have orders to do that, and I fully intend to have them follow through with those orders. It is not an idle threat, sir, but a fact of life. We will not allow it."

"You are crazy, sir. All of your people are crazy. You can't defy the greatest power on earth. We have already destroyed three of your cities. We will surely obliterate you fools. President Rizarre will not stand for this."

"I have advised you as I was instructed. We have no need of further discussion. You tell your sinister president Rizarre that the true greatest power on earth is presently sitting up in the heavens, and I am personally hoping that soon He will heed our call and put you and your republic in the proper cesspools of shit that you belong. Good day, sir. Let's go, Lieutenant."

General Reiner and his aide quickly descended the flight of stairs, and the terminal crew below just as quickly pulled the large platform away from the plane and began to return it to the main terminal storage area. The same flight attendant who had opened the aircraft door was seen closing it again. The tension rose as the military closely observed what the Europeans would do next. The waiting press was furious and in chaos. They had been effectively sealed up in the Lufthansa terminal and now were both out of sight and out of communications with the aircraft. The aircraft sat still for five minutes when suddenly the rear exit door was opened and the emergency exit ramp chute was lowered. The pilot advised the control tower that the Europeans intended to deplane and would do so immediately. Ten seconds later, a United States Army sniper laid ten rifle rounds just below the exit opening. This was meant as more than a warning. Five minutes more passed, and a man was viewed sliding down the emergency ramp. As he landed on the ground and stood up, two sniper bullets cut his legs out from under him. Another five minutes passed by, and the exit ramp was raised back up to the closed position. An army ambulance rushed to the scene and rescued the wounded foreigner. He was the lowest-ranking and youngest man of the two hundred and forty-two people aboard, and it appeared at this point an expendable guinea pig. There was no further communication from Mr. Robles. The Lufthansa requested clearance to take off, and ten minutes later, the big jet was airborne heading east back to Europe.

At twelve noon the same day, David Jefferson advised all Americans living in the major cities of the United States to immediately evacuate their cities and seek shelter. The danger of another nuclear attack was apparent, and there was no escaping the human dilemma that this imposed on all United States citizens.

Chapter 19

So he came near where I stood: and when he came, I was afraid, and fell upon my face: but he said unto me, Understand, O son of man: for at the time of the end shall be the vision.

—Daniel 8:17 KJV

December 17, 2040,
Stuttgart, Germany

Hans Rizarre was extremely angry and beside himself over the American situation. No one was going to shoot one of his diplomatic staff and get away with it. He should have listened to his own inclination to send a sizable number of European troops to Chicago along with the members of the diplomatic corps. Instead, he listened to General Aurielle and his staff. They had consistently advised against the use of any military troops so far away from the European mainland. The general felt that the nuclear detonations in New York, Philadelphia, and Washington, DC, would break the morale of most Americans and they would meekly fall in line. Hans personally loved the idea of nuking the Americans. He and Tony Rondanelli had quite a few laughs when discussing it. However, he certainly did not want to nuke out the whole country. He had already received harsh verbal attacks and great distress and anguish from a good number of the European Republic's Parliamentarians urging against any further use of nuclear weaponry. There would be few people left. Hans wanted slaves to bow down before him, not ashes to blow lonely in the wind. New decisions needed to be made concerning America, and aggressive plans of action would be necessary to subdue them appropriately. At 9:30 a.m. this day, President Rizarre has assembled General Aurielle and his staff in his private study to discuss this very topic.

"Well, General, what do you think of those bastards now?"

General Aurielle knew he was going to be involved in a stormy meeting. The rage of President Rizarre when he heard about the return of the Lufthansa jet was reported by his close advisors as monumental. He was said to have thrown everything he had upon his presidential desk against the walls of his office. In an errant throw, he even bounced a four-pound paperweight off the head of one of his aides who was too slow to avoid it. Second assistant to the president, sixty-three-year-old Wendel Tiersoff, was now resting comfortably in a local hospital. He was suffering from a slight concussion and had eighteen stitches on the side of his head. The general was cautious in his reply.

"Mr. President, you were correct in your initial assessments. We should have sent storm troopers along with the plane. However, my intelligence people have advised me that there were over fifty thousand armed men awaiting the plane in the vicinity of our arrival. If we are going to commit military troops, we need to develop a very carefully laid out strategy."

"That is exactly what I want, General. Those fucking people will be subdued. Look, if you have to use a few more bombs, no nuclear devices, so be it. Just use some of the less powerful types. I've already got some huge flak from our asshole scientific community reminding me of the dangers of fallout to our people over here. I really don't need that shit. Look, you have got two to three weeks to report back here in this office with a new plan of action. As a matter of fact, I'm putting it on my calendar now—January 5, 2041, at 10:00 a.m., General. I want detailed plans with specifics. I don't expect your people to be taking any time off to celebrate this worthless Christmas holiday season either. I can't believe anyone would want to celebrate over a man they nailed to the cross anyhow. He was a rebel. He was one of them—they are the enemy. We must destroy them, put them in their place. Do you understand what I am saying?"

General Aurielle knew it was time for him to depart. He was not about to respond to the blasphemous attack regarding his creator's son and incur or trigger any further wrath from President Rizarre. There was no question the president of the republic was still very upset over the situation. Although he was still personally opposed to a large-scale military invasion of the American continent, if that is what must happen, then so be it. He would prepare well for it and get it over with as quickly as possible.

"Yes, Mr. President. I understand very well. We shall begin this immediately. On January 5th, we shall return with what you wish. Good day, sir. Gentlemen, let's go."

Hans Rizarre smiled as the general departed with his staff. He reached for his private phone and speed-dialed the Vatican in Italy.

"Good morning, this is Monsignor Pacieo speaking on behalf of His Holiness. May I help you?"

"Monsignor, this is President Rizarre. I need to talk to the pope please."

"Yes, Mr. President. Wait a moment please. I will let him know you are on the phone."

Hans chuckled as he waited for his friend to come to the phone. He and Tony had clearly made it to the top of the world. Soon, they would bedazzle the world together.

"Hans, how are you doing? What's going on?"

"Quite a bit, Tony. Look, when can we get together? When are you going to have your papal crowning? What are you waiting for?"

"Well, I'm delaying it on purpose. I want you to be here when it happens. I have a little surprise for you."

"What kind of surprise? What are you up to?"

"If I told you, then it wouldn't be a surprise. Just promise me you'll attend the ceremony."

"I'll attend, Tony. You know I wouldn't miss it for the world. When is it going to be?"

"December 25th, Hans. I couldn't think of a better day."

"You're a sick bastard, Tony, real sick. Hey, how come you haven't chosen a name yet? The whole world is waiting. I'm real curious about this. Is this another surprise?"

"No, not really. I don't know that I will take one. I think I'll be known as the 'pope with no name.' My thinking is this. I want the world to honor you. They don't need to know me. I plan to soon have the Vatican throw in with you giving you the total support of the Vatican."

"Tony, I love you, man. You have really put it together there. We are going to rock the world. They will never know what hit them."

"I think they know right now, Hans. You threw those nukes so quick you caught everybody off guard. The Russians haven't said a word out of line since that happened. That General Aurielle of yours is quite a dynamic individual. Another Napoleon perhaps, maybe a Rommel or Patton."

"You are quite right, Tony. I just ran him out of my office. He is going to undertake one of the greatest projects ever very soon. It should be very interesting. Those assholes in America won't think they are so damn smart when it's all said and done."

"I couldn't believe what they did to your planeload of diplomats. What's holding those people together? They are a whole lot worse off now than when we were taking care of them. What's all this bullshit about 'in God we trust' and 'Divine Providence'?"

"Tony, what the fuck are you talking about? You know more about that than I do. Shit, most of them are members of your great flock. How the hell do you explain it?"

"That's quite a dilemma for me at the moment. We'll think of something when we get together. For the moment I'll continue to badmouth them as rebels and chastise them in front of the rest of the world."

"Okay, Tony. We'll work on it together. General Aurielle will probably resolve that problem for us anyhow. I'm closing for now, so we'll see you on Christmas Day for sure."

"Thanks, Hans. Hang in there. We are on the way to glory for sure. Goodbye for now."

President Rizarre felt much better as he put the phone down. He always felt better after talking to Tony. Soon they would be together again and plot new courses of action. He privately said a prayer of thanks to Lucifersaton and felt an overwhelming inner feeling of something stirring deep within him. He felt these sensations more often of late and sometimes actually felt the presence of a powerful spirit close around him. He thought he knew what it was, and someday soon he was confident the powerful being would show itself to him for he was Hans Rizarre, at the moment, the most powerful man on the planet earth.

Chapter 20

And there shall be signs in the sun, and in the moon,
and in the stars; and upon the earth distress of nations,
with perplexity; the sea and the wave roaring.

—Luke 21:25 KJV

December 22, 2040
Barcelona Space Observatory, Spain

Professor Alonzo Rivera was greatly troubled of late. His primary duty consisted of monitoring the heavens through the latest space orbit satellite telescope put into orbit in 2030 by the European Space Agency (ESA). It was the most powerful telescope yet devised by man. Its high orbit ensured a new look at the heavens for earthlings. It was twice the size and three times the power and range of any telescope previously orbited by mankind in space. He had working with him the finest group of technicians a scientist astronomer could ask for. At age 65, Professor Alonzo had been an astronomer for forty years. There was no one currently in his field who knew more about the universal schematic than he. For the last year and a half now, his team made some new sightings for sure. However, nothing that they found was of such a nature as to cause much of a stir to anyone outside the astrological field until now.

On December 14, the professor noticed a most unusual occurrence. He was viewing the scope late that night as he often did. Through the years, his greatest pleasures in life were derived by viewing the heavens at a time of night and very early morning when most everyone else was sound asleep in their beds. Seemingly alone with the universe, he reveled in his own little world and often dwelled there for hours, leaving the miseries of everyday earth existence shut out from him. Since the ESA spent millions of dollars on this new satellite-telescope, he was even more enthralled. No one person in the entire history of human civilization was known to have ever seen as far into the universe as Professor Rivera. He was scanning the eastern edge of the Milky Way galaxy when he saw it. Suddenly an object the size of what the planet Mars would look like appeared on the scope. It was moving from east to west across the scope. He then observed seven other smaller objects that appeared to be following behind it. Alonzo began an instrument reading off the observatory computer. Many times the eyes played tricks, and the computer set the record straight. What puzzled the professor this date was the fact the computer appeared to be giving out verification data. The printouts from the computer indicated the objects on the screen were visibly there just outside the outer edges of the galaxy. A full equipment systems check was initiated to determine if a computer malfunction occurred. All system monitors read back "Satisfactory—continue online observations."

Alonzo quickly moved across the large observatory room he was in and checked out a less sophisticated telescope. It was one of the primary scopes utilized prior to the newer ESA satellite, somewhat comparable to the two-hundred-and-thirty-six-inch reflector mirror once used at the Special Astrophysical Observatory in the Caucasus in the Soviet Union. The scope showed no unusual objects or unusual movements at all. Professor Rivera went back and checked the newer satellite again. The planetlike object was still visible and moving. In five minutes' time, the entire grouping of objects suddenly took a sharp turn to the right on the screen and sped out of sight.

The week following this event resulted in the same occurrence happening each evening within five or ten minutes of the same time with the objects veering off in a different direction each time. The most astonishing thing happened on the night of the twenty-first of December. There appeared two objects, somewhat larger objects than seen previously, alone without the seven smaller ones following. After four minutes of observation, they veered off in different directions and disappeared off the viewing screen. Professor Alonso and his close knit staff at the Barcelona Observatory were quite perplexed. Professor Rivera had alerted his staff to what he had seen following the night of the fourteenth. This was all very puzzling, and there was no previous data available to justify the existence of these objects.

Alonzo was very hesitant to release these new findings to the government authorities. He wanted first to communicate with other fellow astronomers concerning his sightings. There was just no explanation for it at all. On the night of the twenty-second of December, the most alarming sighting of all occurred. A strange bluish light appeared on the eastern fringe of the Milky Way galaxy. Once again, the computer calculated the distance as just beyond the outer limits of the galaxy. The entire observatory staff of six people were able to view the light on the large scope screen. The blue light did not move but remained stationary for twelve minutes. Then, all at once, it turned from blue to bright red and in five seconds' time, moved from east to west across the scope and disappeared. This event left the entire staff in complete bewilderment. Things like this were just not supposed to happen. Something unknown was moving out there in the vast outer space universe, and its implications were mind boggling to these professionals whose livelihood depended upon monitoring the heavens.

Not a person at the observatory had ever seen anything like this before. UFOs and abnormal celestial sightings were often a topic of normal conversations between astronomers, but these events far exceeded anything this group had ever witnessed. Professor Rivera was sure that his equipment was functioning properly. There was no doubt in his mind that something was amiss. These objects and sightings defied any kind of previously recorded celestial sightings.

On February 25, 2040, following almost two months of Professor Rivera observing movement by unknown objects on the outskirts of the Milky Way galaxy, the ESA placed its highest-ranking official on the observatory grounds, and a special ESA data and technical group set up operations to assist Professor Rivera and his staff. ESA officials officially notified the European government through President Rizarre's office of the sightings, complete with the supporting computer data. The five foremost astronomers in the entire world were invited to Barcelona to witness the events. Government officials at the highest levels of the European government mandated an extremely tight news blackout, and strict censorship was enforced. Knowledge of the sightings was to be restricted only to those on the observatory staff, visiting astronomers, and high government officials on a need-to-know basis only. There was a mood of great excitement within the group, and the expectations of possibly discovering other life within the universe was not beyond the imaginations of this closed group. No one would come out and say it, but this was the closest mankind had come to possibly viewing inhabitants of another world since Jesus Christ of Nazareth had walked planet Earth some two thousand years earlier. At that time, only a small number of humans had recognized and witnessed the fact, and now many thought modern man was tied alone to the Earth with only the popular belief and hope that there might possibly be other benign intelligence somewhere out there in the universe.

When Hans Rizarre first heard the news, he smiled, not shaken at all by it. He thought perhaps they were friends of his. However, if mortal beings truly knew the reason for the UFOs, many would cringe in fear, and great wonderment would cover the earth as a cloud. Mankind was soon to view the most awesome display of power and might since the creation of the universe.

Chapter 21

> Here is wisdom. Let him that hath understanding count the number of the beast: for it is the number of a man; and his number is Six hundred threescore and six.
>
> —Revelation 13:18 KJV

December 25, 2040,
Saint Peter's Basilica, Vatican City, Italy

It was Tuesday, and all of Europe was on a holiday. Antonio Franciscus Rondanelli was to be officially elevated to the Papacy on this date and European Republic President Hans Rizarre had declared a special three day paid holiday for all tax paying citizens of Europe. Live television reports were being beamed throughout the entire world. The "pope with no name" had already achieved great popularity among the people. Armed with outstanding public relations people, Cardinal Rondanelli was being portrayed as the savior of the Catholic Church. He espoused humility and virtuous action and called openly for the restoration of the Holy Roman Empire. He openly preached the subjection of the Church to the State and maintained that the clergy were in a supportive role, not a decision-making directing role. He called the Europeans specially chosen people who had a duty to take care of the planet. He dismissed the past intercontinental European conflicts as nothing more than overzealous sibling rivalry. He presented a handsome, dynamic figure to the public and openly denounced past church practices of accumulating great wealth. Two days before the coronation, he sent Hans Rizarre a check for $10,000,000. It was made out to the European Republic and was specifically donated to assist "our brethren in Europe to ease in any way whatever daily burdens may cross their paths." The press ate it up, and on December 24, it was front-page headlines on all European newspapers:

> Soon-to-Be Pope Rondanelli Turns Riches of Church Over to Citizens of Europe (*Berlin Evening News*)

> No-Name Pontiff Gives Christmas Present to All Europeans (*Paris Morning Star*)

> Viva Antonio, Viva Antonio (*Rome Daily News*)

> Christmas Comes Early, Viva El Papa (*Versailles Register*)

Across the sea in America, the entire episode was being watched with quiet amusement. A three-day European holiday meant no one would be bothering the United States during that time. The American leadership viewed it with relief and continued moving large amounts of the population out of heavily congested urban areas. Thanks in large part to the American military and the Canadian government, things were operating rather smoothly. The whole American continent was a beehive of activity, and time was needed desperately to assist survival against such a menacing foe as Europe. The great struggle appeared to be awesome in scope and each day that dawned without a crisis at hand was viewed as a precious one.

At exactly twelve noon in Italy, Antonio Rondanelli walked his way down the center aisle of Saint Peter's Basilica. With all the pomp and ceremony imaginable, he was consecrated pope of the Roman Catholic Church. In the midst of President Rizarre and all of Europe's highest-ranking officials in attendance, the pope preached a simple sermon. He explained his reluctance to take a new papal name as yet and announced that he was overwhelmed by the true meaning of his new office and that he needed to reflect a while longer on any name that might be appropriate and fitting. He owed it to his large flock of decent citizens around the world. A true shepherd wouldn't arbitrarily pick a name just to meet tradition or a timetable. When the time was right, the announcement would be made.

Following the sermon, a simple low mass was said, and twenty minutes later, Pope Rondanelli and his vast entourage started back down the main aisle. As Tony approached the first row of seats, he stopped. He turned and motioned to two young priests who were standing at a side altar. They immediately came forward carrying a large cloth-covered object which sat heavy on the arms of the two young clergymen. From another side altar came three more priests. One was carrying a microphone, and the others were carrying a platform to stand on.

This was obviously, for the public in attendance, an unscheduled event, and the cathedral was alive with low, whispered voices of a congregation not sure of what was occurring. The platform was set in place right in front of President Rizarre, who seemed obviously surprised by the whole affair. Antonio Rondanelli stepped slowly upon the platform, and as the young priest adjusted his microphone to voice level, he raised his hands in a gesture to quiet the huge throng.

"Children of Rome, children of Europe, take heed of my message. I, Antonio Rondanelli, have before me the greatest symbol of our European strength. It truly represents our earthly destiny. The souls of all those that have previously passed before us shall rejoice at this great event. Young clergymen, remove the cloth please."

A hush fell over Saint Peter's Basilica. No one was prepared for what was about to happen.

"I have before me the original crown of Charlemagne. It has been carefully preserved for this greatest of days."

Without hesitation, Tony hurriedly picked up the glittering jewel covered crown of gold and lifted it high for all to see. He then reached over and placed it upon the head of President Rizarre.

"Long life and victory to Hans Rizarre, crowned by your new pope. Great and peace-loving emperor of all Europeans."

Three times the Vatican choral group shouted this in unison and immediately bowed down in the direction of Hans Rizarre. The new pope stepped down off the platform and bowed down before the European leader. President Rizarre was in shock. He appeared as a man totally caught unaware. For one of the few times in his public life, he was speechless. Tony rose up and motioned to the entourage to begin moving again. The assembled throng was left hushed by what had just happened and seemed hypnotized by the immensity of it all. In a well-staged and well-planned maneuver, Tony gave fulfillment to the longtime dream of Hans.

The mood in Europe was highly receptive to Emperor Rizarre. Hans ruled as a dictator as it was. Now was the beginning of what Hans and Tony both had strived for. Soon they would rule the world together. They were in the right place at the right time. Within two months, the European Parliament would follow the papal pronouncement, and Hans Rizarre would officially be entitled Holy Roman Emperor, No one seemed to notice that the name of God was omitted from the crowning statement, and very few people ever found out what happened at the Tomb of Charlemagne that Christmas Day. The aged caretaker there was dismayed and alarmed when a muffled type of explosion blew the ancient grave stones in the area apart. There was no feasible explanation for it, but when he watched the late night news complete with coverage of Charlemagne's crown being placed upon Mr. Rizarre's head, he immediately went up into the nearby hills to the nearest monastery and intended to spend the rest of his days residing there in prayer.

Chapter 22

And God saw that the wickedness of man was great in the earth, and that every imagination of the thoughts of his heart was only evil continually. And it repented the Lord that he had made man on the earth, and it grieved him at his heart.

—Genesis 6:5–6 KJV

January 12, 2041
Nevaeh

Chareal was the youngest of angels associated with Michel, the greatest of all the archangels. His chief duty was to accompany Marie, the mother of the Great One's son. In the first century AD (earth time representation), she was brought up from earth to the great city body and soul amid great jubilation. The Great One Himself embraced her as she entered the temple. The designation of Chareal to caretake Marie was considered an honor of great distinction. Was she not the single most important human female personage in the universe? Eva, the original lady of love, rejoiced at her arrival. Marie was the true essence of womanhood—loving, caring, supportive, stunning to view. The Great One always smiled when in her presence; so often was seen a twinkle in His eyes at her sight.

As a wondrous epitome of His creative works, the female, was personified by beautiful Marie. As she presently dwelled in Nevaeh, her physical embodiment was perfect in every detail. To look upon her eyes, one could perceive visions of a soul that personified love. She possessed the qualities that represented the true essence of womanhood—an inner strength, a mother's concern for her young, a mother's undying support for her loved ones, the sweet innocence of a youthful soul. Oh, what void or abyss of darkness would man be in without this greatest of creations—woman, a source of all man's inspirations.

The Great One worked His plans of creation to perfection. The male and female, working in harmony together as potentially they could, represented the fulfillment of His universal design for the future. Was He not early on a lonely soul? (In the beginning was the Word, and the Word was with God, and the Word was God.) Who should dwell and rule in this vast universe with Him? Were not men and woman, fashioned in His own image and likeness, being prepared for just such a future everlasting experience? The excitement of this proposition had always stirred the residents of Nevaeh. The hope was that mankind's earthly testing and training would soon be over. The many souls of earth's past departed were anxious and eager to get on with it. The great Mosei was so typical of these restless ones. He often held court in the eastern gardens, espousing all who would listen of the mighty deeds he would perform in the future years. A tower of strength and wisdom, tempered by closeness to the Great One, he would continue to be a potent force in the universe. Just this day, as Chareal and Marie were strolling through the gardens, they viewed him surrounded by over a thousand young souls. Earth's dead children just loved to hear him speak of his mighty earthly exploits—the confrontation with the Pharaoh on earth's Egypt, the amazing parting of the waters, the Great One presenting him commandments etched in stone. He loved the children and never tired of reciting his stories. A five-year-old boy cried out, "Great Mosei, why did the Great One slay the firstborn? Why did He kill the children?"

"My son, a good question indeed. Listen up, young ones. The Great One has told me this…"

Marie and Chareal smiled as Mosei talked to the children as they moved off farther into the gardens.

"Marie, since rumor has spread that Helnoch will soon call for a meeting, the city has come apart somewhat. I've never seen anything like this. Even the Great One Himself walked the streets here last night. I think it was meant to calm everyone down."

"'Tis true, Chareal. So many of these souls have waited a long time for this. The day of the Lord's mission to render justice is soon at hand. My Son shall be arriving shortly. I so look forward to seeing Him."

"I too. I'll never forget Him as a young boy on earth. Remember when you found Him in the temple? Twelve years old and He said, 'How is it that you sought Me? Did you not know that I must be about My father's business?' I was overwhelmed then, even as I am today recalling the event."

"You, Chareal, I found it so hard to believe. My little baby boy standing there before me and Josef, so bold and so sure, knowing then the mission He was on. Only a mother's tears could give me comfort. I no longer had my baby."

"You went through so much, Marie. Now you should rejoice. Your young Lamb has become as a Lion whose mighty roar shall soon be heard."

"Yes, I hope our brethren remaining on earth understand when He arrives. He is their only hope."

"He'll forgive them now as He did when they crucified Him. Remember when He said, 'Father, forgive them, for they know not what they are doing.'"

"Yes, yes, I know. But they'll not crucify Him this time. I pity those who shall defy Him. I know He is a righteous judge. I always hurt when we lose a soul. But souls who disrupt harmony and peace would be the death of us, Chareal. The existence of life demands that we love one another. It is as true as simple math. It cannot be denied. Just as one plus one equals two, if we all do unto others as we would have them do unto us, that ensures the existence of life. Remember the heliographic type message my Son displayed on the inner temple wall. He used His right hand as a sunlike instrument and etched the rule of life for all to see whenever they enter the temple. Everyone who enters the temple can see it. He also etched this same message on the southern face of Nevaeh Mountain so that anyone approaching it will be able to view it, even from great distances. As you can see it on the large rock in front of us now, I am able to display it through telepathic messaging: 'One plus one equals two. Two plus two equals four. Love God plus do unto others equals life, harmony, and peace. Don't love God and don't do unto others equals death, disharmony, and chaos.'

"Come, Chareal, we must continue preparations for my Son's arrival. I told Josef we would be coming by today."

At this moment, in a very remote part of the great city, two awesome souls were deep in discussion, the Great One Himself and Chief Elder Helnoch. Three thousand angelic beings stood guard and listened in awe.

"Great One, it will soon be time to take action. If they keep it up, they'll blow the planet Earth apart."

"I'll stay their hand, Helnoch. My angels are standing by. But you are correct. It will be time soon enough. About another eight years or so earth time. I shall let them play it out to the last act."

"That is truly but a short time for us. We shall be ready, Great One."

"You have always been ready. You've stood by me, as a rock, through the ages. Your devotion and friendship have stood the test of time. Our love is everlasting. You are as a brother."

"I'm a humble man, O Great One. I stand in awe and would perish for your sake. Your kindness and love shall soon be made known throughout the universe. All of us await your son."

"He has saved my project, good friend. You know full well there were times when I thought about destroying mankind. There would have been no further souls created."

"Yes, my Lord. He truly saved mankind by becoming one of us. Only He had faith in your project from the beginning. You were so gracious to create free thinkers. You could have created robots. No one is as loving and giving as you."

"My Son certainly believed in mankind. Yes, He became one of them, went down to earth and lived among them. He has tied the God family and mankind's destiny together for eternity."

"Yes, Lord, and He will show them how to live as you intended us to live. The promise of tomorrow must give you great joy."

"It is true, Helnoch. But enough for now, we must first attend to the details of dealing with Lucifersaton. He has but a short time left to disturb my children."

"Yes, Lord. He is very active on earth. Soon Mr. Rizarre will give up his soul to him. 'Tis a sad plight for him."

"Yes, but as a free thinker, he is still free to choose any option. Lucifersaton had that same choice. I wished to protect mankind from the start. His deception was the highest crime imaginable. He tainted and abused my beautiful children. They were not ready for such a journey."

"Yes, Lord. The universe was flooded with Your tears. Your rage vibrated throughout the galaxies. There has never been such a disruption since. Michel has told me that only the love of Your Son within You and the Great Spirit working within You together prevented You from destroying Lucifersaton then."

"Michel belittles his own role in that affair. I owe him much. It was he who drove the wicked demon and his friends into the abyss they belonged in. The awesome might of his power cut through the low-life betrayers as a mighty sword. He is truly one of the greatest of my angels."

"Michel has told me that You owe him nothing, Lord. He is honored to serve You day and night."

"That, my friend, is the true essence message of the universe. Love God above all else and do unto others as you would have them do unto you. Give with no concern for receiving in return. Love others as you love yourself. That is the simple secret of the universe. If all live it, life and existence is ensured. To defy it brings disharmony, destruction, and ultimately death."

"Your son has left this very message on earth and planted the seed when He was there. You know, although there are very many wicked souls on earth these days, we have never seen so many good souls either. His message has found fertile soil on earth, and the good fruit it has yielded must please You."

"Yes, once again, thanks to My Son. It is a far cry from the days of Noah when we together searched somewhat futilely for a few good souls. I am pleased, Helnoch, and I will not allow My children to suffer much longer. I hear their cries, I see their tears and sorrow. My soul is heavy with their troubles. My angels are already at their doorstep. There is but little sand left in the temple clock."

"We await Your commands, dear Lord. Your children in America especially are reeling at this very moment. The sins of their past will be repaid in full in but a little more time. Your children in Israel will soon face new troubles. The sons of Abraham shall soon meet the Great Deceiver."

"Yes, Helnoch. Make preparations to announce Our meeting. Send for My Son and Michel. When you are ready, make our announcements and we shall proceed. In the meantime, I have angels just outside the Milky Way galaxy doing their vigilance close to earth. I shall be with you always, My brother."

"Yes, Lord. May love and peace come soon to all of our brethren."

With that said, the Great One and Helnoch departed each other, and a huge entourage of angels surrounded the great One. He was off to see the children, and Helnoch was off to do great works. The sand in the temple clock had but few grains left to spill.

Chapter 23

> And they worshipped the dragon which gave power unto the beast: and they worshipped the beast, saying, Who is like unto the beast? Who is able to make war with him?
>
> —Revelation 13:4 KJV

January 26, 2041
Planet Earth

In London, England, this morning, the British Broadcasting Corporation (BBC) interrupted its early morning programming with the following news bulletin: "Syrian, Lebanese, and Libyan military troops crossed the Israeli borders during the night and launched a massive attack against Israel in a vicious attack that has caught the world by surprise. Israeli troops have been rushed into the Golan heights, and early reports received here indicate that the fighting is deadly and fierce. Please stay tuned."

In Stuttgart, Germany, Hans Rizarre called an emergency meeting of the European Defense Command. Gustav Erikson and Marcus Aurielle were summoned to his office immediately.

"Gustav, what will the loss of Israel mean to us? Can we live with it?"

"Certainly not, Mr. President. The current American troubles have hurt us economically right now, and we can't afford to lose the very productive Israeli economy and their access to oil. There is no question or need for discussion about it. We especially need their access to oil reserves."

"General, what happened? Why didn't we know about this or see it coming?"

"Well, Mr. President, our focus has been 100 percent on the America attack plans. The Middle East situation has always been volatile. The Arabs were very deceptive about it. Additional alarming news is the presence of large amounts of Soviet military being monitored just outside of the Afghanistan and Turkish borders. They are supposed to be there on maneuvers and war games, but I fear they may be preparing for a part in this also."

"Look, General, put the America plans on hold for the moment. We'll fix those bastards soon enough. I want European troops in Israel right now. You put a stop to this thing immediately. I want you to personally contact the presidents of Syria, Lebanon, Libya, and Israel. You tell them what we are going to do. They can expect us there very soon. We will destroy anyone who dares to intercede. When you are done with that, contact the Russians also. The message will be the same. Any interference will be dealt with swiftly. If they want war, they've got it. Hurry now and report back to me as soon as you've finished."

"Yes, Mr. President, consider it done."

General Aurielle sprang into action. This was a mission tailored to his training. He rushed to European Defense Headquarters and gathered his aides.

Hans was not sure what to make of this new development. How could anyone be so bold as to disrupt him so, especially with no advance warning or notification. He picked up his phone and dialed the Vatican and left a message for his close confidant, the new pope, to call him. Ten minutes later, he received a callback. Hans took the call and asked everyone to leave his office.

"Hans, what can I do for you?"

"Tony, have you heard the news?"

"About the Mideast? Yes, we have just now been hearing about it."

"Well! What do you make of it? Are they testing out the new Emperor or what?"

"Could be, Hans. However, they know you are concentrating on America right now. Also, the Russians would like to get their hands on that oil access. My bishops in Afghanistan and Turkey tell me there are Russian troops all over the place just across the borders."

"Yes. Yes, General Aurielle just told me. I'm not going to stand for it. We are going in there, Tony. I'm going to stop it."

"Look, Hans, this could be a blessing in disguise for you. What do you think of this idea…"

The new pope and emperor talked for over an hour on the phone, and when they had finished, President Rizarre reached for his office intercom.

"Evelyn, are you there?"

"Yes, sir. What is it?"

"Evelyn, please fix me a drink and please ask everyone to come back in the office."

"Yes, sir. Also, sir, General Aurielle wishes you to call him."

"Fine, fine. Show everyone back in and call the general and tell him to come back over here. And, Evelyn, open the bar for us and have our waiter come over to prepare drinks for us. And also, please order some food for us as well."

"Yes, sir. I'll do it right away."

Hans Rizarre spent the next three hours with his key advisors, and when they had finished with their eating and drinking, they left united to enact a new bold plan of action that would change the political structure of the entire Middle East.

Chapter 24

January 31, 2041
Israel

Tel Aviv radio was the first to break the story:

"During the night of January 31st, in a display of military might, three hundred thousand European troops were airlifted, marched, and driven en route to Tel Aviv, Israel. It was an assault that boggles the mind. Combat ready and mechanized to move, the troops began to move swiftly towards the Golan Heights as soon as they had arrived. An even more startling development occurred when European Emperor Hans Rizarre arrived himself. It is reported he is on his way to Jerusalem to meet with Israeli president Jacob Goth. Reports from the Golan Heights have also confirmed the fact that fighting there between the Israelis and Arabs troops has curtailed. Events are moving so quickly it is difficult to keep up with them."

And so it was, lightning fast and massively mobilized, Marcus Aurielle's army struck as a leopard. No military man could deny his genius at moving men and materials. One day he wasn't there, the next day he was. No warnings given, no time to prepare. His troops descended from the sky as a cloud. Their steady stream of arrival was continuous. He had perfected the art of warfare, and no mission was too difficult for his troops to perform. In three days' time, the borders of Israel outside of the conflict area were secure. The threat of any additional foreign invasion vanished. Syrian, Libyan, and Lebanese troops were observed quickly dispersing back to their borders, and the word from Afghanistan and Turkey was that Russian troops were last seen pulling back and headed in the direction of Moscow.

In Jerusalem, the masses mobbed Hans Rizarre wherever he went. Their new liberator was an instant hero among the people. President Goth hosted him at a state dinner, and the Sons of Abraham awarded him their groups highest medal of distinction. A three-day state holiday was declared, and all Israel celebrated and partied as three hundred thousand European troops stood vigil along their borders.

As the citizens of Jerusalem partied, Hans Rizarre, Gustav Erikson, and Jacob Goth negotiated. Aside from his crowning as Holy Roman Emperor, Hans had never known such exhilaration in his entire life. The power of his position lifted him to new heights. His ego was inflated to the fullest, and those around him catered to his every whim. There seemed to be nothing that could stand in his way to do anything he dared please. You would think the people believed that he was their messiah. On February 7, 2041, he traveled to the airport in Tel Aviv to return to Stuttgart. His mission completed, he stood in front of over a million Israelis at the airport and issued a major statement to the world.

"Citizens of the world, let it be known that Hans Rizarre has offered his protective cloak to the nation of Israel. We have signed official treaties which guarantee her safety and security from this day forward. Any country who threatens her borders will answer to me."

The boisterous crowd went wild with applause. It has been a long time since they had such a powerful friend.

"Thank you, thank you. Also, as a token of appreciation to the fine people of Israel, I have struck a deal with President Goth. My dear people gathered here today, it will cost you oil, but I have great news for you. I have just donated two hundred million dollars to your country in order for you to begin building a new temple in Jerusalem. Not only that, I am leaving behind some of our troops to guarantee the completion of it. You shall have a new temple."

This was more than the crowd could bear. The fulfillment of their dreams would be realized in a new temple. To guarantee its being built was tantamount to being almost messianic. Hans was quickly escorted to his plane. His trip back to Stuttgart was a joyous occasion for his staff.

The potential disaster had turned into a victory of the greatest proportions. Hans had extended his sphere of influence in an area of great previous instability. And in a bold and decisive stroke of military power, he had secured a lock on and access to some of the largest oil reserves left remaining on the planet. The European press hailed him as a conquering hero. Five hundred thousand Germans met him at the airport as he arrived in Stuttgart. He was intoxicated with the worship of his people. They cheered his every move; they crowded into the streets around his motorcade wherever he went. His name was seen everywhere on placards and signs raised high by his followers for all to see. There seemed to be no one man on planet Earth at the moment who could stir the masses in quite the same way as Emperor Hans Adolph Rizarre. Crowned Holy Roman emperor on December 25 by the new pope, officially designated emperor by the European parliament three weeks later, he was well on his way to becoming the most potent leader the world had ever known.

History has recorded many such conquering heroes. Civilization on planet Earth was dramatically affected in each case. Before this man was done, the planet would be shook to its innermost core. No longer did mankind just throw spears at each other, launch catapults, utilize Trojan horses of deception, fire 105 millimeter howitzers, drop firebombs, or detonate A-bombs. No, this was the day and age of hundred-megaton nuclear planet busters, space missiles, and satellite spies in the skies. Was the caveman throwing spears any different than the space-age man firing a laser gun? Perhaps only in the firepower he was unleashing. If left unchecked, would there be nothing left? And the great intellectuals and academicians would have no time left to ponder the question just posed.

Chapter 25

It is during our darkest moments that we must focus to see the light.

—Aristotle

February 11, 2041
Jerusalem, Israel

Jacob Goth had been a busy man of late. Since Israel's new treaty with the Europeans, there were all types of details to attend to. The trade-off of Israel oil access to large oil reserves for the building of the temple was not exactly the most economically feasible of plans. However, the value of a new temple was priceless as far as the average Jew was concerned. Politically speaking, if the temple could be rebuilt, the people wouldn't scream too much over an oil deal that might bankrupt them. Several meetings with European officials were being scheduled, and there was little room on his calendar for new appointments for the next two weeks. His first appointment this Monday date was with the chief rabbi of Jerusalem. No doubt the details of the temple were to be the topic of discussion. At 8:30 a.m., Chief Rabbi Haelem Walloch arrived in Goth's office.

"Good morning, Rabbi. We are about to undertake God's great work."

"Yes, Jacob, the ancients should be smiling upon us. We are blessed and truly chosen ones."

"Our children may see the Messiah. Who would ever think this should happen in our day? The excitement is beyond me."

"Yes, many of our people are in ecstasy. But, Mr. President, we are not totally without troubles. I have just this morning received some distressing news about some new troubles that bear watching."

"What kind of troubles? Surely our people are quite content. Who can question the rebuilding of the temple?"

"Jacob, I don't know if you are familiar with what has been going on up in Galilee."

"Concerning what, Rabbi? I am not aware of any major problems."

"Well, quite frankly, I am not sure what to make of it. As an uncompromising Orthodox Jew, I am appalled at the situation. Within the past year, there has grown a very active messianic movement up north of here in the Galilee area, particularly in Nazareth. Its members openly defy our orthodoxy and maintain that Jesus of Nazareth was and is the true messiah. Their membership is growing, and so is their vocalness. They openly roam the countryside and attack our rabbis as heretics."

"Surely this is nonsense. Now that you mention this, I am familiar with the Jesus Jews group. They have been around for some time. I've never heard of anyone refer to them as being a problem or troublesome."

"That is true, President Goth. But two weeks ago, a young man from America recently immigrated to our country. He has Jewish roots from his ancestors in Poland. I have been told he was actively involved in this American uprising that is currently going on. There is quite a stir in Nazareth where a young religious activist group has openly welcomed him. I don't think your new friend Hans Rizarre would look so kindly on that."

"Good God, Rabbi, we don't need this at all. Look, I want that man watched and scrutinized. I'll get the military involved in this. We can't jeopardize the temple for the sake of a small group of fanatics."

"Such is the nature of our history, Jacob. Look, don't involve the military at this point. We shall closely monitor what is going on up there. I shall increase the appearance of our rabbinical staff in Nazareth and throughout the Galilee area and defuse their efforts. The introduction of the military may only add credibility and further attention to their cause. This man Jesus caused quite a stir two thousand years ago. I can't believe He is resurfacing at a time when we are about to undertake our greatest project. It must be another great test from above. I'll have to return to the Scriptures and try to find the answer to this puzzle."

With that being said, the rabbi and the president talked on for five more hours going over in detail the responsibilities of their new project. Who would give time to anything else? This was excitement personified. There was no time to be given to rabble-rousers who espoused Jesus as their Messiah. Perhaps these people should look to Hans Rizarre. He was the one building the temple.

Meanwhile, this same day, up in the hills of Galilee, a small group of young people gathered to visit with the American who had recently settled within their group. Twenty-one-year-old Rebecca Simons was the group leader, and she made it a point to officially introduce new members to all the other members. The messianic movement locally had grown with rapid speed in the past year. Due to the great increase in natural disasters, plagues, and famines increasing in scope on the planet in the 2030s and the erratic and odd behavior as well of the sun, moon, planets and some stars being observed and reported, it was not surprising to see the growing messianic movement. Jesus Jews, as they were often called, believed the end days for mankind were rapidly approaching and the second coming of Jesus Christ to planet Earth was forthcoming. Orthodox Jews were still waiting for the first coming of the Messiah, and they looked to people like the chief rabbi, Hans Rizarre, and the new pope to lead them in regard to those matters.

Rebecca now had over three hundred very active members in her Galilee group. Three were former hard-core orthodox men who had converted after years of wrestling over the Jesus puzzle. Others such as Zeth Robbins and Jeremiah Montros were typical of the young men represented in the group. Their parents had migrated to Israel from America in the decade of the 2000s. Most of the younger people represented a new breed of Israeli citizens. They openly questioned the past and were full of zeal and dreams for the future.

"Lovely Rebecca, thank you for calling this meeting. We are eager to meet your new friend from America, Issac Pelensky."

"Yes, Zeth Robbins, thank you so much for being here. Please welcome Mr. Pelensky. Some of you have already heard of his exploits in America through Anne Jones. She was here during the nuclear attack against America and told us about Issac and others that were active in what is going on over there. She said that Issac wished to visit and that she was going to help him do so. Anne has visited our country often and has done much to promote our cause."

"You are correct about her, Rebecca. I met her about seven months ago, and she is one of the kindest, most caring human beings I have ever met. In fact, she helped finance my trip over here. I've been quite a lost soul for some years now. Thanks to Anne Jones and Father Ed McCarthy, I have discovered the true meaning of Jesus, and I needed to come here. I need to walk where He walked and be close to the places He lived in."

"Well, Issac, that is the reason we are all here. You are welcome to stay with us as long as you wish. We'll be happy to show you everything you need to see. Anne was telling us that there are those who believe that many Americans are true descendants of the lost tribes of Israel. America was thought to be that new land or new world that they were banished to."

"Well, I don't know about that, but my roots are in the Ukraine. I really couldn't tell you what lost tribe I'm from."

"Issac, it matters not. You are no longer lost. Come to Nazareth with Rebecca and her friends and you'll see firsthand the humble land of Jesus."

"Thank you, Zeth. When will I see you and Jeremiah again?"

"Within a week or two. We want you to get accustomed to our lifestyle first. Then you may accompany us if you wish as we walk these Galilean foothills trying to get through to our stubborn countrymen the real meaning of Jesus Christ."

After bidding proper farewell, Issac gathered up his meager belongings and climbed into Rebecca's Volkswagen van and journeyed on to Nazareth with her friends. In two months' time, he would be a transformed man. The stories of his activity in the Judean countryside would soon make front-page headlines throughout Israel.

Chapter 26

> Sheba and Dedan, and the merchants of Tarshish,
> with all the young lions thereof, shall say unto thee,
> Art thou come to take spoil? Hast thou gathered thy
> company to take a prey? To carry away silver and gold,
> to take away cattle and goods, to take a great spoil.
>
> —Ezekiel 38:13 KJV

February 15, 2041
Paris, France

General Aurielle was deep in thought as he awaited the arrival of Hans Rizarre. He had been summoned to Paris by the ministers of ECOWA (European Council on World Affairs). Acting as an advisory council to the European Legislature, ECOWA wanted an update on the status of American affairs. Urged on by Hans Rizarre, the council had mandated that action be taken against the entire North American continent. The Canadians and Americans had defied European directives, and military action was the primary option recommended by the ECOWA ministers. Since his elevation to emperor, Hans no longer sat as the active council president. He turned over these duties to his handpicked appointee, Francois Derdez of Paris. Because of the crisis occurring in Israel, General Aurielle had delayed the deadline Hans Rizarre had established to present plans for the American situation. Since then, he had turned over the matter to Francois Derdez and ECOWA. In turn, they had insisted that the general announce his intentions by February 15. There could no longer be any delay. In fact, the plans were now complete, and General Aurielle and his staff were prepared to present them to a full meeting of the council. All were ready and waiting for Hans to arrive.

At 10:00 a.m., February 15, Hans arrived and took his seat at the head of the conference table. Fifteen other ministers sat with him, and General Aurielle was summoned before them to discuss his plan for an American invasion. Francois Derdez gave a brief greeting, officially opened the meeting, and immediately addressed the hero general.

"General Aurielle, our express purpose in inviting you here this morning is to seek your guidance concerning our interests in North America. We have unanimously agreed that military action is a necessary option. We have been hurt economically in lost revenues and material resources since their revolution first occurred this past November. The Canadians have defied us continuously for the past four years. We cannot allow the Americans to do the same. We know of your reluctance to commit troops across the Atlantic Ocean and your recommendation that no more nuclear weaponry be utilized. It is our consensus at this point that military force is now a necessary step. Our honored emperor concurs with our findings, and we know you have prepared a plan to deal with the situation. Are you prepared now to advise us of your approach in dealing with this?"

General Aurielle rose from his seat at the table and strode to the center of the conference table and motioned to his aides to activate the audiovisual equipment they had previously set in place. The lights were dimmed, and a full-scale map of the North American continent was displayed on the large screen set high upon the main wall.

"Gentlemen and gentlewomen, we are well prepared to activate your American campaign. Pending your approval, we can move towards implementing it within the next two to three weeks."

A round of applause greeted this statement, and Hans Rizarre beamed with delight. The general was starting off on the right track.

"We shall begin our attack and invasion with a massive assault on the Florida coast."

As he said this, an aide activated a switch that lit up the state of Florida in blue.

"We plan to have that state in our complete control within thirty days. It is ideal for us to start there. They have warm water ports year-round, and we will be able to land men continuously on both sides of the Florida coast. This will neutralize any utilization early on of possible Canadian troops since they would be so far away. The plan is pretty much foolproof. There is no way they can stop us. We will make them believe that initially we will strike the Carolina coast. We will have warships amassed in that area and will actually land a couple of foraging parties to draw their attention. We will also have warships and foraging parties on the west coast of California near Los Angeles as well to draw their attention to that area as well."

Once again, the board lit up, and the Carolina coast and California coast were bathed in a red light.

"Following our initial thirty-day buildup period, we will then strike out in two directions. Major General Ernst Volson will launch an armored attack northward into the state of Alabama with the city of Birmingham as his main objective. General Anzell Dresden will at the same time launch a similar invasion northward up the Atlantic coast with Charleston, South Carolina, as his objective."

Once again, green lights now lit up, two arrows pointing northward up the Atlantic coast to Charleston and the other up to Birmingham.

"We anticipate this area will be sealed up within a two- to three-week period. We will be committing just over a million men and support personnel to this effort. This will consist of military troops, supporting personnel and equipment. I can't conceive of the Americans stopping us at any point. They can't match our firepower or nuclear capability. We have a special surprise in store for the Canadians also. At this time I won't divulge what it is about it, but you will be extremely pleased when you hear of it reported on your daily news broadcasts."

The applause of the ECOWA ministers was loud and boisterous. They cheered their hero, and smiles were evident all around the table. Francois Derdez and Hans Rizarre locked in a bear hug, and it was obvious there would be no negative comments about this operation from those gathered around this table. General Aurielle held up his hand to calm the table so that he could continue. The ministers, finding it difficult to restrain their enthusiasm, slowly sat down.

"Gentlemen, gentlewomen, the loss of life and casualties in this struggle is anticipated to be high. We know that the Americans are willing to pay a high price to prevent what they perceive as our interference in their affairs. However, we truly believe that by the end of 2041, we will control the entire eastern half of the United States of America. Our plan calls for our operations to be in a complete containment stage at that time just east of the Mississippi River. Following that we will move our attack westward, and hopefully they will capitulate prior to total destruction. It is important to note that the placement of over a million military personnel and equipment into a foreign venture will reduce our total efforts in the European theatre. Nonetheless, our manpower needs do not present a problem that we can't deal with. We will still be able to maintain a presence along the Russian border, and I fully intend to maintain our efforts in the Middle East. We presently have the manpower and the resources to wage war anywhere we wish on this planet. It is our goal to have the eastern United States pouring in enough material resources by the end of 2041 to completely finance our military venture over there. We fully expect this to be a long hard struggle."

For the first time during the meeting, the ministers suddenly became quiet. The general had shown them visions of a quick military victory, and now he talked of a multiyear struggle. Emperor Rizarre was the first to interrupt the general.

"General Aurielle, I am confused. You first talk of early two weeks victories and then you suddenly discuss 2042 and beyond. I don't really think the Americans can stop us for any length of time. What do you know that we don't, General?"

"Emperor, sir. It is our belief that if we wage a conventional war campaign in America, it could well be a long struggle. With limited or no nuclear weaponry utilized in the field of battle, we have no choice but to prepare for a long campaign. It is our objective not to destroy the country with nuclear detonations but to gain military control by occupying land mass with our troops and personnel. Our computer readouts have projected presently a two- to three-year struggle if the Americans do not yield and surrender. We have input every conceivable bit of data into our computer programming equipment. We have listed their present military capabilities and the size of what we believe their standing militia to be. The picture that we now paint is quite frankly a worst-case scenario. Our most positive production projections have us completely overrunning the country by the middle of 2042. In fact, we believe that within six months, they will totally capitulate, and that will be the end of that. I would not be properly doing my duty if I did not make you fully aware of all possibilities that exist. We shall strive to shorten the conflict in every possible way. We, at European Defense Headquarters, are ready to move at any time. We humbly await your instructions."

"Well spoken, General. We should have anticipated your exactness with regard to such an adventure. As emperor of our great empire, I see no disagreement among us here. Carry on with your plan and activate it as you will. Don't you all agree?"

The ECOWA ministers all nodded their heads in agreement, stood, and applauded.

"General, you are encouraged to depart and begin this great adventure. I expect to visit you personally in America quite soon. Mr. Derdez, I believe we can bring an end to this meeting."

With that, the general departed with his aides, and the ministers of ECOWA adjourned their meeting. The wishes of Hans Rizarre to crush America would soon be put into decisive military action.

Chapter 27

A good man obtaineth favor of the Lord: but a man of wicked devices will he condemn.

—Proverbs 12:2 KJV

February 25, 2041
Camp Liberty, Mendocino National Forest

Philip Redding had looked forward to his return to Camp Liberty. The rigors of the past three months had taken its toll. When Mary Parker suggested they all return to the northern camps for a few days of rest, the colonel quickly nodded in affirmation. The camps had since been left in the caretake of Sally Watkins and her young friends. Phil looked forward to spending a few days rest in the peace and serenity of the forests he had grown to love. His longtime associate and closest of friends, Harold Baines, was also there to meet him along with John Walker from Canada.

Sally and her twenty-four young people and their entourage of one hundred and sixty-five hard-core Minutemen who had stayed with her greeted Phil and Mary en masse. The exuberance of their youth was a tonic for the colonel. His decision to maintain the camps was logical and sound. The imminent threat of an European invasion meant that all the camps that had been established across the country would have to remain operational. Within the next month, he would spend all his time pouring as much supplies, munitions, and provisions as possible into all the camp areas. General Williamson had appointed him commander-special operations. Now, on the morning of the twenty-fifth of February, he was headed to the subterranean dining hall's main meal table to share breakfast with Mary Parker, Harold Baines, John Walker, and young Sally Watkins.

"Colonel Redding, we in Canada have had much to admire you and your countrymen for. Now we are both tied closely together in what appears to be a real life-and-death struggle."

"John, we couldn't have been successful without Canada's help. You have supplied our people with food and firepower. The trucks that roll south across your borders daily provide us with the lifeline of food and clothing that eases our burden that we presently face. We have moved close to forty million people out of our major cities just during the past two months. This has placed unknown hardships upon all of our citizenry. We owe you an enormous amount of thanks and gratitude."

"Phillip, Phillip, that is pure nonsense. We are brothers and sisters together in this conflict. We share a common foe, and our people all live under the same dark cloud. We have also begun moving our citizens from the larger metropolitan areas."

"Good Lord, John, you don't really think that they'll drop bombs in Canada, do you?"

"Most certainly I do, Colonel. Probably more so now than ever before. We have openly committed to fight together. We pose a real threat to any foreign invasion against North America. We still have a nuclear capacity of our own and your general Williamson has his people working now to properly deploy our offensive weapons. You can believe General Aurielle will be very thorough in his preparations. We have never faced such a threat in the entire history of either of our countries. I am afraid we will pay dearly for our kinship with each other."

Sally Watkins stared across the table with grave concern. Her young face betrayed the anxiety building within her.

"Mr. Redding, do you think we can win? Is there any hope for us?"

Sally had hit the very heart of the matter. This was the main question that was on every American's mind these days.

Phillip Redding was not so quick to respond. He wasn't a man to avoid the truth. It wasn't his nature to give false hope to anyone.

"I really don't know the answer. I must be honest with you. I have always felt we could win. I have believed in America my entire life. Deep down in my heart, I still do. I know we can't prevent foreign troops from landing over here, but I just can't conceive of anyone anywhere totally overrunning us. This country is just too big and full of too many people who will never give up. However, my dear child, there will be a lot of us gone when it is all over with. You should cherish each day that you live free from this moment on. Savor the bonds of trust and friendship that you currently have. Tomorrow may find us all in our graves. I don't wish to sound so fatalistic or portray a future with no hope. As long as mankind lives and yearns to be free, as long as mankind has faith in his fellow man and faith in his Creator, there will always be hope. You young people who have maintained these camps in our absence represent the future for all of us. Keep up your enthusiasm for life, your determination to succeed, your belief in and love for God, your Creator. That is the essence of America's hope for the future. Look also northward to the Canadians. We took them for granted for so many years. We were always the all-powerful ones, the righteous rulers of the world. Now, in our hour of greatest need, our brothers and sisters from the north aid us without question. They feed us, they clothe us, they give us great comfort in our time of need. Follow their example and never, never give up."

The small group assembled finished their meal in silence. There really wasn't too much more to be said. The prospects for the future appeared all too bleak and menacing.

The next four days at Camp Liberty and the northern camps were spent in quiet planning by Colonel Redding and his key staff members. He was convinced his isolated camps spread around the country were going to be vital to the survival of America. Regardless of what may occur in the immediate days ahead, he committed himself totally to supplying the forty-two camps that were now established. He had assigned key men and women from his Camp Liberty projects to be in charge of each unit. Hundreds of America's youth labored many hours each day to build a permanent network of refuge points to serve as clandestine bases of operation and havens from the war zones. When the project was completed, it could later be said that Colonel Redding was a key figure in the fight for the survival of America. Each camp was isolated rurally, completely self-sufficient, and designed to sustain a military-type assault. Depending upon the size of the enemy at hand, the residents could decide to stand and fight, or just as easily escape into the oblivion of the countryside to fight another day. America's former ingenuity was reflected in Phil Redding's work. Nothing was left to the imagination. With the most potent military force ever assembled now threatening America, nothing could be.

Chapter 28

Thou shalt ascend and come like a storm, thou shalt be like a cloud to cover the land, thou, and all thy bands, and many people with thee.

—Ezekiel 38:9 KJV

March 2, 2041
America

From the *Atlanta Daily Journal*'s front-page news on March 2, 2041:

> A massive assault of European Defense troops stormed ashore this morning at Florida's Vero beach on the east coast and established a solid beachhead. At about the same time, thousands of French paratroopers landed north of Cedar Key on Florida's west coast. It appears they are moving towards each other in a race to cut the state in half. Presently there are no American military units in Florida capable of withstanding any kind of major military action. It is anticipated that by nightfall, citizens living in the central and southern part of that state will be isolated. The closest United States military units are stationed presently in northern Alabama, and the United States Defense Department is closely monitoring developments prior to any military engagements.

> This comes on top of reports of a nuclear detonation this morning apparently in the vicinity of Calgary, Canada. It appears that the entire North American continent may be subject to a military conflict. Early morning reports from Charleston, South Carolina, have verified the existence of a huge naval armada offshore. American naval units are presently staying clear of any combat situations. We urge all the citizens of the Atlanta area to be alert to the danger that lurks so close to us. We shall continue to publish for as long as we are able. May God assist us in our desperate need.

The report from the *Atlanta Daily Journal* had recorded the details of the invasion in accurate fashion. However, the horrors of the actual event could only be felt by the citizens of Florida, who had never dreamed such a thing could really occur. When Italian tanks roared through the streets of Fort Pierce, Florida, everyone fled from the streets. By noon the mayor and ten other city officials were hanging by their heels from the top of city hall.

In Melbourne, Florida, Spanish infantry gunned down women and children as they stood helplessly watching. Northward up in Ocala, French paratroopers steamrolled through that city with a vengeance. Any resistance that was met was returned three times over. Interstate 75 and Highway 27 were sealed off with the vanguard of General Aurielle's blitzing armored division. In one day's time, they would be rolling nonstop to the south. Tampa would be a prime target. Possessing the seventh largest port facility in the United States, it was essential. On the early morning of March 3, forty thousand German soldiers landed in Venice, Florida. Supported by French Mirage Aircraft and swift mechanized armored units, the Germans were on the outskirts of Tampa shortly before nightfall. Unfortunately for Florida, the old MacDill Air Force Base which once served as command headquarters for the United States military had been closed down six years earlier and relocated to Louisiana in a big cost-cutting budget move and was now an upscale neighborhood for some of Tampa's wealthy citizens. Outside of occasional sniper fire along Interstate 75, there was no noticeable resistance. American troops were mobilized in northern Alabama, waiting to see where else General Aurielle would strike. It would be necessary to give up much American ground before any major effort could be made to win it back. The citizens of Florida were actually in a helpless position. They would have to fend for themselves. Where was the American Navy? Where was the American Air Force? It was clear that the American military was ceding Florida to the enemy so as to properly set up a defensive posture in the states north of there and leave a lengthy supply line that would run for hundreds of miles and leave the Europeans vulnerable to disruption.

At 5:00 a.m. on the fourth of March, the mayor of Tampa was executed outside city hall. Southward the people of Miami were preparing to capitulate totally twenty-four hours prior to any troops arriving in their city. French warships sat in Biscayne Bay while German fighter jets flying overhead ensured no commercial flights would dare test their missiles. South Floridians were in the midst of the hell that is war. The last occurrence of foreign troops fighting on American soil was so many years ago. There was nobody alive in America today who could say he or she ever experienced such a thing on American soil.

In Montgomery, Alabama, American general Williamson was holding a council of war. The anticipation of waiting to see where or when the Europeans would strike was over. Tactically speaking the general felt that an invasion of Florida gave him a better defense posture to work with. He had a million and a half men at his disposal. The manpower was sufficient, but the firepower might not be. The United States Air Force currently had more than three thousand five hundred operational aircraft and hundreds of military satellites. It was time to use them to start fighting back. They had for the most part been directed away from coastal areas and large cities to protect them from nuclear attack. The United States Navy was still a power force to be dealt with. Over four hundred ships were in active service. Aircraft carriers to destroyers to submarines were in abundance and currently reassigned to northern ports on the East Coast and Canada and West Coast ports running up to Canada as well. The problem was with firepower. Following the economic crisis of 2037, the Europeans greatly reduced the budgets of the US Air Force and the US Navy to include the US Marines. Dollars for munitions, missiles, and new technology was reduced to the bare minimum. Both service agencies had all they could do to stay viable. Despite this, General Williamson had a sort of ace up his sleeve so to speak. The United States Coast Guard had stayed pretty much fully funded during this period. Its search and rescue operations were utilized and respected throughout the world. The Coasties, as they were sometimes called, had over fifty-five thousand personnel to include active duty, reservists, and civilian employees. They currently had over two hundred coastal and oceangoing patrol ships, tenders, tugs, icebreakers, and over one thousand five hundred smaller boats as well an aviation division consisting of more than two hundred helicopters and fixed wing aircraft. Although their public image was one of safety and water rescue operations, from a military standpoint, they presented the general with a formidable military option that not many realized or knew about. He knew he was going to use them soon enough.

As chief of staff for the United States military, General Williamson was in agreement with his associates that the United States should fight a defensive war, utilizing offensive operations only in the most carefully thought out battles. Americans were fighting on home turf, and it would be extremely difficult to keep the Europeans boxed up in Florida. General Williamson would not allow his troops to get sucked up in that kind of trap. He would have to be content to keep the enemy confined to the coast and continuously attempt to cut off their lines of supply and free movement.

In the late afternoon of March 4, General Williamson ordered the First, Second, and Eighth Armies to mobilize in the Talladega National Forest north of Montgomery, Alabama. The city of Montgomery was ordered to evacuate with all major highways and interstates to be dynamited immediately following the removal of all citizens from the city. The United States Army Fifth Armored Division and the United States Marine Eighth and Tenth Divisions were deployed halfway between Montgomery and Tuskegee to the east. It was the intention of the American high command to establish a line of demarcation that they would not let the Europeans cross. The imaginary line on the huge wall maps in the war room behind General Williamson's council chair ran from the west starting at Mobile, Alabama, and eastward to include Montgomery, Alabama, Columbus, Macon, and Augusta, Georgia, and Columbia, South Carolina. North of this, the Appalachian Mountains provided strongholds of defense that no enemy could penetrate very easily. One of the things about America that few foreigners knew was despite her world reputation as a land of prized wealth and advanced civilization, she was still a land of geographically rugged terrain and immense rural land mass. Destroy her main roads and one was soon face-to-face with the elements. Mother Nature still reigned supreme in the countryside, and the forces of nature were a real factor to be reckoned with. General Williamson and others in his command were counting on this to be a decisive intangible that would slow down their potent adversary. The rougher the terrain, the better for the Americans. The worse the weather, the better so. The good general put the word out to all his clergymen to pray for the worst spring weather ever.

"Snow, rain, sleet, come on down," roared General Williamson. "Anything to make these uninvited guests yearn for the comforts of their own homeland."

For the next three weeks, while the Americans maneuvered troops in key areas along its demarcation line, Generals Aurielle, Volson, and Dresden concentrated on solidifying their hold on Florida. Hundreds of ships sat offshore near Tampa Bay and Merritt Island, Florida, and a continuous flow of men and supplies came on shore. There appeared to be no major resistance encountered anywhere. There were a number of reports of sniper fire and small guerilla-type attacks against the Europeans to be sure. But these were as gnats or pesky mosquitoes as far as the generals were concerned. The whole state of Florida was ripe for the taking. It appeared that the planning that went into this venture was paying off in big dividends. The Americans so far had not chosen to fight. General Aurielle was somewhat displeased at this event. The flat terrain of Florida was ideal for his swift moving armor. It was a pity Americans chose not to test him.

By March 30, 2041, the state of Florida was in the control of European hands. The cities of Jacksonville, Tallahassee, and Pensacola were the last to fall. Most Americans had fled these areas. And there was little or no resistance encountered. Most Floridians fled northward into Alabama and Georgia. But still, many stayed. There were thousands of elderly citizens who decided to stay where they were. Others fled into the countryside where they hoped to avoid foreign troops. Armed American guerillas set up operations deep in the Florida Everglades of south Florida and the Ocala National Forest in northern Florida. General Aurielle wasn't about to waste his time and energy bothering with them either. He was already a week behind his schedule and was anxious to strike to the north. General Volson was poised east of Tallahassee and ready to begin his move toward Birmingham, Alabama, through Montgomery. Four hundred and fifty thousand troops stood ready to move as soon as the orders for battle were announced. To the east, Anzell Dresden amassed another three hundred and fifty-five thousand troops just west of Jacksonville, Florida. He anticipated a swift move up the coast. He bet Marcus Aurielle a steak dinner they would be dining in Savannah, Georgia, within two days. There were warships and planes sitting off the coast to ensure this would be done. The ease with which America was falling gave great encouragement to the European troops. Their morale was high, and they started to get the feeling they were invincible. Daily messages of encouragement from Hans Rizarre from across the Atlantic Ocean were broadcast to the men and women in the war zone.

"Your mission is of the greatest importance to your brethren back home. We urge you on towards victory. Soon we shall be masters of the entire planet. Let nothing deter you from the task at hand. The riches of America shall be yours shortly."

This was the typical tirade that Emperor Rizarre delivered each day. He wanted to crush America in the quickest fashion possible. His troops were ruthless in obeying his orders. American citizens were facing their wrath daily all throughout the state of Florida.

Troops raped and murdered at will. Americans were subhumans as far as they were concerned. On March 30, the *Paris Morning Ledger* carried a half-page photo on the front page of its morning edition. It showed Major Genersl Volson presenting the decapitated head of one of Orlando Florida's Disney World characters to Marcus Aurielle. The graphic photo made it clear that a human head was still inside the familiar costume. So much for the decision by some greedy Americans who felt they could still operate the huge amusement park and make a profit off the Europeans. Generals Aurielle and Volson were not amused. They razed half of the park, and three hundred and fifty men and women were murdered there. The blood of Americans was spilling at an alarming rate. No one had been prepared for this type of onslaught. Americans had read of this kind of thing happening to other people. History was full of the tragic experiences of war. How could it happen here? What went wrong? In the short span of four years, so much had gone haywire. America's world flip-flopped, and the accompanying psychological trauma it brought to its people was devastating. Used to living in comfort and luxury, half of the American population was now encamped in rural tent cities wondering if tomorrow they might face their death. Able-bodied men and women everywhere were off in the military, and families were torn asunder. No one could really be sure they would ever see loved ones again. This was a totally new experience for Americans of this generation. No one could tell if these modern-day citizens had the same strength of character as their early ancestors. Only time would tell.

April 4, 2041
Uniontown, Alabama

Jethro Winters sat uneasy this spring morning. As he sat in his field tent, he worried about the rain that was presently pounding around him. As commanding officer of the First United States Air Cavalry Division, he was assigned a key role in stopping Ernest Volson's drive through Montgomery, Alabama. American troops were already amassed on the northern edge of the city. In three hours' time, the United States Marines Eighth and Tenth Divisions were going to strike full force into General Volson's east flank. The United States Army Fifth Armored Division would provide a spearhead for the assault, and it would be America's first major test in the field of combat. Two hours following the initial assault, The United States First, Second, and Eighth Army units were to swoop out of their strongholds in the Talladega National Forest. Their instructions were to charge headlong into the west flank of the enemy in a do-or-die assault. During the height of the battle, Commander Winters was to spring his two thousand air cavalry troops into action. Mounted on death-dealing helicopters, he was to land south of Montgomery for the express purpose of cutting off the European supply lines and harassing their rear flanks. Now as the rain fell, Winters felt a growing worry begin to burn in his stomach. He just had to get his men into this fracas. The success of his mission could help turn the tide of the battle. It was now 5:00 a.m., and at 10:00 a.m. his machines had to fly. The weather forecast called for showers to fall intermittently throughout the day. America needed a victory badly. So far she had been bloodied up. General Dresden was already in Savannah, and word had it he was starting to move against Charleston already. General Williamson couldn't delay any longer. Ernest Volson was at his doorstep, and it was time to answer the loud knocking on that door that was being heard around the world.

America had a good thing on its side this day. It was simply the element of surprise. Ernest Volson had four hundred and fifty thousand European troops at his disposal. He didn't know, however, how many American troops were facing him around Montgomery. His intelligence-gathering group knew about the marines and mechanized armor to the east. It was too obvious to miss. The initial attack would most likely come from the northwest. Volson knew there were Americans in the forest. He just didn't know how many. But nobody knew about the air cavalry. General Winters had flown them east of Uniontown, Alabama, close to Selma, during the night from Columbus, Mississippi. Flying safely just above treetop level all the way, his air machines slipped in close to Uniontown completely unnoticed by the Europeans. Their advance scouts had ventured only as far west and south of Selma, Alabama. It was in this town at 2:00 a.m. that American troops and European troops had their first engagement. In a fierce fifteen-minute firefight, the Americans drove the fifty man German advance unit back toward Montgomery. Casualties were light, with five Americans and twelve Europeans dead.

When this action was reported to General Volson, he was not convinced the Americans would strike from the northwest. His field commanders were advised to react accordingly and the line of battle was set.

At 9:00 a.m., Commander Winters assembled his flight leaders. The rain was still falling, but its intensity had leveled off.

"Colonel Roberts, what is the firing status of our machines?"

"Commander, we are ready to move. We are not at maximum stress levels as far as weather is concerned. We have three hundred choppers available for backup if we have machine failure."

"That's excellent, Colonel. We've been monitoring the battle as best we can. The assault on the east flank has been going on for over an hour now. It's too early to tell anything. In an hour's time, the Eighth Army will lead the charge out of the forest. We will have to be ready to fly then, Colonel. It'll take us a good hour to get there."

"We're ready, Commander. The men are a little wet, but their appetites to strike at our enemy is wetter yet. We will fly, General, regardless."

The battle in and south of Montgomery raged on for an additional eleven hours. When it was over, the Americans could say they tasted their first victory. However, it was a win that was ever so costly. American casualties were listed in the thousands, and the city of Montgomery, Alabama, was left a rubble of brick, concrete, and ashes. The superior European troops held their own up until about 4:00 p.m. It was then that Commander Winter's air cavalry began to make the difference. His troops had successfully landed twice at the rear of both enemy flanks. Troops at each flank delivered swift destruction and chaos to enemy supply trucks and support troops south of Montgomery. He then airlifted additional men smack into south Montgomery and completely caught the Europeans off guard. General Ernest Volson was torn in half as a low-flying Cobra attack helicopter blew his jeep into oblivion. Within an hour and a half, the cavalry was back in the air and flew southwest of the city just before the onrushing crush of the retreating Europeans could have swept them away. The European retreat took Volson's troops about halfway to Dothan, Alabama, north of the Florida border. There an additional ninety thousand troops had rushed up from Tallahassee, Florida, to support General Volson. This action and the death of General Volson represented an initial setback to General Aurielle's American campaign. It certainly didn't spell defeat for the Europeans by any means, but merely confirmed the general's early observations the struggle for America would be long and hard. However, the fury of Hans Rizarre and his associates in Europe would be difficult to contend with. He would just have to proceed slowly north toward Montgomery and try to gain more ground. It was the only soothing salve he could think of to heal the wounds of Montgomery.

Following their success at Montgomery, General Williamson gave orders to his troops to immediately pick up their dead and wounded and return to their initial staging areas. It was not beyond the Europeans to bomb the area with a few low-yield nuclear devices. The general, as it turns out, was correct in his views regarding this tactic. Thirty-five minutes following the departure of the last American units from the Montgomery area, French Mirage jets dropped three bombs in the battle zone area in an attempt to eradicate large masses of American troops. The only thing the bombs did for the Europeans was to incinerate the bodies of the dead corpses they had left behind. The Americans were wise to the ruthless barbarous tactics of the enemy that had invaded their homeland. General Williamson kept his men moving and well spread out. He could not afford to leave his units vulnerable to modern-day nuclear devices or aircraft that could decimate his troops instantly. His commanders' first reaction following the battle at Montgomery was to linger and bury their dead. They weren't prepared for the general's strange orders to pick up and run away. After the visit by the French planes, they would not question the general's wisdom again.

Chapter 29

> Scornful men bring a city into a snare:
> but wise men turn away wrath.
>
> —Proverbs 29:8 KJV

April 6, 2041
Meridian, Mississippi

All across America the news was out.

The success at Montgomery was the tonic that was needed. There was at least a real hope now. Since the initial invasion of Florida and right up to the nuclear blast in Canada, the overall picture looked bleak. It mattered not that General Dresden and his troops were now on the outskirts of Charleston, South Carolina. For the moment, the American troops had showed well in their first major engagement. Even though it was for the most part a draw, the Americans stood firm and caused the Europeans to withdraw and fall back from the battle. American troops in the field felt it wasn't to be the last time that was going to happen either, and everyone in the world could count on that. Also reports coming in from Canada were confirming that the nuclear detonation in Calgary, although the city was immensely damaged, the event did not take the number of lives that the Europeans thought it would. The casualty count was nearly one hundred thousand citizens hurt and some twelve thousand deaths estimated. The Canadians had been busy relocating their citizens as well out from the larger cities. The potential for so many more deaths and wounded was avoided. Also additional news reports were now detailing how American and Canadian fighter jets caused a great deal of damage to European aircraft engaged in this bombing run followed by more reports of US Naval and Coast Guard units engaging with and harassing the European Pacific Fleet that was off the coast of California. Suddenly the news was good for a change. It may not last for long, but it felt damn good.

This day, April 6, in Meridian, Mississippi, General Williamson had summoned David Jefferson to an urgent meeting. The event had all the appearances of a victory celebration with many high-ranking officials entering the city. At 6:00 a.m. Jethro Winters sealed off the city with his air cavalry troopers, and no one was allowed into the city without authorization from General Williamson's personal staff.

At 10:00 a.m., David Jefferson landed on a small field outside the Meridian city limits. His twin-engine Cessna had flown straight through the evening and early morning hours to arrive here on time. He was somewhat puzzled by the urgency of General Williamson's message. It was understandable that the most should be made out of America's good showing at Montgomery, but the unusual nature of the message seemed out of the norm by Jefferson. Two armed US Army Rangers greeted him as he stepped out of the plane, and when he questioned why, they responded, "Just following orders, Mr. Jefferson. We are to personally escort you to Meridian."

As Jefferson started to walk away from the aircraft, the sky was suddenly filled with low-flying helicopters. Twenty-five air cavalry choppers swooped down and engulfed the small airfield. David Jefferson was suddenly surrounded by some two hundred heavily armed troopers. A young soldier with the markings of an army captain strode forward to greet him.

"Welcome to Meridian, Mr. Jefferson. Please excuse the nature of your greeting party."

"What is the meaning of all this, Captain? What is going on?"

"I'm not at liberty to discuss it with you, sir. My orders are to bring you and the army rangers with you safely to General Williamson. We should not linger here. If you please, sir, your choppers are waiting."

Jefferson could see he was in no position to question anything at this point. The tight security was certainly impressive, but the front lines were quite some distance away, at least he thought so.

Johnston Williamson waited anxiously for the arrival of David Jefferson. His aides had set up a temporary headquarters for him at the local Ramada Inn. Lieutenant General Andrew Waverly was with him as he waited. Lieutenant General Waverly was presently commanding general of the US Army I Corps. With forty-five thousand troops assigned to its two divisions, I Corps was responsible for sealing off the southern perimeter of the Washington, DC, nuclear detonation zone. No Americans were authorized to enter the contaminated area because of the high radiation readings still present. Despite this ever-present danger, it was a full-time job keeping stragglers and curiosity seekers from viewing the ruins of the nation's capital. People could not understand that there was so much damage done. For twenty-five miles or so, the area was littered with broken buildings, rubble, and ashes. It looked so much like a war zone.

An additional division assigned to Waverly's command was the Fifth US Army Special Forces Brigade. Their responsibility with its three battalions and four thousand troops was to defend the underground military complex established in the rugged Virginia mountains deep in the confines of the George Washington National Forest. First established as an underground communications network to operate during the event of a nuclear attack, it had evolved into a vast underground complex. It served not only as a military communications center but also a haven for high-ranking civilian politicians and their families.

On March 18, Special Forces Sergeant Hanover Manquin came to General Waverly with some startling information. It seemed that US Senator Newton Gether of Virginia, a lifelong personal friend of former President Carlson, had been observed making some unusual trips. Carlson, Gether, and two other US senators had been sharing assigned spaces in the underground Virginia complex since the beginning of the revolution in November of 2040. Although peace had been declared with the American rebels and America seemed united as one, Carlson, having relinquished the power of his presidency, never appeared to have his heart totally in the struggle against Europe.

It was by accident that Senator Gether's actions came to be suspicious in nature. He was involved in a freak boating accident on March 15 off Bloodsworth Island in Chesapeake Bay. A US Coast Guard vessel reported the incident. It appears there was a collision of two boats just off the coast, and the incident and the actions of the two parties involved were immediately communicated to the US Defense Communications Center in the Virginia Mountains. Apparently Senator Gether, somewhat unfamiliar with the boat he was piloting, rammed into a larger craft he was obviously meeting. A amateur ham radio operator sitting in his cabin on Bloodsworth Island, having witnessed the accident and believing the smaller boat to be in trouble, radioed a distress message to the US Coast Guard. The message he gave read simple enough. A twenty-five-foot Trojan Sedan fiberglass cabin cruiser with at least two men aboard had just been rammed by a smaller twenty-foot Chris-Craft with at least one man on board. By the time the coast guard had arrived, the larger craft had left the area and traveled southward. Senator Gether showed his credentials and dismissed the incident as minor and headed back up the Potomac River to dock his boat. However, unbeknown to the parties involved, the twenty-five-foot Trojan Sedan cruiser had been the subject of very recent Coast Guard and US Military investigation teams. The boat had been monitored making varied trips out of Chesapeake Bay out into the Atlantic Ocean. It was believed the boat was meeting with European warships stationed off the coast. All this information had been routinely communicated to the communications center in the Virginia mountains.

Hanover Manquin was an expert communications operator. Fifteen years in the army and currently a member of the Special Forces Brigade, he was assigned to the Virginia Complex because of his computer expertise. He never missed a message. Every bit of data that pumped out on the terminal printouts were read by his eyes. Half of the stuff pumped out on the terminals was boring and routine. It was computer coded and routinely sent to whichever department it applied to. At 2:00 a.m. of the sixteenth of March, Manquin was working the 11:00 p.m. to 7:00 a.m. shift. Everything was quiet at his duty station, and he was routinely reading the printout messages. The connection between Senator Gether and the mystery men in the boat hit the sergeant square in the eyeballs. He was quite familiar with the information concerning the Trojan cruiser. The idea that a meeting had taken place alarmed him to take immediate action.

"What the hell was the old fart doing out alone in a boat anyhow?"

Sergeant Manquin realized he was talking to only himself, but he knew just how to handle this. He had been in the military long enough to know that things like this had to be handled in a nonroutine fashion. He could cut across chains of command and get to the heart of a matter with the best of anyone. He used his Special Forces credentials to the fullest and found that when he wore his Green Beret, he could pretty much talk to anyone he chose. This particular matter needed to get to the attention of General Andrew Waverly. As commanding general of I Corps, he had an impeccable reputation. His men idolized him, and although he gave the outward impression of a stern taskmaster, he was easily approachable by his men.

Two days later, Manquin sought him out following a weekly briefing session. Their discussion was short and to the point. Two hours later, a security team was assigned to monitor Senator Gether and his associates. The results of their efforts are what brought General Waverly to Meridian to seek out General Williamson.

"Andrew, how widespread is this plot?"

Andrew Waverly was very perplexed at the moment. He didn't like reporting to his commanding officer on something he wasn't totally sure of. Perhaps even the great general was a possible target. It was a difficult decision to report the matter at this point in time.

"General, I honestly don't know. I've come to you because you were the man who took a stand five months ago. You put your life and career on the line for your country. You stood by Mr. Jefferson and defied the scum that had overran our country. All I know is that Mr. Jefferson's life is in great danger, and perhaps yours also. We had no time to let this linger any longer. When these things happen, you really don't know who to trust or confide in."

General Williamson was deeply touched by what he had just heard. Through the years, he had heard of Andrew Waverly, but they had never officially met. He knew that when you consistently received favorable comments about a man that spanned a decade or more, they were usually true. Career officers, utilizing good public relations techniques, could perpetuate their fine reputations over a short period. The true test was the test of time. Andrew Waverly had passed that test over the twenty-two years he had served in the army since his graduation from West Point. Johnston Williamson was impressed.

"My good general, I'm sorry we have not had the pleasure of meeting sooner. The country owes you a great deal of gratitude."

"At this point, General, I'm concerned only with the safety of Mr. Jefferson and yourself."

"As commanding general, Andrew, I will continue to do my duty. I am a soldier, a fighting warrior. I shall simply double my guard until we put this matter to rest. However, Mr. Jefferson must be hidden away for the moment. He should be here shortly. I have sent my men to bring him here."

The two generals were interrupted by the deafening arrival of the air cavalry. There was no mistaking the churning whine of their engines as they descended upon the Ramada Inn parking lot and surrounding grounds. Within five minutes' time, David Jefferson was greeted by General Williamson at the front door of his command office.

"David, David. It's so good to see you again."

"The same to you, General. Congratulations on your efforts in Montgomery."

"Thank you. Come inside please. I have an office set up here in the main conference room. General Andrew Waverly is waiting there for us."

Once again Jefferson was surprised at the tight security in effect. Armed air cavalry troops had positioned themselves both inside and outside of the building. His army rangers were excused by General Williamson, and he was hurriedly ushered into the general's office where he was introduced to Andrew Waverly.

"It's been a long time, Andrew. It's good seeing you."

"Yes, sir, I'm honored. The last time I saw you was during your last term in Congress. I think I've had six different assignments since then."

"Well, I'm glad to see you on our side. You were well spoken of back then. Did you have anything to do with Montgomery?"

"No, Mr. Jefferson. Unfortunately, I was unable to be of any assistance to us there."

At this point, General Williamson interrupted and asked the two gentlemen to be seated.

"David, General Waverly is just being overly modest. The overall communications network we have in place is the result of his great support folks in Virginia. They have made sure our commo is a first-rate operation. David, let me get quickly to the reason we have summoned you here. It has nothing to do with our success at Montgomery. I am sorry that we could not advise you of what is going on. General Waverly's command group has uncovered something that needs your immediate attention. Andrew, would you please brief our esteemed leader on your findings."

As General Waverly turned to speak, the three gentlemen were interrupted by the loud ring of the telephone on General Williamson's desk. It was immediately apparent that the message received was alarming in nature as the general hollered for Andrew Waverly to pick up the other phone to listen in.

"Major, please repeat what you've just told me. I have General Waverly on the other line."

Both men listened without responding for almost a minute. Then General Williamson thanked the caller, and both men put down the phones.

"Andrew, we must move quickly. Please advise David of what is going on. I will make arrangements to get him out of here."

With that, General Williamson hastily departed the room, leaving David Jefferson all the more bewildered as to what was going on.

"David, we've uncovered a plot to assassinate you. We are not sure of all the players involved. We know that Senator Gether has had meetings with the European general Dresden. We truly believe your coleader, former president Carlson, may also be part of this. We have been able to intercept some private communications that indicate you are a target for assassination, as well as General Williamson. We have been unable to get absolute confirmation of this, but some of the communication we were able to hack points back to Senator Gether and Mr. Carlson. The phone call we just received was from my intelligence group leader Major Francis Sanders. Apparently, Mr. Carlson is arriving here this afternoon to participate in an unknown as yet victory proceeding following our positive performance in Montgomery. He is being escorted by members of the Second Brigade out of Virginia. Those troops are part of my own command. The problem is that no one of my staff has advised me our men were escorting Carlson, and it appears to be possibly a rogue move that we need to attend to. The problem is, we can't be sure how deep the plot runs. It will take only one man and one bullet to put you away sir. General Williamson is making arrangements to send you into temporary hiding."

David Jefferson was not prepared for this kind of development. He had meant to take full advantage of any celebration proceedings. It was important for him to be as publicly exposed as possible. He wanted Americans to see him on the local news reports and the front pages of the daily papers. It was important for them to have their morale lifted. It was a critical time for the country. After so much tragedy and hardship, a great perceived win could turn the tide and bring a new spirit that could spread from coast to coast.

"With all due respect, sir, we can't afford to lose you. You are the heart and soul of our cause. We would be remiss in our duty to the citizens of this country if we did not protect you."

David Jefferson knew these men were sworn to protect him, and they would not be budged. The depressing idea that there were traitors in the ranks swept over him, thoroughly rendering him temporarily speechless. His previous jovial mood was replaced by a new dread that left him a shaken man. It seemed such an unfair fate. There was sufficient time indeed set aside for the perils and pitfalls that life provided. Somehow, in this day and age, there was to be no time allotted for spending time on things considered fortunate and good for his country, America.

It was ten minutes before General Williamson returned to the room. In the meantime, Andrew Waverly left David Jefferson to his thoughts and then stepped out of the room momentarily to ensure that security on the building was doubled again. He was thankful he had his loyal troops along with him on this trip. General Williamson and Andrew Waverly reentered the room together. With them were several officers from the First Cavalry's Airborne Brigade. Williamson did not hesitate. He was a man quick to take action during a crisis.

"David, these men are going to escort you to Camp Liberty. At the moment, it's the safest place we can think of. As soon as we clear this mess up, we'll get you out of there."

"Johnston, what can I say? I'll wire you when we get to the camp. I understand that your duty is here. Please resolve this quickly."

"Most certainly, David. The whole thing leaves a bitter taste in all of our mouths. General Waverly, sir, the plan is to move all those choppers outside to a different staging area about a mile from here. Following this maneuver, Major Collins will slip away with ten choppers and Mr. Jefferson and head west to safety."

With that, David Jefferson was presented with some army khakis, a helmet, and a weapon. When the First Cavalry made their move fifteen minutes later, he was in the middle of it all, and no one looking could tell that America's foremost leader was in the midst of ten choppers that swiftly departed from the grounds of the Ramada Inn. Within an hour's time, David Jefferson was more than eighty miles away from any celebration event he so very much wanted to attend.

Chapter 30

An unjust man is an abomination to the just, and he that is upright in the way is an abomination to the wicked.

—Proverbs 29:27 KJV

April 7, 2041
Paris, France

The early morning edition of the *Paris Morning Star* sent stirring news all across Europe with shocking headlines:

> AMERICAN LEADERSHIP IN DISARRAY AS EXPLOSION RIPS THROUGH HEADQUARTERS COMMAND POST

> A HUGE EXPLOSION OF UNKNOWN ORIGIN LEAVES AMERICAN GENERAL JOHNSTON WILLIAMSON IN CRITICAL CONDITION IN AN AMERICAN HOSPITAL

> EARLY REPORTS INDICATE THAT EX-PRESIDENT CARLSON, NOW AN ACTIVE LEADER IN THE AMERICAN TRIUMVIRATE, HAS BEEN CONFIRMED KILLED

> TROUBLE ERUPTS DURING A VICTORY CELEBRATION OF SORTS THAT WAS TAKING PLACE IN MERIDIAN, MISSISSIPPI. IT WAS NOT PRESENTLY KNOWN THE STATUS OF DAVID JEFFERSON.

The information was received with great elation by Hans Rizarre in Paris. He had arrived in Paris to attend a meeting with

French delegates who were summoned by Gustav Erikson to determine the role that France would play in accumulating oil through the Israeli access to the oil reserves. French technicians were far advanced among Europeans in their abilities to economically extract oil deposits. Their particular expertise had already done much to add wealth to the European economy. It was at the end of his first day in Paris that he had learned of the American performance at Montgomery. The loss of General Volson had momentarily jolted Hans Rizarre. He excused himself from a key meeting and went into the executive restroom and retched into the commode. It was fifteen minutes before he could gather himself together enough to return to the conference room. He immediately adjourned the meeting, and he and Gustav Erikson closeted themselves in Han's hotel room until he was able to contact General Aurielle in Florida. It was only after talking with the general for two hours that he was able to calm down. General Aurielle had assured him that it was only a temporary setback. Soon General Dresden would be marching up the East Coast of America, and plans would go on as scheduled. Also he had some positive feedback from their old friend, ex-President Carlson. He let it be known that he was very receptive to working out a peace settlement. There was talk of eliminating David Jefferson and General Williamson. With those two key individuals gone, the scenario was much simpler. The only thing Carlson wanted was his old position back. There had already been preliminary meetings with General Dresden on one of the European warships east of Savannah, Georgia. If Emperor Rizarre would just be patient a while longer, positive results would soon be forthcoming. One battle certainly did not win a war.

Now that the news was being broadcast about the American leadership in Meridian, Mississippi, Hans and Gustav ordered in a breakfast to the presidential suite so they could sit and watch the television broadcasts of the news from America.

"Gustav, Marcus Aurielle is a man of his word. General Williamson put out of action is a major stroke of good fortune. Old Mr. Carlson back as president would be very good for us. An America without their three leaders working together leaves them a country in serious trouble and very vulnerable. A couple of quick wins on the battlefield by us and we may be able to negotiate a quick surrender by them."

"It is certainly good news, Hans. I wonder what became of Mr. Jefferson? He seems perhaps to have escaped this."

"Don't be too sure about that, Gustav. We haven't learned all the details. We know he was in Meridian when this so-called victory event, must say a short-lived event at that, occurred."

"Perhaps you will be able to attend a victory party over there of your own, Hans."

"That is a day I am looking forward to. Actually Gustav, I am glad you brought that topic up. As soon as things become a little more stable with the war effort, I want you to take a trip over there. We already have Florida pretty much in line. I want you to coordinate the economic effort. There is no reason we can't put those people back to work. We need it to support all those troops in the field."

"I'm very anxious to get things started over there, Hans. These meetings should be pretty well completed within a week. I'll begin then to prepare for it. You know our own people are already spending money in South Florida. There were two vacation junkets that flew out of Germany two days ago. Some of our people wanted to see war firsthand and close up. You know, it's a shame Aurielle destroyed Disney World. We could have made a fortune with that."

A loud chuckle of amusement by Hans Rizarre almost caused hm to spill the coffee cup he held to his lips.

"Yes, it's truly a shame. I guess that's an example of the general's true hatred for America. You know he didn't really want to send his troops over there. That's one of the pleasures a general may take during combat. I would just as soon have him get it out of his system anyhow. We'll just rebuild the place. We'll resurrect Mr. Mickey Mouse."

"General Aurielle does not have the vision you do, Hans. How can you rule the world if you keep your soldiers at home all the time?"

"That's exactly correct, Gustav. It's just as well our generals don't have that kind of vision. Just let them do as we tell them. Today

Aurielle is in America. Who knows, next month I may have him in Africa. Good Lord Gustav, it was just last month I had him in Israel."

"What's going on in Africa, Hans?"

"Absolutely nothing, Gustav. I was just making a point. It's that overall concept of vision we were talking about. We have to be prepared to be at any area of this planet whenever it becomes necessary."

The two men chatted on for some time. The animation of their conversation reflected the aggressive aspirations of men seriously involved and committed to yet unfulfilled goals. There was no question about the intensity of their purpose.

Chapter 31

What you get by achieving your goals is not as important as what you become by achieving your goals.

—Henry David Thoreau

April 11, 2041
Tel Aviv, Israel

Issac Pelensky was feeling more alive than at any time he could recently remember. In the short time he was in Israel, he had become as a man reborn. Two days earlier he had received word that the Israeli Knesset had officially approved his citizenship, and he traveled to Tel Aviv to receive his official paperwork along with several others. He was now free to rejoin his friends Zeth Robbins and Jeremiah Montros in Galilee. Rebecca Simons had arrived from Nazareth to pick him up. The day was still early, and she recommended the two join each other for early morning coffee and breakfast at one of her favorite neighborhood cafes, the Castel Café.

"Well, Issac, are you ready for Galilee?"

"Rebecca, I am ever so ready. As a new citizen I feel like a man upon a mission. I'm afraid, however, that I won't be accepted without a fuss."

"That's foolishness. You've been very well accepted. Your citizenship is proof of that."

"It was pretty much a mandatory acceptance, Rebecca. Anyone who can closely verify their Jewish roots must be granted citizenship. The fuss I'm talking about is Jesus. Most everyone here practices the Jewish faith in one way or another. We believers in Christ as the Messiah are in the minority. I worry that may bring us trouble."

"We've not let that deter us previously, Issac. Now that we know the temple is to be built, we must press on even harder."

"Press on we will. The temple is the key. I worry we will offend many, and I remember Jesus's words from Matthew: "Jerusalem, Jerusalem! Thou who killest the prophets, and stonest those who are sent to thee!" I don't know how ready I am to feel the wrath of those who may want to do us bodily harm. It's kind of crazy anyway. We are all working from a common ground, Rebecca. Both sides believe in the Messiah. The difference is that we believe He's already arrived once before."

"Well spoken, Issac. If we approach it from that viewpoint, we may find a way to lessen the antagonism of our adversaries."

"Well stated. We can all wait for the Messiah together. The frightening thing is that some of these misguided souls act as if Emperor Rizarre is exactly that. Even the pope is encouraging that kind of thinking. It tends to weaken our own credibility when the leader of Christ's church on earth espouses such nonsense. It tends to make us seem like we are somewhat out of touch, certainly out of touch with their reality."

"Issac, another subject. I don't understand why Cardinal Rondanelli has yet to choose a papal name. He told the Italian press last week that he was 'the true servant, a humble man' alongside the great emperor, Hans Rizarre. I find it hard to believe he could say such a thing."

"Rebecca, since the time of Peter, our church has been victimized by some men of corruption. Forget about hypocrites that sometimes sit at the top and mislead so many. The people are the church. Remember Christ said, 'For where two or more are gathered together for my sake, there am I in the midst of them.' This is what we are about. We'll just try to reach as many as we can. That is all we can do."

"We should be going now, Issac. The young ones in Galilee need the strength of your wisdom. Sometimes their youth and exuberance get them into trouble. Last week Zeth openly challenged the chief rabbi in Nazareth during the Sabbath prayer meeting. It has created quite a commotion."

"I will do my best, Rebecca. Sometimes young people, such as yourself, are wiser than what you give yourself credit for."

Rebecca and Issac spent another fifteen minutes at the quaint café. Between sipping their coffee and enjoying each other's company, they talked of the group up in Galilee. There had been two articles prominent in the Israeli newspapers just this past month about them. Israel was beginning to take notice of these newly titled zealots. Their increased activity in the Galilean Hills was causing considerable discussion. The seventy-five to eighty percent Jewish population in Israel of over eight million was itself a diverse group. From the most severe orthodox to the less rigid liberals, there was quite a difference of opinion regarding the correct interpretation of just what was required of a true believing Jew. Now, with over two thousand years of history behind her, the Christian Jew was in full impact mode. One journalist described it as a recent phenomenon, another test for the "chosen people." In a most recent article, a Bethlehem editorialist was bold enough to say that "it was possibly time to consider the issue more closely. The building of the new temple seemed as a prodding spur to the Jesus believers. They felt time of was of the essence and that soon their hero may return."

It seemed that biblical prophecy had nothing left to fulfill but the end-time writings. Even the Orthodox Jews were saying this. There was a certain feeling now among most all Jews. It was almost a tangible thing. Perhaps Daniel's prophecy was occurring before their eyes. The final fulfillment of the days of the end times seem to be upon them. One Israeli editorialist even entertained the bizarre notion that Hans Rizarre and Pope Rondanelli could well be the prophesized two witnesses coming into place.

Rebecca's van arrived southwest of the Sea of Galilee in the early evening hours of the next day. There was great joy and celebration among Zeth and Jeremiah and their friends as close comrades were reunited once again. At dinner that night, almost a hundred followers of Jesus planned their future course. They would soon vocalize to their brethren countrymen the need to prepare. Their Messiah would soon be knocking at their door.

Little did these well-meaning souls know what the future really held for them. Within the next five years, over seventy-five of them will have been murdered for the message they bought. Do unto others would take a menacing direction down a one-way street at the orders of the rulers of the European Republic as mercenary soldiers at their direction would cause much murder and mayhem. Men who acted as sheep would be nothing more than easy prey to the wolves that would roam the earth at their direction.

CHAPTER 32

When you reach the end of your rope, tie a knot in it and hang on.

—Franklin D. Roosevelt

April 10, 2041
Savannah, Georgia

At 3:00 a.m. on Wednesday, April 2041, the citizens of Savannah, Georgia, experienced a shaking and jolting that was severe enough that most got up and ran outside from the homes they were sleeping in. A 6.8 Richter scale rated earthquake had just struck about eighty miles east of Savannah, Georgia, south of Wilmington Island in North America. Ships from the European Defense Fleet sustained damage and were forced to withdraw back south and east in the Atlantic Ocean to safety. Tsunami activity was felt from Charleston, South Carolina, to the north and south to Jacksonville, Florida. Twenty-foot waves caused a great deal of chaos along that section of the coast line and any supplies or additional support from the European naval forces were going to have to be suspended for two or three days until calm was restored to the ocean waters. On land, General Dresden and his staff, just west of Savannah, Georgia, would spend two days calming his European troops after they were so were so violently awakened in their tents atop the shaking earth beneath them. They would have to pause and determine just exactly where and when their next advance to the north would be.

Just southwest of Montgomery, Alabama, in Boykin, Alabama, General Williamson and his staff were contemplating their next assault against the European troops south of them near Dothan.

PLANET EARTH

Plans were being made to send raiding parties out to attack the Europeans from the rear flanks south of Dothan in a series of aggressive, violent quick strikes. It was designed to force the Europeans to slow down their forward north movement and cause havoc to their supply lines, resulting in requiring them to have to concentrate more troops to defending their rear flank positions in rural country they were unfamiliar with. The tremors from the earthquake were multiple in number, but neither the Americans nor the Europeans troops to their south were adversely affected. It did cause all parties to pause their activities and closely monitor the quake.

Within four hours of the Savannah area earthquake, the BBC (British Broadcasting Corporation) broadcast an alarming and astonishing news bulletin on its noon world news report. Eleven major earthquakes of 6.5 and higher had been reported occurring throughout planet Earth all within the nine-hour period starting at 3:00 a.m. in Savannah.

Special BBC News Bulletin

An earthquake assault on planet Earth has shaken eleven communities around the world in a major way. Thousands are reported dead, and tens of thousands have been injured in an astonishing earthquake swarm event of great magnitude that has occurred almost simultaneously in various places throughout planet Earth: Savannah, Georgia, 6.5 quake; Anchorage, Alaska, 7.1 quake; Nagasaki, Japan, 6.8 quake; Vladivostok, Russia, 6.7 quake; Wuhan, China, 7.3 quake; Northern Mariana Islands, Guam, 6.5 quake; New Delhi, India, 7.5 quake; Erbil, Iraq, 7.1 quake; Kayseri, Turkey, 8.1 quake; Bogota, Colombia, 8.0 quake; Concepcion, Chile, 7.9 quake. The magnitude of these shifting tectonic plates were sending seismic shock waves, tremors, and tsunami waves rumbling throughout the planet. In Savannah, Georgia; Anchorage, Alaska; Osaka, Japan; Vladivostok, Russia; Guam; and Concepcion, Chile all of the quakes were close offshore events resulting in flooding coastal conditions and tsunami wave conditions.

Chapter 33

*The most difficult thing is the decision to
act, the rest is merely tenacity.*

—Amelia Earhart

April 13, 2041
White River National Forest, Colorado

David Jefferson waited in his jeep along the White River. His twenty army choppers and two-hundred-man escort from the First Cavalry Division set down here at Camp Belden five days ago. It was to be a short refueling and rest stop before traveling onto Camp Liberty. A late spring snow blanketed the White River National Forest with over two feet of snow the morning following their arrival. It was to be two more days before they could move. Jefferson was awaiting the arrival of Anne Jones. She was driving in from Denver, Colorado, where she had been visiting General Williamson. He had been flown into Mercy Hospital there following the assassination attempt. From the information received from General Waverly in Meridian, it was a miracle that Williamson was alive at all.

The second night following Jefferson's Meridian departure, all hell broke loose. A young army commando from the Sixth Virginia Brigade, while delivering a message from ex-president Carlson to the general, walked into Williamson's office at the Ramada Inn and immediately dropped two hand grenades across the general's desk. One army bodyguard shot him to death instantly, and another flung himself on top of one of the grenades. The resulting explosion left the room a mass of tangled and wounded bodies. One bodyguard and two other officers died in that room. General Williamson was rendered unconscious, and his left leg was severely injured. Amid the resulting chaos that immediately followed the explosion, General Andrew Waverly took it upon himself to lead a team of army rangers to personally question ex-president Carlson. The ex-president wouldn't hear of it and ordered his own group of army troopers to send the general on his way. Waverly was not deterred and initiated a fearsome gun battle that resulted in the quick demise of Mr. Carlson. Subsequent investigation revealed correspondence in the ex-president's possession that clearly implicated him in the assassination plot. Meetings were now going on to determine who would take General Williamson's command position in the field. It was essential to replace General Williamson right away in order to maintain a viable military operation. There was no doubt capable replacements that were available, General Waverly included, that could step in and capably give direction.

The sound of approaching vehicles stirred Jefferson from his deep thinking, and Major Bobbie Collins pulled up alongside him in his jeep followed by five other military vehicles.

"Mr. Jefferson, you really should not be sneaking away from us like this. I know you like your privacy, but I would be very embarrassed if we lost you."

"I'm sorry, Major, I apologize. It's very important to me to be alone sometimes. I was thinking how pleased I am that the plot has been put to rest. Carlson is dead, and Senator Gether behind bars in Virginia was very good news. However, the earthquake events are very troubling to ponder. Don't know quite how to deal with that information. I thought for the moment I would sit out here, try to enjoy the scenery, and wait for the group from Denver to arrive."

"We have made contact with their convoy. They are about twenty minutes away from us. They cleared Interstate 6 east of Glenwood Springs just a short while ago. When we couldn't find you, we were worried you might be driving out to meet them."

"No, Major. I wouldn't do something like that without telling you. If ever I'm missing, I truly won't be far away. I promise you that."

"Fair enough, sir. Look, I'm going to meet that convoy. I'll take one of these other jeeps with me. The other vehicles will stay here with you. We'll be back shortly."

Forty-five minutes later, Major Collins appeared at the White River crossing with his convoy. David Jefferson could not remember seeing Anne Jones look so beautiful. It was difficult to explain. She was covered head to foot in winter gear, yet the beauty of her smile was as a warm glow. He knew he acted as somewhat of a schoolboy when he was around her, and he was uncomfortable about that. It wasn't liked he lacked in available female admirers. Since his divorce six years previous, there were several that vied for his attention. The fact of the matter was, he simply wasn't interested. He had got to the point in his life that meaningful relationships were the only type that appealed to him, and he was on the road so often, traveling, he never had the time to develop any real close acquaintances. Although he appeared to be a lonely man, he was married to the cause of a new free America. He knew it would have been unfair to a woman to entangle her in his private obsession. This effort now consumed his life, and he still believed there was great hope for America.

Yet Anne Jones, standing there before him in the snow, looking somewhat as a schoolgirl herself, seemed to work a magic on the man. He was suddenly feeling emotions that he had known only so many years ago. This was the excitement that a young teenage boy feels when caught in the midst of female infatuation. Jefferson found it necessary to take a couple of deep breaths to clear his head. Having steadied himself, he greeted Anne warmly with a welcoming embrace.

"It's so good to see you, Anne. You look radiant as usual."

"Thank you, David. It's so good to see you too. We have been worried about you. The way things are going, we don't know which of our friends we'll lose tomorrow."

"Sadly, that's the way it is with war. How is our General Williamson doing?"

"He is much better today, David. He told me to give you his regards and to tell you he'll be back out in the field in under two months' time. They were able to save his leg, and he is able to stand on his own and is already in a rehab mode. He says he still does not remember what happened that day."

"This is good news, Anne. Did you talk to his doctors? C'mon, climb into my jeep. I'll drive you into camp."

As the two drove the short distance to the camp, Anne Jones filled David in on the general's condition. The general had suffered a severe concussion from one of the hand grenade blasts and severe lacerations to his left leg where pieces of shrapnel tore into his thigh. But the general was correct. His doctors maintained that in about two months' time, they felt he could probably return to the duties of directing his troops.

This was heartening news to David. There was received initial reports out of Mercy Hospital that indicated the general might never walk again. It was out of the question at that time to even speculate when he would be able, if ever, to return to the war. The initial effort had to be concerned with saving his life and then his leg. Anne went on to fill David in as to the conditions all the wounded soldiers faced after the battle at Montgomery. There simply wasn't enough hospital space available to accommodate so many injuries. School gymnasiums and auditoriums were being utilized as emergency patient care facilities. Anne appeared to be simply exhausted from overexposure to the human pain and agony she witnessed by visiting all the areas that housed these victims of war. To make matters worse, her companion of many years, Mr. Jones, had mysteriously disappeared. He had been on a plane carrying medical supplies to remote villages in Brazil, South America. The twin-engine plane they were flying in never reached its intended destination, and the six people on board were feared lost. Brazilian authorities had searched extensively but were unable to find any trace or clue as to the whereabouts of the plane. The dense jungles of Brazil had swallowed up whole many a man. It was not unusual to conduct a short search and rescue operation, conduct a quick memorial service, and move on altogether and forget about it in a couple of days. It was a rare occasion when someone emerged from the jungle alive. The usual occurrence was that Mr. Jones always communicated in the past despite the situation. His failure to do that now rang as an ominous sign that a disaster of some kind had occurred or he had been called upon to participate in another mission. Anne was inclined to believe that he had been called on to participate in another mission. Whether or not it was on planet Earth or elsewhere, she would not speculate.

Jefferson parked his jeep adjacent to the entrance of the communications center. He assisted in helping Anne as she stepped out of the vehicle. He had made arrangements to have her housed in the underground suite originally set aside for one of the post commanders. It was obvious she was fatigued and needed a prolonged rest. They quickly descended into the earth beneath Camp Belden. The communications center housed two of the ten underground entrance points that were positioned throughout the camp. The rugged mountains of Colorado provided underground quarters that were in some cases akin to hotel accommodations. The residents of Camp Belden took great pride in the highly skilled workmanship that went into the building of their camp. Their underground city covered an area that was the size of a big city block. Visitors usually needed escorts to prevent them from becoming lost due to the complex layout. There were many exit points provided to enable its residents a quick escape to flee in the case of an unwelcome attack by armed and unwelcome enemies.

Jefferson escorted Anne to her assigned room, bid her good day, and hung a Do Not Disturb sign over her entrance. She was soon sound asleep and would not rise until the following day when her worn-out body decided it had rested long enough.

Jefferson returned to the communications center. He was anxious to receive additional news from the East Coast. He wired his recommendation that Andrew Waverly replace General Williamson until he was able to return to active duty. It was his wish that American troops keep very active in the southeast. Prolonged inactivity in remote staging areas could be detrimental to America at this point. He sent off a cable to Waverly urging him to pursue an aggressive posture against the foreign troops. Constant harassment against the enemy supply line was essential. It was becoming apparent that General Aurielle might shift his attack to the west toward New Orleans. He had quickly replaced General Volson since his swift demise at Montgomery. French general Louise Gagnon was now commanding Volson's troops. He had already moved his half a million troops one hundred and fifty miles west of Dothan, Alabama, and had advance units setting up camp just east of the Alabama River. The citizens of Mobile had already begun their evacuation westward into Mississippi. America was fast becoming a country of refugees. Homes and memories were quickly left behind to escape the menacing foe that breathed impending disaster upon her fragile neck.

By 1:15: p.m., all the American generals had wired their unanimous affirmation approving Jefferson's recommendation. General Waverly would soon move his troops out of the Talladega National Forest and begin an aggressive campaign in an attempt to stall the drive of the Europeans. Plans of action were now being developed, and Jefferson would be kept advised.

Throughout the day, Jefferson kept himself busy roaming the grounds of Camp Belden. Something was unsettling him, and he couldn't quite put his finger on it. It wasn't until he lay down to sleep late that evening he realized the cause of his unrest. She was sleeping peacefully two doors down, and he dreamed great dreams as sleep finally took him.

April 14, 2041

As the morning sun began its slow rise over the high-peaked Rockies, it was obvious that spring was settling in. Fast-melting snow was causing the White River to rise and the residents of Camp Buford were forsaking winter parkas for light jackets and similar spring wear. It was clear that by the end of the day, Jefferson would be able to travel on. The thought of Camp Liberty and the serenity of its surrounding forest stirred him with a special yearning. It was there six months ago that his awesome project was officially launched into motion. It seemed sometimes like six years ago instead. And Laytonville, on Redwood Highway, he would surely stop there. He felt it was home to such a sturdy people. Redwoods and lumberjacks combined with mother nature's rough exterior and challenge to survive. A chance to forsake the big city for the serenity of Mendocino National Forest environment and quiet calm seemed so appealing to him.

Jefferson arose and dressed quickly. There would be much to do today, and he hoped to be in the air toward Laytonville come nightfall. He would begin with breakfast and then spend the next four or five hours planning his departure. He hoped to spend some time with Anne if it was at all possible. He strode off to find Major Collins to make final arrangements.

Since her arrival at Camp Belden, Anne Jones had been fighting a certain excitement that was stirring within her. There was no doubt it was connected with Jefferson. He was a man who made it quite obvious through the years that he was attracted to her. He was certainly a man who showed his feelings and let others know exactly how he felt about them. His outspoken ways got him into trouble on various occasions. Truth was often difficult to deal with. When you lived in a world of contradictions, hypocrisies, social mannerisms, and etiquette that were designed to obscure certain truths, a man who could cut through the opaqueness of the bullshit was sometimes offensive. Refreshing yes, but sometimes offensive. There had never been any realistic opportunities for Anne to get to know this man. They had both controlled their inner urges and developed a relationship of trust, admiration, and deep respect that had endured through the years. She knew now that her beloved friend, Mr. Jones, may be gone from planet Earth forever. She also felt he was being taken care of. If there was truly a heaven and his earthly mission completed, then he would be there. There could be no denying that. Years of helping fellow human beings could not and would not go unnoticed. Anne had never revealed the secret she kept concerning Mr. Jones. His angelic characteristics were well known to her. She had accused him once of being her guardian angel. He denied that he was, but he never denied that he was of the angelic mode, as she was certain he was.

Anne finished dressing, tried to settle the butterflies swooning within her, and went in search of David Jefferson.

David waited nervously in his room. He was sipping his bourbon slowly and hoped he would be able to prepare a drink for Anne as well when she arrived. The knock on the door put an end to his worrying about it. Before he could turn around, she was in the room. Major Collins closed the door behind her and hollered, "Thirty minutes, Mr. Jefferson, the choppers are almost ready to roll."

"How is it that I rate such an official escort, David? The good major advised that I had been summoned to your quarters."

"I certainly hope it's not an inconvenience, Anne. I simply wished to see you before I left. I must say your beauty startles me at the moment. You have consistently radiated it through the years. Will you join me in a drink please?"

"It's not an inconvenience at all. As a matter of fact, I was out searching for you when he found me. I'd love to have a drink, thank you. I prefer scotch if you have it."

"I do have scotch. Let me get it for you."

The two looked into each other's eyes as David gave a toast to Anne Jones.

"To one of the loveliest ladies on planet Earth. The majestic mountains that we now stand upon pale beside her magnificence. The creatures of the planet are in awe of her presence."

"David Jefferson, please don't embarrass me."

"What I speak is the truth. I speak what I feel, and through the years you know I've never wavered very far from espousing principles and opinions that I believe are true and correct. By the way, I am very sorry about Mr. Jones. I grieved and sorrowed for you when I heard of it."

"Thank you, David. I have much sorrow but no regrets. He was doing what he enjoyed doing so much, bringing aid and comfort to those who needed it. My fate lies in whatever my God has in store for me. I believe and have faith that I will be guided in the right direction."

"My belief is the same, Anne. The Good Lord knows the dreams that I dream. Look, Anne, my time here is very short. I will speak bluntly. If you wish, just tell me to shut up if I speak too openly. To start with, I find you so devastatingly attractive. Standing before me, I see one of God's loveliest creations. My very soul rocks and stirs with the excitement of your presence. I don't know what the future holds in store for us, but I hope, even though this is so bold and forthright, that when this life crisis has passed us by, I may be able to be a valuable part of your life."

Anne set her drink down and faced David.

"I find no fault with what you say, David. To tell you the truth, you have caught me off guard. You have made me feel very good, I must say. The future is certainly a precarious proposition at best right now. I will tell you this though. I will entertain your dreams for the moment. Who can say what the future will bring to us. For the time being, your country needs you. Go to Camp Liberty, and I shall be praying for you here. I shall keep in close touch and pray that we shall both survive this."

The warm embrace that followed brought David and Anne together in each other's arms. The closeness of her warm body left David weak in the knees and unable to speak for a moment. He could hardly think straight. Here was a man who could fearlessly stand in the face of the dreaded armies of Europe and defy them openly. Yet now he trembled in the arms of this woman, at a loss for words. He felt strange, and as he tried to speak, a soft moan was all that he could utter. As they looked deep into each other's eyes, their lips briefly touched each other. Both were left in a weakened condition. Powerful forces of nature were taking their toll on two very unique human beings. David dropped his arms and withdrew slightly.

"Anne, I've just experienced a taste of heaven. It's not often a mortal man is blessed so."

Before Anne could respond, the loud knock at the door by Major Collins returned them both to another world. They both quickly embraced once again before David gathered up his things.

"Please keep in touch, Anne. I need to hear from you. You don't know how important it is to me."

"I will, David. Please take care of yourself. My love goes with you. I will stay here until I hear from you."

"Love you, Anne. Stay safe until we can be together again."

With that, David was out the door and on his way. He seemed to be a man renewed and inspired. There was no mistaking the sudden change that had come over him. He was filled with a new vigor of life and great hope for the future. Anne Jones remained in David's room for some time. She lay upon his bed and prayed to God to spare them both. She hoped it wasn't too much to ask, just some time put aside in the days ahead to spend with a man she truly cared for.

Chapter 34

Lord, make me an instrument of thy peace.
Where there is hatred, let me sow love.

—St. Francis of Assisi

April 18, 2041
Glendale, California

Kevin McIntyre lay awake in his bed on the second floor of Glendale Fire Station number 3. It was 4:00 a.m., and he had another eight hours to go to finish his work shift out. Although the vast majority of people had been evacuated from the Los Angeles area, it was felt it was still necessary to maintain some semblance of police and fire protection. He had stayed behind voluntarily. At age 25, he had endured two years on the force already. A degree in fire science and the fact that he was a single parent had earned him an exemption from military service. His three-year-old daughter, Kelly Marie, was presently resting securely in the hands of his parents. In another week's time, he planned to move her further inland with the city relocation efforts in its final completion stage. In the meantime, the child lived in an environment of grandparents, day care centers, and precious little time with her dad. Kevin was looking forward to the party the Montebello Day Care Center was hosting on the twenty-first of April. It would be a day to spend some happy enjoyable time with his daughter. No one knew where her mother was. She had left to visit her own mother on December first, about four and a half months ago, in Kentucky. Since the nuclear detonations of December 7, Kevin had heard not a word from her. Authorities in her hometown of Elmrock, Kentucky, said the family was gone, and no one knew where they were. As Kevin lay thinking, he tried to imagine what nightmarish event had occurred to his wife, Tricia, that would cause her to vanish like this. They were too close to each other. He knew that if she were alive and able, she would communicate with him somehow. He personally feared the worst had befallen her, but deep in his heart, he dared to keep the hope alive that perhaps she was still okay and well and would soon make contact with him. At least the thought of this helped him to maintain his sanity and function normally one day at a time. To make matters worse, there were now rumors floating about that European warships had been spotted a short distance off the coast of California out in the Pacific. With American ground troops concentrating all their efforts on the fighting in the east, this was not good news to hear. All the firemen carried weapons now, and Kevin didn't relish the idea that they might have to soon use them. Causing problems on the West Coast by the European military could certainly affect the American military effort in the east. There was no doubt that the Europeans were pulling out all the stops in their effort to subdue America. It would take a determined effort to stop them. In the meantime, Kevin McIntyre would do the best he could to play his part in helping America to survive this crisis.

Camp Liberty, Mendocino National Forest, California
Same day

    At 6:00 a.m. the majority of the residents of Camp Liberty were preparing to rise. The arrival the prior evening of David Jefferson and his two hundred air cavalry troopers stirred everyone with a sense of excitement and hope. Phil Redding and his dedicated group of young people had greeted their guests with joyous enthusiasm.
    They were pretty well isolated from all that was going on in the country although they kept abreast with everything almost instantaneously via the camp communication center. To have David Jefferson and his men in camp with them was an exciting change of pace. A huge meal was prepared, and the underground dining area hosted

an evening of exchanging stories and information. Philip Redding had worked long hard hours day after day to ensure his many camps were well supplied and ready to use by combat troops when needed. This visit presented him with an opportunity to test just how well his small group could interact with and sustain a two-hundred-man combat contingent that must stay prepared to depart at a moment's notice.

A special project was also in operation this day. A two-thousand-truck convoy was traveling down Interstate 5 to bring provisions and supplies southward to the displaced citizens of Los Angeles. Almost daily convoys of varying sizes were traveling southward from Canadian cities, helping to bring necessary and life-sustaining materials, as well as arms and munitions, to a number of American checkpoints along the northern border. Canadian cities such as Kelowna, British Columbia; Lethbridge, Alberta; Weyburn, Saskatchewan; and Fort Frances, Ontario played key roles in allowing their cities to continuously be thoroughfares for keeping America supplied. Colonel Redding was to meet the convoy of Canadians at Red Bluff, California. Instead, he would dispatch soldiers from the air cavalry unit to meet them, pay their respects, and pick up the specially designated military weapons the colonel had requested. Especially important were the ten trucks carrying nuclear-tipped missiles which were earmarked for a secret project. Colonel Redding was to ensure they arrived safely at Stewarts Point, north of San Francisco. From there American naval ships were going to make a raid on the European warships south of Los Angeles and attempt to sink them. The United States was rapidly preparing to accelerate their military activities. The strike against the warships would hopefully take place within the next two weeks, and United States naval units on the West Coast were anxious to attack. Submarines had already discovered the exact location of the ships they were targeting, and it was now a matter of delivering the missiles to the ships that could do the job.

It was a good time for David Jefferson to be on the West Coast. From Camp Liberty's Communication Center, he could instantly contact key individuals who were directing US military tactics and mobilizing the vast civilian population. It was his intention to soon have a one-hundred-thousand-man army encamped between Los Angeles and San Francisco. Time was needed to get this done. The more, the better. Just give America a little more time and it would be possible to drive the terrible foe away. It would be possible to rebuild and have a chance once again to be a free nation. Some days surely looked better than others, and this was one of them. The morning was spent primarily on the phone giving directions and receiving updated reports from around the country. Especially interesting was a message concerning a top secret dispatch from the government in Mexico that was on its way route to his location. Americans in the southwest were extremely nervous about reports of military buildups in that country. David decided to spend the rest of the day meeting with as many of his advisors as he could. Conference calls and satellite hookups were essential to keeping all the key players working together, operating from the same plan.

2:00 p.m., same day
Saltillo, Mexico

Captain Durango San Luis waited nervously in his jeep along Mexico's Interstate 40. He commanded the vanguard of the one-hundred-fifty-thousand-man army that President Miguel Nieves had assembled to move into Texas. The debate to go to the aid of America had raged on now for four months. All the old wounds regarding the Americans had risen to the surface rapidly, and some Mexicans had even urged assisting the Europeans and attacking and occupying parts of Texas, New Mexico, and California. In the end, a decision was reached that later on would surprise many Americans. As a point of fact, many Mexicans had relatives in America and their sense of duty to family ties overrode old bad memories. A feeling of kinship spread across Mexico, and very quickly an army was assembled, and Mexican generals converged in Monterrey to begin drawing up battle plans. Confidential dispatches were sent out to Jefferson in America, and now the Mexicans sat waiting for their secret plans to come into view before his eyes. Captain San Luis knew he could be sitting near San Antonio within a few hours' time. He welcomed the opportunity of the hero's role. He had two uncles in Austin, and he longed to see the joy in their eyes as their saviors from the south passed by with their troops. In another two months' time, there could possibly be another fifty thousand added to join them. It was a glorious day, a day to ride north on wings of steel and prove to America the real stuff of what her southern neighbor was all about.

The perception that America had treated her so bad through the past two centuries since the Mexican-America War of the 1840s was a source of hurt and dismay to the average Mexican. Soon America would realize her great errors, and perhaps hurts of long ago could be mended in full. For now the young captain had all he could do to restrain the enthusiasm that was pumping his adrenaline beyond normal limits. He and the thousands of men with him anxiously awaited the orders that would send them moving northward.

4:00 p.m., same day
Jackson, Mississippi

General Waverly paced steadily in front of the small group he had assembled. The seven most senior officers of the United States military stood in silence before him. They stood in the study of an historic old Southern mansion five miles northwest of Jackson, Mississippi. If the walls could talk, they might tell of other such meetings held here by perplexed and worried warriors of another war fought so long ago. The Civil War fought in the States seemed to some in the South as a conflict that somehow still lived, although hidden and obscured somewhere below the surface, yet somehow still not dead. Andrew Waverly felt it was time now for America to flex its military muscle. The entire eastern seaboard south of Norfolk, Virginia, was in European hands. The deep south was under ominous threat along its entire southern front. It was time now to strike back viciously at the hounds that were hard on its heels.

"Gentlemen, shortly we shall strike back once again. At 7:00 a.m. on the twenty-third, we shall launch attacks in six different areas along our southern front. We shall hit hard and then withdraw. Exactly two days later, we shall strike exactly the same way and in the same areas and then withdraw. It is our intent to create as many widows and grieving kin in Europe as possible. We have worked up and talked through these plans over and over. We will be successful. The South fell once long ago. It shall not happen again. The difference now is that we fight together as brethren in a cause that transcends all that ever separated us. We shall come together as we never have. In four days' time, it is our plan to gather again in Atlanta to analyze our efforts. Perhaps we shall celebrate then the death of Marcus Aurielle. Two assassination squads are sitting outside Savannah right now. May God guide them to their mark. If any one of you have reservations, speak them now. If not, we shall adjourn, and may God go with each of you."

Silence hung over the study, and each general in turn saluted, turned, and withdrew from the room. Andrew Waverly was left alone and knew that his men were ready for the struggle that lay ahead. A bit of excitement stirred within him. He knew that if things went well that great success and military advances could be made. He also knew that it was wise now to temper his enthusiasm and proceed forward with calm determination.

9:00 p.m., same day
Stuttgart, Germany

Gustav Erikson was in a jovial mood as he placed the phone back down on the receiver. Hans Rizarre had just established April 21 as the date for a most important meeting. Only those considered close to him on the highest levels of the governing republic would be present. The great world leader, dictator of the republic, would be holding private court among his advisors. It would be a most historic occasion. Even the pope would be in attendance. The power brokers of Europe were once again determining the fate of the world. Millions of lives could be affected by the decisions reached at such a meeting. Gustav knew he sat close to the heart of earthly power. He struggled to maintain his composure at the thought of his own position of power and status. It was difficult to conceive what lay ahead. It certainly appeared that the greatest things were yet to come. The pinnacle of European power throughout the world had not yet been reached.

The meeting of the twenty-first would be a time to set in motion the decision-making processes that could lead Europe to greater heights. No one seemed to particularly care about the price that was to be paid, and up to this point, it hadn't been too bad at all. Aside from a few thousand soldiers being buried in their graves, the great republic hadn't suffered much at all. The great outcry against the use of nuclear weapons seemed now to be quieted as Hans Rizarre had now given assurances that they would no longer be used. Europe was prosperous, and the opportunity to become wealthier was bright indeed. The one main major real problem seemed to be just how stubborn those misguided Americans were going to be. Certainly they couldn't hold out much longer. They didn't appear to be the kind of people that had the stomach for a long fight. With this thought in mind, Gustav retired to his study to prepare his own list of suggestions on how to deal with the Americans. He looked forward to traveling there, and as he sat reflecting, he couldn't help but begin envisioning an America, conquered and subdued, enthusiastically welcoming him as he toured the cities of that distant country.

Chapter 35

A new commandment I give unto you, that ye love one another; as I have loved you, that ye also love one another.

—John 13:34 KJV

April 20, 2041
Camp Liberty, Mendocino National Forest, California

News had been filtering into Camp Liberty all day concerning the war in the east. American troops were fighting an aggressive and determined enemy. General Waverly was still scheduled to initiate attacks along a broad southern area on the twenty-third. This morning initial reports coming into camp reported that it looked as though the Europeans on the East Coast were prepping for a northern move continuing up the coast and that their troops to the west may be moving westward in a possible New Orleans maneuver. One good piece of news was received midday when it was reported a large American naval party had successfully engaged several European naval ships in the Gulf of Mexico south of Tampa, Florida, and caused major damage to ten warships. A combined US Navy and US Coast Guard battle group came up from Merida, Mexico, where they had been harboring since the initial European landings in Florida. It was a quick strike engagement, and the American ships fled south immediately after the engagement. Reports were that it appears two of the American ships may have been lost in the battle. America was in for a long hard fight. It was difficult to comprehend just how it was all going to end. David Jefferson was now making plans to leave Camp Liberty and head eastward to be near the fighting. He had met all day with his friends to establish his itinerary. It was his intention to pass through and visit as many cities as possible and boost the morale of as many people as he could. It was now 8:00 p.m., and David called an end to the long day of meetings and established April 23 as the day to begin his trip. He prayed it would be a round-trip affair, and not a one-way trip into oblivion and disaster.

As Jefferson left his friends, he retreated into his room to meditate and ease his mind. Of late it was necessary for him to do this. The survival of mankind was at stake, and it required the most out of any man. Lately in his room, whenever he felt the need, he reached for his father's last letter. In 2028, he had passed away at age 73, his body ravaged with cancer. He wrote to his son for the last time. He deeply sympathized with his son's views on America and on life. He encouraged him to remain strong when so many others were weak. He knew his son's battles were an uphill struggle, but worthy and honorable. The planet needed righteous men in order to survive. Tears filled David's eyes as he remembered the early years with his dad. Times were so much happier for him then. Innocent days of youth, worrying more about soccer and Little League baseball, spent in careless frolic and ignorance of the world. His eyes always wandered to the last page of the letter. His dad seemed to know the troubles that lay ahead for mankind, and in his dying struggle, he gave pen to insightful visions. Jefferson would read his words often.

> Is there not any hope for man? Will the Great One intervene in time? There is an Ancient Book on earth that tells the story. So many discount it as that, a story. A story made up by men. Men, in fact, who lived so long ago we find it very difficult to verify scientifically their data. Who has time for such fairy tales? We are a progressive people in a modern day advanced society. So advanced we do so many awesome things, some awful awesome things as well, such as spend billions of dollars on nuclear weapons and modern-day firearms. They are nothing more than as sophis-

ticated rocks, things we use to slay each other, a Cain-and-Abel kind of thing. We pollute our lakes, our drinking waters, and our oceans and then wonder why we have cancers. We sit and listen to stories of millions of our earthly brethren affected by famine, yet feeding our people is not our highest priority. Murders and assaults are commonplace occurrences, and yet we say we have never been so civilized. Illiteracy is on the increase, and our leaders hedge when education is discussed at budget hearings. The list of troubles can go on and on. It seems odd that these same types of human stories are mentioned in the Ancient Book. This same book talks about the solution to man's problems here on earth: "Do unto others as you would have them do unto you. Love thy neighbor as thyself." These represent fundamental universal principles that can't be denied. They are as simple as one plus one and even as mathematically sound. As our math becomes more and more complex, the solutions may be difficult and complex but always result in one true answer. It is the same with man. As life's problems become more and more complex, the solution is also always the same true answer—love of one another. It stands out as a beacon in the night. It cannot be denied. With it, there is life. Without it, there is death. O Great One, hurry. Your children are in need.

Jefferson set down this oft-read letter, left the room, and found his way above ground to wander into the serenity of the deep woods. As he passed one of the night sentries, he could see that the night sky was clear, and as he came upon a small rise, he viewed the countless stars in the heavens. Alone with nature, he suddenly lifted his voice and cried out in despair to the heavens.

"O Great One of whom my father speaks, heed the call of Your children on earth. We are desperate for Your help. If You exist, You surely know of our plight. We shall not make it without you. Can You stand by and let wicked men destroy us all? A madman presently runs loose with his friends. Our lives are considered as nothing. Do not forsake us, Your children. The Ancient Book tells us of Your earthly visits of long ago. Please return, O Great One. We need You now as we never have before. Heed our crying call."

Jefferson was ready now to return to his room. He had never quite vented his feelings so openly to his Creator. The experience was uplifting and inspirational. This was the time of night that David usually spent writing to Anne, and he turned about to head back to camp This was a most important part of his day. Although he wasn't able to be with Anne physically, he could be with her for a couple of hours as he would write of the day's events and particular incidents that would occur. David knew now that his feelings for Anne were very deep. He had never devoted so much concern for any one woman in his life. He needed to see her soon. He just needed to see her, to be around her.

Suddenly in the eastern sky, David noticed something unusual. A blue star appeared suddenly and was moving westward in the sky. It turned green, then red. It stopped for a moment and suddenly sped across the heavens out of his sight. It was the first time in his life he had seen a UFO (unidentified flying object). He thought it quite odd, and it left him a little troubled. David started back through the woods and wondered how his friends would deal with all the tomorrows that forebode disaster and sorrow. Perhaps a story about a UFO would be a good topic of diversion to occupy troubled minds that yearned for something other than daily bad news.

Jefferson lowered his eyes and surveyed the woods around him. He spotted the pathway that brought him to the clearing and now casually began to stride back to camp.

"Jefferson, David Jefferson, wait a moment please."

David was momentarily confused. The voice was clear, but its location was not readily evident. Suddenly a blinding light appeared to his left, and the power of its radiance knocked him off his feet.

David had known of laser weapons, and the first thing that flashed across his mind was that the Europeans had landed and he was suddenly a victim, a casualty of war.

"Be calm, David. I mean you no harm."

There was something in the voice that reached into David's soul. The power of its message washed over him as a cloud. He immediately felt at peace, and his racing adrenaline slowed to a calming pulse. The light that blinded him suddenly reduced to a barely visible glow. He saw in front of him the figure of a man, a young man. As his eyes properly focused, he realized the person now in front of him as a strangely unique man. Handsome of face, he was dressed in a robe of fine linen, white and pure. This was certainly no man of war, no man who meant to slay him. David, realizing he was still on the ground, suddenly found himself in an embarrassing position. He slowly raised up on his feet and brushed himself off.

"Young man, who are you? Where did you come from?"

"I have come to deliver a message to you and your friends."

"A message. What kind of message, and from whom?"

David was confused and somewhat irritated. He was in control of most situations, but for some reason he felt totally inadequate in the presence of this young man.

"Pay close heed to what I now tell you, David Jefferson. My name is Chareal. I have been sent by the one you and your father refer to as the Great One. My time with you will be very short and my message quick and to the point. The Great One wishes you to know this. Concerning the Ancient Book, it is written for a purpose, an aid to man. Know that it contains words which are trustworthy and true. The Great One sends his messenger Chareal to tell His children what shortly will come to pass. The Great One shall send His Son quickly, for the time is near at hand. He who does wrong, let him do wrong still; and he who is filthy, let him be filthy still; and he who is just, let him be just still; and he who is holy, let him be holy still. Behold, the Great One's Son comes quickly! And His reward is with Him, to render to each one according to His works. He is the Alpha and the Omega, the first and the last, the beginning and the end. I shall not forsake my children. As a sign, He will soon send two men who will witness for Him. They shall fly in the face of your enemies, and *fear* shall be a word they know not. The Ancient Book shall play to the last scene."

Chareal stopped, and a warm glow surrounded him as an aura. He raised his right hand, and suddenly the trees overhead were showered in light. Something stirred overhead, but David couldn't see what it was. Whatever it was stayed out of view and did not pass over the clearing. David sensed immediately that he was in the presence of some powerful being and bowed to a knee before the young Chareal. As if in shock, young Chareal rebuked David Jefferson.

"Thou must not do that. I am a fellow servant of thine, and of your brethren, and of those who follow the Great One. Worship only Him."

David slowly raised up. He was trembling in awe. Chareal moved off into the woods in the direction of the lights.

"Farewell, my friend. Until we meet again."

Chareal waved and disappeared into the night. Through the trees, David caught a glimpse of a new light. A blinding flash raised from the ground upward from the direction of where the young man went into the forest. The ground shook under David's feet, and he almost went down again. The lights overhead now wavered as if movement was imminent. In an instant, the clearing was bathed in soft white light. Looking upward, David could not see anything behind the light to determine the identity of its source. Suddenly the white light changed to the purest blue that one could imagine. The awful silence that instantly prevailed assailed David's brain. The only noise that he was aware of was the crashing of his brain waves against a mind that couldn't compute the data that was being input into it in a swirling rush. Despite the shock of this experience, David determined now to face this great light, stood straight up with arms lifted, and continued to peer directly skyward trying to see beyond the light that hovered over him. In an instant, it shot straight upward and streaked skyward and disappeared. David now realized he had been lifted two feet off the ground and suspended there for more than a second or two. As he gently floated back down, the light was out of sight and out among the stars. David Jefferson collapsed on the ground and remained there sitting for some ten minutes, attempting to assess the experience he had just gone through.

The quiet of the night was again broken by voices behind him. As he turned, once again lights were visible through the trees. David knew what the source of these lights were. Three flashlights searched for him from the edge of the clearing. Phil Redding, Sally Watkins, and others called out to him.

"Over here, I'm over here."

David got to his feet and walked toward his friends. Sally was first to reach him. She ran toward him in an excited rush.

"David, David, we've seen some UFOs. The whole camp is in an uproar."

"Calm down, Sally, calm down."

"It's true, David. I saw them myself. It's the most incredible thing I have ever seen. Three of them passed right over the top of the camp. They were flashing multicolored lights and darting all over the place. Never even made a noise."

"I know, Philip. I know."

"Sally rushed out to find you, David, just about twenty minutes ago. They disappeared up in the stars somewhere. We caught a good glimpse of them as they got higher up. I saw at least three of them. Did you see any? It was unreal."

As David spoke to his friends in the quiet serenity of the beautiful Mendocino, deep within the bowels of the planet Earth, a great being was heard gasping in despair, and so, so many light-years away, the Great One was seen smiling as news of the imminent return of Chareal filtered into the deepest recesses of the temple gardens at Nevaeh, true home to the guardians of the planet Earth.

> But of that day and that hour knoweth no man, no, not the angels which are in heaven, neither the Son, but the Father. Take ye heed, watch and pray: for ye know not when the time is. For the Son of Man is as a man taking a far journey, who left his house, and gave authority to his servants, and to every man his work, and commanded the porter to watch. Watch ye therefore: for ye know not when the master of the house cometh, at even, or at midnight,

or at the cockcrowing, or in the morning: Lest coming suddenly he find you sleeping. And what I say unto you I say unto all, Watch.

—Mark 13:32–37 KJV

About the Author

Bill Doherty is a first-time author with the publication of *Planet Earth: Period of Crisis*. He has a 1972 bachelor of arts degree from Syracuse University at Utica College majoring in government administration. He has great interest in prophetic novels and literature. He spent three years in the US Army, serving his last year as a member of the US Army's Old Guard Presidential Honor Guard Unit at Arlington National Cemetery. Subsequently Mr. Doherty spent five years with the state of Illinois penal system as a corrections officer supervising incarcerated adult female felons. Following twenty years of service enforcing housing and environmental codes, he retired from the city of Tampa, Florida and has begun a new career of authoring books.

www.ingramcontent.com/pod-product-compliance
Lightning Source LLC
Chambersburg PA
CBHW051923310125
21209CB00011B/746